# PRAISE FOR HELENA HUNTING'S NOVELS

"Perfect for fans of Helen Hoang's *The Kiss Quotient*. A fun and steamy love story with high stakes and plenty of emotion."

—*Kirkus Reviews* on *Meet Cute*

"Bestselling Hunting's latest humorous and heartfelt love story . . . is another smartly plotted and perfectly executed rom-com with a spot-on sense of snarky wit and a generous helping of smoldering sexual chemistry."

—*Booklist* on *Meet Cute*

"Entertaining, funny, and emotional."

—*Harlequin Junkie* on *Meet Cute*

"Hunting is quickly making her way as one of the top voices in romance!"

—RT Book Reviews

"Sexy. Funny. Emotional. Steamy and tender and so much more than just a book. *Hooking Up* reminds me why I love reading romance."

—*USA Today* bestselling author L. J. Shen

"Heartfelt, hilarious, hot, and so much sexiness!"

—*New York Times* bestselling author Tijan on *Shacking Up*

"Helena writes irresistible men. I loved this sexy, funny, and deliciously naughty story!"

—*USA Today* bestselling author Liv Morris on *Shacking Up*

"Fun, sexy, and full of heart . . . a laugh-out-loud love story with explosive chemistry and lovable characters. Helena Hunting has done it again!"
—*USA Today* bestselling author Melanie Harlow on *Shacking Up*

"With that perfect Helena Hunting flair, *Shacking Up* is the perfect combination of sexy, sweet, and hilarious. A feel-good beach read you won't want to miss!"
—*New York Times* bestselling author K. Bromberg

"A look into the world of tattoos and piercings, a dash of humor, and a feel-good ending that will delight fans and new readers alike."
—*Publishers Weekly* on *Inked Armor*

"A unique, deliciously hot, endearingly sweet, laugh-out-loud, fantastically good-time romance!! . . . I loved every single page!!"
—*New York Times* bestselling author Emma Chase on *Pucked*

"Sigh-inducing swoony and fanning-myself sexy. All the stars!"
—*USA Today* bestselling author Daisy Prescott on the Pucked series

"A hot roller coaster of a ride!"
—*New York Times* and *USA Today* bestselling author Julia Kent on *Pucked Over*

"*Pucked Over* is Helena Hunting's funniest and sexiest book yet. SCORCHING HOT with PEE-INDUCING LAUGHS. All hail the Beaver Queen."
—*USA Today* bestselling author T. M. Frazier

"Characters that will touch your heart and a romance that will leave you breathless."

—*New York Times* bestselling author Tara Sue Me on *Clipped Wings*

"Gut wrenching, sexy, twisted, dark, incredibly erotic, and a love story like no other. On my all-time favorites list."

—Alice Clayton, *New York Times* bestselling author of *Wallbanger* and the Redhead series on *Clipped Wings*

# A
# SECRET
## FOR A
# SECRET

# OTHER TITLES BY HELENA HUNTING

## *PUCKED SERIES*

*Pucked* (Pucked #1)
*Pucked Up* (Pucked #2)
*Pucked Over* (Pucked #3)
*Forever Pucked* (Pucked #4)
*Pucked Under* (Pucked #5)
*Pucked Off* (Pucked #6)
*Pucked Love* (Pucked #7)
*Area 51: Deleted Scenes & Outtakes*
*Get Inked* (crossover novella)
*Pucks & Penalties: Pucked Series Deleted Scenes &*
*Outtakes*

## *THE CLIPPED WINGS SERIES*

*Cupcakes and Ink*
*Clipped Wings*
*Between the Cracks*
*Inked Armor*
*Cracks in the Armor*
*Fractures in Ink*

## SHACKING UP SERIES

Shacking Up
Getting Down (novella)
Hooking Up
I Flipping Love You
Making Up
Handle with Care

## STAND-ALONE NOVELS

The Librarian Principle
The Good Luck Charm
Meet Cute
Felony Ever After

# A *SECRET* FOR A *SECRET*

## HELENA HUNTING

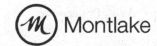

Text copyright © 2020 by Helena Hunting
All rights reserved.

Published by Montlake, Seattle
www.apub.com

Amazon, the Amazon logo, and Montlake are trademarks of Amazon.com, Inc., or its affiliates.

ISBN-13: 9781542023382
ISBN-10: 1542023386

Cover design by Eileen Carey

Cover photography by Wander Aguiar Photography

Printed in the United States of America

*For the restless souls searching for some calm within the chaos and for the ones looking for a little chaos to temper the calm.*

# PROLOGUE
## MOMMY ISSUES

*Kingston*

I have six different drinks in front of me, ranging from very expensive scotch to some kind of carbonated fruity cocktail that's so sweet I'm positive I'll get a cavity if I finish it. Despite the variety, I'm still having trouble getting drunk. Mostly because I'm not a fan of the way alcohol tastes, so I've only had a couple sips out of each glass.

"Excuse me, is this seat taken?" A soft, slightly smoky female voice draws my attention to the left, where the stool next to mine sits empty.

I notice several things as her gray-blue eyes, ringed in navy, lock and hold with mine: she's pint size and stunning, with long chestnut hair pulled up in a loose ponytail, high cheekbones, full lips, and thick lashes that don't appear to be coated in mascara. But beyond how beautiful she is, she looks sad.

We match.

"Uh, no, it's all yours." Regardless of my sour mood, I push back my stool and stand, partly to make space for her, since the stools are crammed in close together.

She climbs into the one next to mine before I have a chance to offer my assistance.

"I'm Queenie." She holds out a hand, and when I do the same, she slips hers into my palm, sending a jolt of unexpected energy through me. The way her eyes flare makes me think she's felt it too. Maybe there's something in the air.

"Queenie?" I smile. "I'm Ryan." I don't know why I introduce myself this way. No one calls me Ryan except for my parents. Even my siblings call me by our last name most of the time. In part because of my career choice, where my last name is what most people recognize. It's too late now to backtrack. Maybe I don't use my last name because my entire identity has been brought into question thanks to today's events.

"Hi, Ryan." Her gaze darts down and then back up. Our palms are still connected. And I'm still staring at her.

I release her hand and instantly want to find a reason to touch her again.

The bartender is quick to spot his new customer. I take my seat again while Queenie orders. "I'll have a vodka martini, extra dirty, extra olives, please. Actually, make that two."

The bartender's eyebrows rise, but he gets out his shaker. She stops him when he reaches for the bottle on the shelf behind him and asks for well vodka instead. I'm not sure what the difference is between the two, but that gets another eyebrow raise from the bartender. He fills two martini glasses and drops a skewer of olives into each one. He looks to me before he moves on. "You still doing okay?"

"I'm fine, thank you."

I try not to stare at Queenie, but I can see her reflection in the mirrored bar. She takes a sip out of one glass and makes a face, then does the same with the other one. She transfers one of the skewers of olives to the other glass and downs the whole thing in two gulps.

Her shoulders curl in, and she turns her head away, coughing into her elbow.

"Are you okay?" I ask.

She holds up a finger and coughs a couple more times. When she finally looks my way, her eyes are watery and her cheeks are flushed. "Fine, thanks. Well vodka isn't very smooth going down."

"Oh." I don't know much about vodka. "Why didn't you have the other kind, then?"

"Because it costs twice as much, and I just lost my job, so I have to get drunk on the cheap stuff." She plucks one of the skewers of olives from the still-full martini glass and pops one in her mouth.

"I'm sorry that you lost your job."

She gives me another wry smile. "Thanks. I kind of sucked at it, though, so it's not much of a surprise. Plus, serving tables isn't my end-game, so this is sort of a wake-up call to figure out what I want to do with the rest of my life." She motions to my lineup of drinks. "What's going on here?"

"I'm trying to get drunk too."

"You'd have a lot more success if you actually drank them."

"Yeah, I know. I'm not big on alcohol," I admit.

She scans me slowly, her grin growing wider once again. "Can't really say I'm surprised to hear that. You look like you got lost on your way to a Boy Scouts meeting."

"I used to be a Boy Scout." I run a hand over my chest. I'm wearing a white polo and khakis, which is my usual attire. "I was even a camp counselor when I was a teenager."

She throws her head back and laughs. "God, you're adorable. And I mean that in a good way." Queenie props her cheek on her fist. "So tell me why a former Boy Scout and camp counselor would need to get drunk by himself."

"It's a little complicated." I pick up one of the glasses in front of me and take a hefty gulp.

"I'm the queen of complicated. Hit me with it."

I bite the end of my tongue for a few seconds, debating. "It's pretty messed up."

3

"That's okay. I'm pretty messed up too. How about this: you tell me why you're getting drunk, and I'll tell you why I'm a mess, aside from the fact that I lost a job." She holds up her pinkie finger. "And we can pinkie swear that whatever we tell each other tonight, we'll take to the grave."

I link my pinkie with hers, and again, that jolt of energy hits me. Like the static in the air that comes with a thunderstorm. "A secret for a secret?"

"Exactly."

"Okay." I nod once and blow out a breath. It's probably easier to tell a stranger this than it is to tell someone close to me. I bend so my mouth is close to her ear and say quietly, "I found out my sister is actually my mom."

Queenie leans back and rapid blinks several times in a row. "I'm sorry . . . what?"

"My sister is actually—"

She waves her hand in the air. "I heard you. Oh my God. I don't even know what to say to that. Are you . . . okay? Never mind. That's a stupid question. Obviously you're not okay. Do you want to . . . talk about it?"

"Uh, not really. Is that okay?" I almost feel bad that I don't want to share more, especially since she's expressing genuine concern. I do feel a little better about the whole thing, considering her shock and empathetic expression.

"Of course it's okay. It also totally explains why you have a line of drinks in front of you." She chews the inside of her lip. "I feel like my secret is kind of lame in comparison."

"I'm sure it's not. And you don't have to tell me if you don't want to." I won't be the least bit surprised if she finishes her second martini and leaves, considering my revelation.

"I want to. Tell you, I mean." She slurps her second martini and exhales a long breath. "I have dependency issues."

"On alcohol?"

She laughs again. "God, I love you." Her eyes flare. "I don't mean that literally. I just mean you're cute. The things you say, just . . . anyway . . .

4

I'm not dependent on alcohol, apart from at this moment. I'm dependent on my dad."

"That's not necessarily a bad thing, though, is it?"

Queenie pops another olive in her mouth and chews thoughtfully. "He was only twenty when I was born, and he ended up having to raise me on his own. So lots of trial and error in the whole how to deal with raising a kid alone, you know? And I'm really good at messing things up, and he's really good at bailing me out every single time, so I've perpetuated that dependency, and he sort of inadvertently feeds it." Her nose scrunches up. "Sorry, I'm basically unloading all my baggage on you, and you already seem to have enough of your own to deal with."

"Please don't apologize. It's good to know I'm not the only one with problems."

"I've never actually admitted that out loud before, so it kind of feels good to unload it, even if it's with a virtual stranger, if that makes sense."

"It does. Make sense, I mean." I feel like fate has obviously thrown us together tonight for a reason, so I decide I'm willing to share a little more. "I'm actually the product of a teen pregnancy too. My biological father wasn't in the picture, and my grandparents decided it would be best if they raised me as theirs to give my sister . . . mom . . . and me a better chance at a normal life."

"So I guess that means we both have mommy issues."

"Looks that way, doesn't it?" I agree.

"You know what we should do, Ryan?" There's a hint of mischief in her eyes, the kind I might have shied away from before today.

"What's that?"

"You game for getting drunk and forgetting about our mommy issues, at least for tonight?"

"I'm game."

She pushes my scotch toward me and clinks her glass against mine. "After we knock back all your drinks, we can do shots."

◆ ◆ ◆

My head is pounding.

The last time I had a hangover like this, I was seventeen years old.

I crack a lid and groan when the light streaming through my bedroom window hits my eyeballs. I drag my hand down my face and freeze. Because it smells like sex.

I glance to the right, noting the rumpled sheets and the head-dented pillow. I roll over—which makes me nauseous—and breathe in the sweet scent of vanilla shampoo.

*Queenie.*

After we polished off all my drinks, we did shots. Which, based on how I'm feeling right now, was definitely not a good idea.

And then I brought her home.

I throw off the covers and sit up. I'm naked. Again, this is atypical. I usually sleep in a T-shirt and boxer briefs. I find a discarded pair on the floor and pull them on so I can go in search of Queenie.

I get as far as the hallway when a yellow Post-it stuck to the door-jamb catches my eye.

> Thanks for taking my mind off of my mommy issues
> last night. And this morning. ;)
> Xo
> Queenie

I peel it off, hoping she's left a phone number on the back, but it's blank. Which is when I notice the scrap of fabric hanging from the knob. I untangle it and realize that it's a pair of women's underwear.

A thong, to be exact. A *ruined* thong.

And this, right here, is the reason I don't drink. Or bring random women home. Because now I get to feel equal parts guilty and mortified that last night's sexual-therapy session has only warranted a Post-it goodbye note.

# CHAPTER 1

## FIRST DAY

*Queenie*
*Six weeks later*

"Honey, you ready? We needed to be out of here five minutes ago."

"Coming!" I slip my feet into my heels, check my reflection one last time, make sure I have my laptop bag and purse, and rush down the hall. The last thing I want is to make my boss late for work my first day on the job. As his assistant.

He's standing in the kitchen, dark hair styled neatly, athletic frame wrapped in a navy suit with a gray tie that matches his eyes and the hints of gray at his temples—that I'd never mention exist. He looks far more put together than I feel. He glances up from the phone in his hand, and his smile fades. "What are you wearing?"

"It's called a dress." Like his suit, it's navy, with cap sleeves, belted at the waist. Classic, simple, and stylish, or at least that's what the salesgirl said when I tried it on last week. And then charged it to my boss's credit card. The perks of living with the guy who runs the show.

"Maybe you should change into pants."

I prop a fist on my hip. "Weren't you just yelling at me to hurry up, and now you want me to change? What the hell?"

He waves a hand in my direction. "This isn't work-appropriate attire."

It's my turn to frown. "How is this not work appropriate? It has sleeves and a high neckline, and the hem falls below my knees. I look perfectly professional."

"You're going to be in a roomful of male athletes, primarily in their twenties and thirties."

"And a few in their forties." I motion to him. "Your point being?"

He tips his head to the side, regarding me with something like frustration. "Don't pretend you don't know what the issue is."

I know exactly what the issue is. My dress is tailored; it hugs my curves. It's professional and also maybe a bit sexy. But all of me is covered, apart from my arms, and my legs from knee to ankle. "This isn't the sixteenth century. I shouldn't have to hide in a burlap sack. Are you telling me these guys are so barbaric they're unable to control themselves in the presence of women? I should be allowed to wear whatever I damn well please, and what I'm wearing is tasteful and completely appropriate. Besides, the second they find out I'm your daughter, they'll avoid me like the plague, especially if you're wearing that scowl." I poke him in the cheek. "Now stop being archaic and overprotective. We're going to be late." I grab our travel mugs, which are filled with the coffee I made this morning, and head for the door.

My dad sighs, aware this isn't a battle he's going to win. I'm twenty-four. I'm athletic, curvy, and female. I refuse to hide my shape because men might happen to appreciate it. Although I do understand why my dad does not love the prospect.

He locks up behind me, and his Tesla beeps once as he presses the key fob.

My dad is the general manager of the Seattle NHL team. When he was a teenager, he showed real promise as a player. He even played in the minors and almost got called up, but then he got my mother pregnant and became a father at the ripe old age of twenty, which changed everything. Especially when my mom decided being a parent was too much for her and took off, leaving him to raise me on his own.

He still could've played for the NHL. My grandparents would have helped take care of me during away games. But he didn't want me to be without both parents for a good part of the year, and my mom had proven to be completely unreliable. By the time I was two, he had full custody. So he set aside his NHL-playing aspirations and took a lower-level administrative job instead.

Over the years he's worked his way up the ladder—taking positions inside the organization that required minimal travel.

But the opportunity of a lifetime presented itself when Seattle took on an expansion team and they offered my dad the general manager position. We were living in Florida at the time, and I'd already trans-ferred colleges once (and lost an entire semester), so I decided to stay behind, hoping I could prove myself capable of adulting. I also wanted my dad to put himself first for once. He didn't love that I was on the other side of the country, and honestly, neither did I, but I wanted him to have a life that didn't revolve around me.

So I stayed in Florida and went to school. And for a while it worked. Until it didn't anymore. I was one semester shy of graduating when the bottom fell out. Again.

So I moved to Seattle, because that's where my dad was.

I managed to secure a job and got an apartment on my own. Not a great job, or a great apartment, either, but at least I could afford it without help from my dad. I tried a couple of college programs, but neither of them was a good fit. Even still, I was managing okay on my own until I lost another job, and all my prospects dried up. And now here I am, living in my dad's guesthouse and working as his assistant, until I can figure out what exactly I want to do with my life.

"Should I call you Mr. Masterson, or do you want me to call you Jake?" I ask as we pull out of the sleepy suburbs and head toward the arena.

His brow furrows for what seems like the tenth time this morning. This might be a bit of a rough transition. Sure, I worked for my dad when I was a teenager, running errands and getting coffee, but it's different now. I'm an adult and a woman who should be self-sufficient but am not. Also, as close as we are, my living in his guesthouse and working with him every day might be more than we can both handle.

"That's a joke, right?" he asks, attention shifting back to the road.

"I can't call you Dad in front of your staff and the players."

His hands flex on the steering wheel. "Yeah, you can."

This is *definitely* going to be a rough transition. "How professional will that sound?"

His cheek tics and he sighs. "Fine. Everyone calls me Jake, so I guess you can, too, but only in front of them. Otherwise I'm Dad. For the most part they're nice guys, but a few of them are all over social media for being womanizing assholes."

"Got it. Jake in front of the players and Dad otherwise. Stay away from the womanizing douches."

"Not just the douches. Don't get involved with the players, or the staff," he adds.

"Is that a rule that everyone has to follow or just me?" I'm only sort of being snide.

"It's an unofficial policy, not a rule. We both know how much you love rules." He half smirks.

"Don't worry, Dad, I won't date your players." The last time I dated a hockey player, it blew up in my face. That was years ago, but the experience still haunts me. So much so that I haven't watched the sport since my first year of college.

"It's not you I'm worried about, if I'm totally honest. You're beautiful, just like your mother. Boys couldn't keep their heads around her, and they're exactly the same with you."

I shoot him a glare. "You had to compare me to her, didn't you?"

"I'm sorry. It's not intended as an insult. I didn't mean it in any way other than you got your mother's looks." He gives my shoulder a squeeze.

"I get it. I just wish I had it together." What I really mean is that I wish I were less like my mother in this regard. Looking like her is one thing, but I have far too many of her less-than-awesome personality traits. I seem to have inherited her penchant for poor life choices.

She's always been aimless, flitting from thing to thing, and place to place, and man to man. She was never consistent in my life. But when I was in college in Florida, she wormed her way back in for a short while. She's always had the uncanny ability to get under my skin like a porcupine quill, and no matter how hard I try, I can't seem to get her out.

She was the reason I ended up dropping out in the final semester of my dual major of art and psychology after being told repeatedly—by her—that I was wasting my dad's money on a pointless degree, since I'd never be good enough to get my work into a gallery and I was too fucked up to help people. She told me I'd be better off finding someone who could take care of me. And that was the last time I spoke to her.

I hate that I believed her. I also despise that I did exactly what she said I should: I ran back home and let my dad pick up my pieces. But what's worse is that I've been so afraid that she's right about how screwed up I am that I haven't even tried to finish what I started.

This year I was hoping I could work on some business-related courses, because that sounds practical, but there was a mix-up with my transcript, and by the time the problem got sorted out, I was late applying and ended up on a wait list. My marks are decent, but it's a competitive program, and not exactly what I'm passionate about, so it's probably better that it didn't work out.

"You're only twenty-four," my dad says gently. "You have lots of time to find your passion, Queenie. I don't want you to feel like you have to pursue something because you think it'll get you a job in a better pay grade. The money isn't important. I want you to do what you love, and I'll take care of the rest."

"I wish I knew what that was." I know he means well, and that we've relied on each other for a lot of years, but I don't want my dad to take care of me for the rest of my life like a pampered brat. Besides, he's only forty-four. He has all his hair, he's in great shape, and he's an awesome person with a killer sense of humor. It'd be nice if he could find someone who could appreciate all those things about him, aside from me. Since we spend most nights hanging out, I know he's not actively dating. He doesn't even have an app on his phone.

"You'll figure it out, kiddo, and in the meantime we'll get to spend more time together. It's pretty much a win all the way around, isn't it?"

"Total win, Dad." And I mean it. Mostly. I love spending time with my father. I just worry that working for him isn't going to be quite as easy as we hope.

# CHAPTER 2
## SOMEONE'S BABY GIRL

*Kingston*

"Hey, momster, how's it goin'?"

Hanna chuckles and shakes her head. "Should I start calling you bro-son, or sother?"

"I told you that nickname would grow on you."

"Like mold?"

I pause in my mission to clean my breakfast dishes so I can meet her gaze in the two-dimensional screen. "If it bothers you, I won't call you that anymore, Hanna."

"It doesn't bother me. I actually kind of like it."

"I can hear the *but* in there." I set my cereal bowl in the drying rack.

Morning video chats have become a new part of our routine at least twice a week. It's our way of getting in one-on-one time as we adjust to the new dynamics of our relationship. That's how the therapist put it. Really we're just working out the awkwardness and weirdness of the whole thing. Nothing has changed, but everything has changed.

"We know each other too well." Hanna sighs and sips her coffee. "I just . . . don't want Mom to feel like it makes her role any less important. And I don't know if I deserve a special nickname, all things considered."

"You deserve a lot of things, including a special nickname. We've always been tight, and it doesn't diminish her role in either or both of our lives. It can just be our thing, if that would make you feel better."

She laughs quietly. "Listen to you. Who's the parent and who's the child here? I should be the one giving the support, and more times than not it's you supporting me."

"You had to give up something, though. And I've had two amazing female role models in my life, so for your loss I had a significant gain. How you experience this revelation and how I do are going to be different."

"I know, and like every other situation, you've handled it incredibly well. Anyway, I didn't call to get all philosophical with you about a nickname. I just wanted to wish you good luck this morning. How are you feeling about the beginning of the season?"

I pull the plug and let the sink drain before wiping down the sides with a sponge. "Pretty good. I was a little restless last night, but otherwise fine. I worked out a lot with my teammates this summer, and we've had enough time together that we're smooth on the ice now."

"Your friend and the team captain are still getting along? I know that caused a lot of problems for a while."

"Oh yeah, Bishop and Rook are good. For the most part. I mean, Bishop is always going to be Bishop, so he often misses the concept of tact, but the rivalry on the ice is long over, which is better for the team."

"I'm glad to hear that. I know that kind of thing weighs on you."

"Well, we both know how much I love internal dissension."

We laugh, because I'm 100 percent the guy who addresses an issue as soon as it arises. Hence the reason I put Hanna on a plane the day after I learned that she was my biological mother. We dealt with it together, and then when we were ready—or as ready as we could be—we flew home to Tennessee and dealt with it as a family. Because that's how we've always done things. No point in letting wounds fester. The best way to heal is to get rid of the rot, even if it hurts at first. And this one hurt a lot, although I've done my best not to put that on Hanna.

"How about you? How are you handling everything else?" I'm referencing the divorce, which hasn't been easy for Hanna, especially with my finding out the family secret that our mother had apparently planned to take to the grave. Instead, Hanna's vindictive jerk of an ex-husband took it upon himself to send me the adoption papers citing Hanna as my biological mother.

"I'm okay. Better now that the house is sold and I'm in a new place without my mistakes from the past haunting me on a daily basis."

"Has Gordon backed off? Do you need any more help with the lawyer stuff? Do you want me to come out there? My weekend should be pretty open."

"No, no, you don't need to do that. You're at the start of preseason training, and I'll be flying out in a couple of weeks."

"Are you sure? Family takes precedence. I always have time for you if you need me."

"I appreciate the sentiment, but I've got things handled. Between Mom and Dad, and some work friends who live close by, I've got loads of support. Me and a few girlfriends are planning a rom-com movie night on Saturday, and I know how much you love those."

"Jessica used to get so mad when I'd fall asleep on her." We both chuckle.

"How is Jessica? Are you two still talking, or . . ." She lets it hang.

It's been seven months since I broke things off with Jessica. It wasn't an easy decision to make, but it was necessary. "She calls every once in a while, and we were a part of each other's lives for a long time, so I don't feel like I can cut her out of my life altogether. But I don't think the whole being friends thing is easy on either one of us, since I'm already over it and I don't think she is." We didn't see a lot of each other apart from occasional visits and a few uninterrupted weeks during the off-season. But we've been an integral part of one another's lives for the better part of a decade, and my family has always treated her like a daughter—more than hers ever has—so I understand the challenge that comes with feeling like she's lost more than just a boyfriend.

"Mmm, I think you might be right about that," Hanna agrees.

"What's going on? You're doing that lip-tapping thing." It means she wants to say something but isn't sure if she should or not.

"Mom told me Jessica stopped by more than once with some of your things, but the timing was suspect, since it's been around dinnertime on Sundays."

"Did she stay or drop stuff off and go?"

"You know how Mom is. She's not going to turn her away."

"No. Of course not." I rub the back of my neck. Our mom has always been Team Jessica and wants nothing more than for us to reconcile. "Did Mom say anything else?"

"Just that she seemed to be a little nostalgic. I'm sure she'll move on, though."

"Hopefully they both will," I mutter.

Hanna laughs, but it's a half sigh. She gets what I mean. Our mom is very much about making things work. "You two were together for a lot of years, so it makes sense that she's having trouble letting go. And you know how Mom is. She doesn't love change. Anyway, what about you? Any hot dates lined up?"

"Uh, no. No hot dates. I'm just getting my head back into the hockey season. I don't have much time to dedicate to dating." It's not a complete lie.

My alarm goes off, alerting me that I need to leave in the next ten minutes so I can pick up Bishop and make it to the arena on time. "The team meeting starts in less than an hour, so I gotta run."

"Don't think I don't notice that every single time I bring up your love life you suddenly have somewhere to be."

"I really do have somewhere to be, though."

"I'm just giving you a hard time. Have a great day. I'll talk to you later in the week."

"Sounds good. Message if you need anything."

"I will. I love you, Ry."

"I love you, too, momster." I end the call and stare at the blank screen for a few long seconds, hoping she really is okay, and that our family isn't making this divorce more difficult for her instead of less.

◆ ◆ ◆

Thirty-seven minutes later my teammate and best friend, Bishop Winslow, and I push through the front doors of the arena, ready for the first team meeting of the season. I inhale the familiar scent of cleaning products, rubberized mats, ice, and—no matter how much they bleach—the slightly stale smell of hockey equipment.

"What are the chances that Waters *won't* throw a preseason team party this year?" Bishop asks.

"Slim to none, I'm thinking." I'm not opposed to the preseason party. It's a good way to get to know the new players and catch up with the ones I haven't seen in the off-season in a less formal environment. "It boosts team morale, and the new guys feel more comfortable with the team."

"Why must you always be so damn positive about every fucking thing, King?" Bishop gripes. Bishop is a bit of a pessimist and not much of a people person.

"Because you're negative about everything, and we all need balance in life."

"It's a fucking miracle that I have friends and a wife, isn't it?" He gives me a wry smile.

I clap him on the shoulder and grin. "Not at all. I consider myself one of the lucky few who actually know what's under the surly exterior."

He rolls his eyes and knocks my hand away, but he's still smiling too.

My phone buzzes in my pocket, and I slip it out, checking to see who it is. My family text has twenty-five missed messages—which is not unexpected, since I was driving and everyone is chatty first thing in the morning. There are also three from Jessica.

Bishop glances at the phone and then at me. "Everything okay?"

"Should be. Probably the usual 'Have a good day' stuff." At least, the family group messages should be like that. Every morning at nine my mom—it still freaks me out to think of her as my grandmother—posts her quote of the day, usually taken from her daily "words of inspiration" calendar. My dad—uh, granddad—chimes in with a funny meme, and then we all see if we can post something funnier or mess with Mom's quote.

The messages from Jessica I leave for now, because once I respond there's a chance she'll call. Since I'm going into a team meeting, I won't be able to manage the situation in a sensitive manner should it be necessary. There have been a few occasions in which she's called and then ended up in tears. It can take a while to talk her down, and I don't currently have the kind of time I may need to explain, gently, why our relationship wasn't working for either of us and that getting back together is a bad idea.

"Jessica's still texting you? Is that a regular thing?" Bishop asks, glancing at my phone screen.

I shrug. "She's having trouble letting go."

Bishop blows out a breath. "Dude, if my ex was still messaging me, Stevie would shit a brick."

"I don't have a girlfriend or a wife, though, so I don't have to worry about anyone else's feelings getting hurt."

"Not right now, but you'll have a new girlfriend eventually. How do you think Jessica's going to react when that happens?"

"I don't know. I'm hoping I won't have to deal with that scenario."

Bishop's brow creases. It's not an unusual expression for him to wear. "Are you planning to get back together with her or something?"

"No. Definitely not." Jessica was under the very misguided impression that once we got married I would quit playing professional hockey. When I explained that I would continue with my NHL career for as long as they kept renewing my contract, she got upset, accusing me of putting my career before her.

And in some ways she was right. I had put my career before her. But she hadn't proven to be very supportive over the years, always talking about our life together *after* hockey.

At thirty I have some solid years left in the game. Goalies can have long careers, and I signed on with Seattle for seven years. I won't even be in my midthirties by the time my contract is up for renewal, and as long as I stay in good shape and keep my stats up, I'm hoping for more years after that. I didn't want to continue in a relationship that felt like it was on hold until I was done with hockey, since realistically I can't imagine ever being finished with it. I realized that no matter how much history we had, she was never going to be able to handle my career, so I broke it off.

We arrive at the team meeting room. A catered hot breakfast buffet is spread out along one end of the room. Half our team is already seated at the tables, shoveling food in their faces while they catch up after off-season. Bishop and I grab a plate and load up.

"Shippy, King, have a seat!" Rook Bowman, our team captain, gestures to the two open seats at his table.

"Always with the Shippy bullshit," Bishop mutters.

Bishop and Rook loathed each other with the fire of a thousand burning suns during the team's first season. It got a lot worse when Rook found out Bishop was dating his younger sister. They had it out behind a garbage dumpster—I mediated—and now most of the time they get along.

"Keep calling me Shippy, and I'll tell you all about your sister's favorite positions in the bedroom," Bishop mutters as he takes the seat across from Rook.

Rook half chokes on his sausage link, and Chase, one of our teammates, who's sitting on his other side, gives him a couple of slaps on the back. He waves his hand away and shoots a glare at Bishop. "You wouldn't."

Bishop gives him a *you-try-me* look. "Only your sister is allowed to call me Shippy, so unless you're going to start snuggling with me during movies and fondling my—"

I slap the table to prevent Bishop from finishing that statement. Also, Rook looks like he's about to launch himself over the table. My shirt is white, and I would prefer not to walk around all day with remnants of my breakfast splattered on it.

"It's too early for this nonsense. We don't need the team captain scrapping with teammates on day one in front of the actual rookies." I nod in the direction of two very fresh faces standing by the door, watching their new captain and his brother-in-law get into it. They're too new to know that it's just two guys giving each other the gears. Mostly.

"We're good." Rook shovels in a forkful of scrambled eggs and pushes away from the table. He wipes his mouth with a napkin and tosses it at Bishop before he heads for the new guys.

"Man, I'm glad I don't have to be all friendly and peppy this early in the morning like he does." Bishop picks up a strip of bacon and folds it accordion-style into his mouth.

"I'm not sure peppy is something you could achieve, even if you mainlined energy drinks and ecstasy," I offer.

"Probably not." Bishop looks around the room and tips his chin up. "You think our GM got himself an assistant?"

I follow his gaze to the front of the room. Standing at the desk with her back to us, arranging papers, is a woman with wavy chestnut hair that nearly reaches her waist. "Maybe an intern?"

She's wearing a navy dress that conforms to her very feminine form. I trace the dip of her waist and the curve of her hip, skimming down to where the hem of her dress hits the bend in her knee. Her calves are bare, athletic, and toned, and her heels boast a little bow on the back. Classy, yet sexy. "Possibly."

"I hope the eye candy is gonna be permanent," someone at the table behind us says, loud enough for everyone close by to hear.

"I wouldn't mind if she helped me with my jockstrap," one of the other guys chimes in, eliciting a loud chuckle from the rest of the table.

I glance over my shoulder and pin them with an unimpressed glare. I recognize Foley from Tampa, and Dickerson is an LA trade. They're notorious womanizers. "Watch your mouth and have some respect. That's someone's daughter."

"Take it easy, King. It's not like we'd actually say that to her face," Foley says.

I don't have an opportunity to reprimand him further because the GM, Jake Masterson, and our head coach, Alex Waters, enter the room through the side door. The GM crosses over to the woman, whose back is still turned to us, and he gives her a smile that seems . . . overly warm. He leans in and squeezes her shoulder as he says something with his mouth close to her ear.

"Maybe she's not his assistant. Maybe she's his new girlfriend, 'cause that looks pretty damn friendly to me." Bishop jams a sausage link into his mouth.

"Maybe," I agree.

She turns slightly, giving me a glimpse of her profile. Her cheeks are flushed pink. I blink a couple of times, because she seems incredibly familiar.

"I think I know her," I mumble, more to myself than to Bishop.

"Not as well as our GM does, by the look of things."

It hits me like a puck in the chest without pads on. I do know her. *Queenie.* My one-night stand who bailed the next morning and left a

Post-it and panties hanging from my doorknob. *Destroyed panties.* "Oh God."

*Did I sleep with the GM's girlfriend?* Memories come barreling into my brain, and I want to sink into the floor. My behavior that night was highly atypical. *Everything* about that night was. I chalked it up to the alcohol, the family drama, and the fact that she seemed to be a very eager and willing participant in our adventures. *Do not think about the things you did to her.*

I'd be lying if I said I haven't thought about Queenie and our night together. I've even considered driving by the bar where we met, but I don't know if she's likely to show up there. And it's not as if I can ask the bartender about her without looking like a creep. Besides, if she wanted me to have her number, she would've left it.

"Are you okay? You look like you're about to hurl," Bishop asks.

I cover my mouth with my palm, not because I'm going to be ill but to hide the fact that it's hanging open and I can't seem to close it. Although my stomach is starting to do those awful somersaults that will soon turn into full-on nausea. The kind I used to get when I'd first hit the ice for a game.

This is bad. Really bad. I've never had a one-night stand before. I've always been in committed relationships, and I prefer to get to know my bed partners before they actually get into bed with me. Teen pregnancy was pretty common where I grew up in Tennessee, because there wasn't much else to do apart from playing sports or getting into trouble with drugs and alcohol—my brother, Gerald, went the latter route. I obviously fit into the sports category. By the time I became a teenager, my parents had finally learned their lesson. It was drilled into me to never become that kind of statistic, or to turn my girlfriend into a mom before she was ready to take on more than senior-level algebra.

Ironic how my actual mother would've been one of those girls had my grandparents not made the choices they had.

"King?" Bishop nudges me. "You're staring, man."

Jake whistles with his fingers, causing the woman beside him to cringe but then quickly school her expression into an uncertain smile. "Who's ready for a new season?"

He's rewarded with a chorus of cheers from the players. Waters stands off to the side, clapping enthusiastically. He generally runs all team meetings, but Jake is a hands-on GM, so he always manages first-meeting intros before he hands it over to our coach.

Jake waits for everyone to settle down and take their seats before he continues. "Gentlemen, I'd like to introduce you to my personal assistant, Queenie." He throws his arm over her shoulder and pulls her into his side.

A hot spike of anger rushes down my spine—it's a foreign feeling. I'm usually very levelheaded. But not right now. It's obvious by the way Jake and Queenie interact that there's a relationship there. *Is she a cheater? Did she make me one?* There's a definite age gap. He's young for a GM, but he's in his forties, and I'm pretty sure she's in her midtwenties.

"She also happens to be my daughter, so don't get any ideas, boys." He somehow manages to wink and glare at the same time.

And it just went from bad to worse.

My one-night stand isn't my GM's girlfriend; she's his daughter.

# CHAPTER 3
## I WISH THE FLOOR WOULD
## SWALLOW ME

*Queenie*

This is not happening. I blink several times, hoping that my lack of sleep last night is causing me to hallucinate. It's not.

My hookup from six weeks ago is sitting front and center amid a sea of hockey players.

*What are the freaking chances?*

My mouth is suddenly dry and my nipples harden as the memories wash over me. Such a pretty boy. So nicely dressed, so polite. So very, very respectful. But good God, get that man's clothes off and get him into a bed, and it's a whole different story. One I'd like to write a few more chapters in, or maybe an entire novel—a long one. I took the Boy Scout out of the polo and unleashed a very dirty man.

Based on his wide-eyed, horror-struck expression, he's as shocked to see me as I am to see him.

For the past six weeks I've replayed that night, and the following morning, in my head. I can't believe I left a Post-it and my destroyed panties behind. I wonder if he threw them out. Or kept them.

I wonder if he was as disappointed as I was that I didn't bother to leave a number. I still have his address, thanks to the Uber ride from his place to the diner my dad and I frequent every single Saturday.

The father who I now work for.

Who manages this guy's team.

Who told me not to get involved with any of the players. It's day one, and I've already inadvertently gone against the one request he made.

This isn't a great situation, and, based on how pale Ryan's face has gone, I'm thinking he feels exactly the same way.

I'm so stunned I forget to be embarrassed about the fact that my dad pulled the father card in front of the entire team.

"Queenie?"

I drag my gaze away from my one-night stand—I've been staring at him—and give my attention to my dad. I smile questioningly. "Yes, Jake?"

His right eye twitches, like he has something in it. But he doesn't. It means he's irritated, likely because I'm calling him by his first name, and there's some annoyance in my tone. I'm sure I also appear mortified, but not for the reason he probably thinks.

He passes me a stack of folders. "Can you hand these out, please?"

I want to say no, because that means I'll have to make some kind of purposeful eye contact with Ryan. But since I'm my father's assistant, my role is literally to do every single menial task that could potentially distract him from anything important. Which means I get the job of handing things out to the team, and collecting them and filing them. Riveting work, really.

If I'd been on the ball this morning, which I was not, I would've had the forms already set on the tables to make it easier on myself and the players. And then I could avoid some up close and personal embarrassment.

"Of course." I take the folders with clammy hands and start on the left side of the room, setting one in front of each player. I get a lot of mumbled *thanks* and brief, uncomfortable smiles.

Maybe my dad was right about the dress not being the best idea. Most of these guys are wearing some kind of casual pants and T-shirts. A few wear jeans. Ryan has on a pair of gray casual pants and a white polo. I try to keep my breathing even and a smile plastered on my face as I hand him a folder. We make eye contact. My nipples harden further. Thank God I'm wearing a padded bra.

His lips part and his tongue peeks out to wet the bottom one. I remember, very, very vividly, how it felt to have that tongue circling my bare nipple, among other places. Some kind of sound, halfway between a groan and a sigh, slips out of my mouth.

His eyes widen and his cheeks flush. I'm still holding the folder, and he's trying to free it from my hand. All of this takes place over a few short seconds, but I feel like there's a spotlight on us and that every single person can read the thoughts in my head.

His deep, rich voice feels like a caress between my thighs when he murmurs thank you. I'm about to step away when his fingers wrap around my wrist to stop me from moving on. His hand is just as big, warm, and rough as I remember. I don't expect the contact, so I jolt and nearly lose my hold on a few of the folders.

He releases my wrist. "You dropped something." He leans down and picks up a piece of paper. I have no idea what I could've possibly dropped, since all I'm holding are folders. He slips the fallen piece of paper into my hand and mumbles something about needing to talk. I give him a strained smile before I move to the next table.

He's certainly right about the talking part, but there's no way it's going to happen in a roomful of his teammates with my dad watching.

During the meeting—which lasts a good two hours—I find out my hookup's last name is Kingston and he's the team goalie. That certainly explains his incredible flexibility. It would be fantastic if I could stop thinking about the time we spent together while naked.

After the meeting there's a team workout led by the coach, Alex Waters. He appears to be younger than my dad, by five years or so if I had to guess. He's built the same as the hockey players and looks like he should be an underwear model or something.

I don't have a chance to check the piece of paper Ryan gave me—or "King," as everyone else seems to call him, including my father—because I'm too busy trying to decipher the players' barely legible handwriting. Except for Ryan's, which is ridiculously neat.

I don't even have time to look Ryan up on social media because I'm too busy transcribing notes, making copies, and getting my father coffee. By five I've decided I need to wean him down to fewer than six cups a day, or at least alternate between decaf and caffeinated since he drinks so much of it. And I'm going to try to switch out the cream for milk to save his poor arteries.

I set the one-sugar, one-cream coffee on his desk. "Can I get you anything else?"

He peers over the frames of his reading glasses—they're new, and he hates them. "I think I'm good for now. You did a great job today, Queenie. You should be proud of yourself."

I feel like a glorified lackey in a pretty dress, but I appreciate his trying to make me feel good with the compliment. "Thanks, Dad."

He smiles and taps the end of his pen on the desk. "I've got another hour or so of paperwork to finish up, but you can head out if you want."

"I can wait; it's not a big deal." I'll just internet stalk my hookup.

"No point in you hanging around for nothing. You can take an Uber, and I'll meet you at home."

"Sure. Okay. That sounds good."

I leave my dad to his paperwork, quickly tidy my desk, order an Uber, and head for the front doors of the arena. It's quiet in the building, the team workout long over, and most of the administrative staff have already left.

The car is already waiting for me, so I slip into the back seat. Uber Man is super chatty. I *Mm-hmm* and make other affirmative sounds while he regales me with his plan to open up his street-taco shop. At least he has a dream and a plan to go after it. By the time he drops me off at the house, I'm craving tacos.

I walk around the side of the house and down the short path to the guesthouse, which is a one-bedroom miniature bungalow—it's three times as big as my previous apartment and much, much nicer. Not that I need the space, or the luxury. In fact, I'd trade it in a heartbeat if it meant I'd be more self-sufficient and would have a real direction in life. At least my dad is understanding, and he likes having me around.

As soon as I'm inside my apartment, I flip open my planner and retrieve the piece of paper Ryan gave me this morning. It's actually a grocery receipt. I get caught up in scanning the items he purchased. *Four gallons of milk?* Geez, he must really love dairy.

I flip it over and scan the rushed but neat writing on the back. Receipt paper is notorious for smudging, and my hands were clammy when I took this from him, so the ink is smeared across the white paper, making it difficult to read. I think it says *Please call me*, and there's a phone number, but I can't tell if the second number is a three or a six or a nine, or what.

I drop down on the couch and squint at the receipt some more. I definitely need to figure out how to handle this. The last thing I want is my dad finding out I messed around with one of these guys, when he specifically asked me not to.

I exhale a long breath and watch the ceiling fan spin for a minute. How the hell am I going to see this guy every single day and *not* think about all the amazing things he did to my body?

# CHAPTER 4
## CREEPING CREEPER

*Kingston*

"I think it might be better for both of us if we didn't talk for a while."
I cringe and turn down the volume as Jessica's sob comes through the
surround sound. I've been sitting in my car for the past hour. At first I
was waiting for Queenie to leave the arena, but Jessica called, so now
I'm trying to explain, again, why her texting me every day isn't in either
of our best interests.

"D-d-don't you still care about me?" she says between sobs.

"Of course I still care, Jessica, but this is making it impossible for
either of us to move on."

My response is followed by more sobbing. I spend the next ten
minutes trying to reassure her that it's not her, it's me, and that not
talking for a while doesn't mean we'll never speak again. I'm so busy
talking her down from the emotional ledge that I nearly miss Queenie
leaving for the day.

As it is, I watch her get into an Uber. I don't want to wait until
tomorrow to talk to her, so I hastily end the call with Jessica and follow
the Uber, hoping I can catch her. I have to drive over the speed limit
and run a couple of stale yellows to avoid losing her.

Based on the neighborhood, and the direction we're headed, I have a feeling she might live with her dad. I've been to Jake's a couple of times for team get-togethers over the years. He lives on the corner, so I pass the driveway and make a right before parking on the street at the side of the house.

Jake is still at the arena, although I have no idea how far behind Queenie he'll be, so I need to make a move. I wipe my sweaty palms on my thighs and cut the engine. After stepping out of the vehicle, I round the corner and knock on the front door, then ring the doorbell, but no one answers. It's a nice day, so maybe she's outside.

I have limited options, so I follow the driveway to the back of the house, past the detached garage, and down a short path that leads to a quaint bungalow. Beyond that is an Olympic-size pool.

My phone buzzes in my pocket, scaring the crap out of me, and I nearly stumble into a rosebush. I check to see if maybe it's Queenie messaging, finally, but it's Hanna. While I'm generally pretty open with her about things, I never mentioned my one-night stand, and I've been avoiding the family chat today because I'm freaked out. I'm sure she's noticed.

I tuck my phone back in my pocket and knock on the door of the bungalow. After thirty seconds, no one answers, so I knock a second time but still get nothing. Maybe she's by the pool. I round the back of the bungalow. A small table and a pair of lounge chairs are arranged close to the back door.

I scan the pool area, but it's empty of Queenie. She has to be inside.

I approach the back door and have to step over a potted plant and some empty containers. I open the screen door, which groans on its hinges, and knock for the third time. Curtains cover the windows, but there's a small gap in the gauzy fabric, allowing me an inadvertent glimpse inside.

The floor plan is open concept, so I can see from one end of the small bungalow to the other. The place is messy, dishes littering the counter, clothes layered over chairs. In one corner of the kitchen is an easel draped with a paint-streaked white sheet.

I'm poised to knock again, when Queenie appears in the narrow gap. Between one blink and the next the pretty navy dress she was wearing today slips over her shoulders, exposing her bra straps. *She's undressing in the middle of her living room.*

I take a quick step back, aware this is a horrible invasion of privacy. I trip over a ceramic flowerpot and stumble into one of the lounge chairs. It tips over, landing on the stone patio with a loud crash.

I freeze as the curtain is yanked open. One of her arms is barred across her chest, covering most of her bra and her cleavage. Most, but not all. The top half of her dress hangs loose around her waist. It takes an incredible amount of willpower to keep my eyes from dipping down, away from her face.

Queenie's gorgeous wide eyes meet mine through the glass. Her perfectly shaped eyebrows pull down and then shoot up. "What the fuck?" Her voice is slightly muffled through the glass, but I can still hear her as clearly as I can see her.

The curtain drops, and her form moves away from the window. I hope she doesn't call the police on me.

"Queenie?" I knock on the window and whisper-yell. "I'm sorry. It's not what it looks like!"

A few seconds later the lock clicks. The storm door flies open as Queenie appears, again. "So you weren't watching me get undressed?"

"I knocked a bunch of times, but you didn't answer. I didn't know you were getting changed. I'm sorry." I've raised a hand to cover my eyes when she lowers the arm barred across her chest. I'm not quite fast enough, so I catch a glimpse of pink lace cups before my hand is in place and my lids are closed.

Several very long seconds later, she tugs on the back of my hand. I allow it to drop but keep my eyes closed. "Are you decent?"

"You didn't seem to be too worried about my decency when you were peeking in my window."

"It was an accident. And you were changing in your living room."

"Usually there aren't random hockey players spying on me. And you can open your eyes."

I crack a lid, relieved to find she's wearing a wrinkled tank top. "I'm so—"

"Sorry, yeah. You keep saying that. What're you doing here?"

"I followed you home." That sounds far worse coming out of my mouth than the actual act of tailing her felt while I was doing it. "I mean, I waited for you in the parking lot, but you got into the Uber before I could catch you. We need to talk. I promise I'm not a stalker."

She rubs the space between her eyes, but after a few seconds she steps back. "Well, come in then."

I cross the threshold and find myself submerged in her scent. It's a combination of a subtle floral perfume, lotion, and her vanilla shampoo. My sheets held that combination after she spent the night. In my bed. Naked. With me. *Which I need to stop thinking about.*

Her dress is still hanging off her hips. She crosses over to a small dining table and grabs a pair of shorts draped over the back of one of the chairs. I avert my eyes again as she pulls the shorts up her legs. She tugs the dress past her hips, and it drops to the floor. Queenie steps out of the puddle of fabric, nabs it from the floor, and tosses it over the back of the chair. Maybe she doesn't own a laundry hamper.

"So . . . I didn't know you were a hockey player."

"I wouldn't have brought you home if I'd known you were Jake's daughter." I cringe. "I don't bring girls home. Women, I mean. Especially not when we're under the influence and not thinking clearly. It wasn't . . . I'm not . . . I don't—"

She raises her hand, and I take it as a signal to shut up, which is probably a good idea since everything coming out of my mouth seems to be making this worse instead of better. "I don't need you to apologize or justify your actions. I don't usually hook up with random guys, either, so we have that in common. Is it awkward that my dad is essentially both of our bosses? Yeah, but neither of us knew that until today."

"He lives there." I thumb over my shoulder to the main house. It has zero relevance to our current discussion, but it's what popped into my head and consequently came out of my mouth.

"Uh, yeah. I can't afford a place like this on an assistant's salary." She blows out a breath. "He won't be home for a while, though, and we don't talk about my sex life, so you don't need to worry about him murdering you or anything."

"That's good. That he's not home, and that he's not going to murder me for the things I did to your body. To you." I wish I could stop saying the first thing that comes to mind. Another inconvenient memory surfaces: me on my knees between Queenie's spread legs, warm and wet and—I slap a palm over my mouth to prevent me from saying anything further.

But then I remember I didn't find any condom wrappers the next morning.

"We didn't use protection."

# CHAPTER 5
## DIRTY BOY SCOUT

*Queenie*

Ryan, or King, or Kingston, or whatever people call him, looks absolutely horrified. And ridiculously hot, but mostly horrified.

"I'm sorry, what?" I ask, because whatever he said came out all garbled and unintelligible.

He drops his hand. "A condom? Did we use one?"

"Seriously?" I don't know whether he's joking or not.

"I didn't find any the next morning. Used ones, I mean. There were two on the nightstand, still unopened. Oh God." He grabs the back of his neck and paces the length of the kitchen. His face is the color of a beet. "I'm never this irresponsible. Ever. Or do the one-night-stand thing. That's not how I operate. I date." He stops pacing for half a second, eyes flaring even wider, if that's possible. "What's wrong with me? I didn't even buy you dinner."

"You bought me a lot of drinks."

"That's even worse!" Now his hands are in his hair, messing up his perfect part. "Have you gotten your period since we . . . were together?" He doesn't give me time to respond, instead barreling on with more questions. "Should we go get tested for . . . things? I mean . . . I'm clean and I'm not saying that you're not, but just . . . it would be a good idea for peace of mind, don't you think? I can take us to a clinic that will be discreet. We could see the team doctor."

I hold up a hand. "There is no way I'm going to the team doctor to be tested for *things*. Besides, we didn't have sex."

He ceases his relentless pacing and stops in front of me. He's a big man. Broad, with thick shoulders and bulging biceps, ropy veins lining his forearms. I remember what it was like to have him between my thighs, one hand cupping my ass to tilt my hips up, the other cupping a breast so he could thumb my nipple while he licked and nibbled and sucked me to orgasm. More than once. Ryan Kingston is very, very skilled at oral and very, very giving. So giving.

"We didn't?"

I can't decide if his apparent relief should offend me. "No." Although we got close—very close. Closer than we should have without a condom on. And we sure as hell covered every other conceivable foreplay option available, multiple times.

My lady parts clench at the memory of how unreal his stamina was that night. They also seem unaware that his proximity does not mean it's going to happen again. It can't. No matter how much I might want it to.

His brow furrows. Even that expression is fairly adorable on his distressed, pretty face. "But I remember . . ." He trails off.

"You remember what?" He was definitely far more intoxicated than I was, although I can admit now that I was tipsier than is generally safe when out alone with a strange man. And while parts of that night are fuzzy—like the last shot we did and the glasses of water we chugged—most of what happened between and on top of his sheets is not.

"I was . . . we were . . ." He's back to pacing. "You were under me, weren't you?" His eyes move over me, causing my already alert nipples to peak.

"That's correct." Our eyes lock, and some weird energy passes between us. "I was under you."

"We were naked." His voice is gravelly and low.

"Very naked, yes." And I sound like I'm ready to get naked all over again.

If he weren't a hockey player on my dad's team, I wouldn't be opposed. But he is. The level of complication is too high, and engaging in additional foreplay activities will not make this bad situation we're in any better. No matter how good it will feel.

This is my internal argument as I hold on to the counter behind me to keep from doing something like grabbing the front of his shirt and biting his neck. He really liked that. A lot.

His brow creases again. He seems so confused.

"How much do you actually remember?" I ask.

"Uh, bits and pieces of everything? I think . . . apart from the sex, which you're saying we didn't have?" It's more question than statement.

"Not technically, no," I explain.

He takes a step closer, bringing him inside my personal-space bubble. I have nowhere to go, since I'm pressed up against the counter. I inhale, getting a whiff of his cologne and his deodorant. "What does that mean, 'not technically'?"

Oh God, when he said we needed to talk, I didn't think he meant rehashing all the down and dirty. "Well, uh . . . you went down on me—"

"I remember that." He rubs his bottom lip, like maybe he's recalling it in vivid detail.

"Do you remember what happened after that?" I have to tip my head back to look at him because he's so close.

"I made you come with my mouth."

"And your fingers."

"And my fingers." He nods his agreement. "You seemed to enjoy that quite a bit."

Oh, Jesus. Here he goes again with his color commentary on my reaction to his foreplay skills. "I did. Like it, I mean. A lot."

"So did I." His tongue drags across his bottom lip. "But it gets murky for me after that."

It's definitely not murky for me. He'd prowled his way back up my body. Kissing bare skin, stopping at my nipples on the way back up to my mouth. He'd wanted to kiss me so I'd know *what it was like for him to have me in his mouth and down his throat.* A warm shiver works its way along my spine and pings around between my thighs at that lovely memory. He'd propped his huge body up on one forearm so we could make out while he fondled my boob.

I'd been the one to wrap my legs around his waist. I'd also adjusted my position so our sex parts could line up and we could achieve some mutual friction. Was it the smartest thing I'd ever done? Definitely not. Did it feel really good? Hell to the fuck yes.

"We wet humped," I explain.

"'Wet humped'?"

"Yeah, you know, like when you were a teenager, you'd dry hump someone through their clothes, but if you do it with the absence of clothing it's considered wet humping."

"Did we almost . . ." He trails off, as if he might be finally remembering that part of the night.

"You slipped low once."

"Yes. I did. By accident."

We nod at the same time, both of us obviously mentally taking a trip down wet-hump memory lane. The feel of his shaft gliding over my clit. Our lips brushing as he rolled his hips. His heavy groan when the head nudged my entrance and slipped inside, just the tip.

We'd both stilled for a moment, clearly aware that it wasn't a good idea, or safe, but it had felt really good. He'd rushed to correct himself, and that was the point where he told me that as much as he wanted to have sex with me, he didn't think it was a good idea because we were both still under the influence, and he didn't want either of us to regret it. Or not remember it. It was incredibly sweet.

So instead we wet humped the living hell out of each other, several times.

We're both breathing heavily, kind of like we were that night.

His expression becomes horror struck again. "Did I come *on* you?"

I can feel the heat in my cheeks. "On my stomach, yeah." I motion a little higher. "And my chest."

His eyes slide closed, and he shakes his head. "Good Lord. I am so sorry."

"Why are you apologizing? You were pretty into it, and so was I."

"It's not normally something I would do."

"Me, either, but I had fun, and I'm pretty sure you did too." Sadly, it's the only fun time we'll ever get to have.

His face turns a more vibrant shade of red, which is impressive, considering how red it already was. "But you left."

"I was late for a thing with my dad. We always go for a run on Saturday mornings, and then we have brunch together. He was worried, and you and I had agreed the night before that we weren't making this a thing, so . . ."

He jams a hand in his pocket. "So it had nothing to do with my performance?"

"No. Your stamina is legendary and your performance was exemplary. You probably devoted a good hour or more to providing oral pleasure, which is more than I can say for any guy I've ever been with before." I need to stop talking; instead I keep rambling, trying to erase the concerned look on his gorgeous face. "Plus, I came a million times, and we didn't even have sex. And you needed almost zero recovery time before you were ready to go again." I stupidly motion to his crotch, drawing attention to it. I also happen to notice that the fabric is tight there—indicating this conversation might be making him as excited as it's making me, based on the hardness of my nipples and the very noticeable ache between my thighs.

Not that I'm going to do anything about it, even though I kind of want to. Okay, I definitely want to.

"That's good. About my performance, I mean. And having legendary stamina." One side of his mouth quirks up, the first hint of a smile since I caught him lurking outside my window. "You were great too."

"Thanks?" I'm not sure if he's tacked on the compliment just because.

"I've thought about your mouth a lot since that night."

I'm not sure if he's referencing my blow job skills or what. "That's . . . good."

"My ex-girlfriend wouldn't do that . . ." He cringes and trails off.

"Whoa, wait. She wouldn't do what?"

"Uh." He motions to his crotch, which is kind of hilarious, since he's very much a graphic talker when he's getting down and dirty. Politely graphic, though. "Use her mouth on me." He mumbles the last part, so it's hard to hear.

"Your ex wouldn't blow you?"

He jams one hand in his pocket and rubs the back of his neck with the other. "She had a sensitive gag reflex."

"Did she even try?"

"Like, once or twice. It wasn't . . . enjoyable for either of us."

"I guess that relationship didn't last long, huh?"

His cheeks puff out. "Uh, actually we were together for a long time."

I'm totally enthralled with the turn this conversation has taken. "How long is a long time?" I dated a guy for almost a year once, and it was on and off during that time. It was during college, when I also almost completed my art degree.

"Around eight years."

I'm very glad I'm not drinking anything; as it is, I almost choke on my own spit. "You went *eight years* without a blow job?"

"Sorry. I probably shouldn't have told you that."

I wave away the apology. My curiosity about this guy has shot up several levels. That chick must have really had him by the balls for him to go without oral for that long. "I mean, I guess I can see how she might've been a little overwhelmed, because you've got a lot going on in that department." I gesture to his crotch again. "But it's not like you'd try to force the whole thing down her throat without some baby steps first."

I fight a smirk because I rocked the hell out of deep throating all that length and girth, and it's a significant amount of both. My nosiness takes over, and I can't seem to control the questions that come out of my mouth. "Did she even like, lick it? Kiss it? Suck on the head, at least?"

Kingston blinks several times in a row and then swallows thickly. "Uh, no. She didn't."

"Wow." She seems like a prissy bitch. I don't like her. All she had to do was lollipop it, even if she couldn't get more than the head in. Mostly I think it's an excuse not to be a giver. I keep that to myself, though, in case he's the kind of guy who stays friends with his exes. For some reason that makes me jealous. I'm just a notch on his blow job bedpost. "How long have you two been broken up?"

"Um, more than half a year." He shifts around, like maybe this is making him uncomfortable.

"So you've had lots of time to make up for all those missed BJs, then." I'm being tongue in cheek. He's a hockey player, a professional one, although maybe not super high profile, considering I had no idea who he was until today. Granted, my dad offered me the job two days ago, right after I got passed over for yet another service industry opportunity, so I didn't have much time to prepare, or to study the members of the team. Also, I've been avoiding hockey since my first year of college, not because I hate the sport but because of the memories I associate with it.

"You're the first. Since college."

"You're shitting me, right?"

"Uh, no."

"Wow. I hope I did okay, then."

"You did better than okay. You were amazing. It was . . . I haven't been able to stop thinking about it." He turns his head and coughs.

"Me, either, if I'm being completely honest."

"I wish you weren't related to Jake." Ryan's voice is gritty and low.

"If you didn't play hockey for the team my dad manages, I would totally get on my knees for you again." I need to cut this honesty crap. I still feel bad for the poor guy. Being in a relationship for almost a decade with a woman who refused to blow him is reprehensible, really.

Ryan makes a sound somewhere between a groan and a growl. He's so close I can feel his breath caress my cheek. I'm half-afraid and half-hopeful he's going to try to kiss me. I don't think I'd have the willpower to stop him if he did, and I'm banking on his Boy Scout morals to keep that from happening.

I settle a palm on his chest to keep him from getting closer. "Ryan."

"It's King, or Kingston."

"You introduced yourself as Ryan."

"Only my parents call me Ryan." He covers my hand with his, and a warm shiver trickles down my spine as the hair on his arms stands on end. "Do you feel that?"

"Feel what?" My whole body is on alert.

"The same thing happened last time. Like there's electricity in the air."

My phone buzzes on the counter behind me, startling us both. His eyes flare and he raises both hands, stepping back so we're no longer touching each other.

"It's your dad," he croaks. "What the heck is wrong with me? I shouldn't be here. With you. Alone. Unsupervised."

I put a finger to my lips, clear my throat, and answer the call. "Hey, Dad, what's up?"

"I'm on my way home now. I figured we could go out for dinner, celebrate your first day." A horn honks in the background.

"Or you could pick up takeout on the way home." I glance at Kingston, who's standing frozen a few feet away.

"I made a reservation at our favorite place for seven, but I can cancel if you'd rather I pick something up." I detect disappointment over that possibility.

"How close to home are you?"

"About' five minutes away."

"I guess I better get ready, then." And get Kingston the hell out of here.

"Sounds good. See you soon."

He ends the call, and I drop the phone on the counter. "My dad will be home in five minutes."

"I need to leave. Your dad can't find me here." Kingston takes a step toward me and then backs up again. "I'm so sorry. I just wanted to talk things out. I didn't mean to get all up in your personal space, or make you rehash our night together."

"Why don't we just forget any of it ever happened?" I'm trying to give us both an out.

"Forget it happened?" He frowns.

I lift one shoulder in what I hope is a nonchalant shrug. "It was meant to be a one-off, right? Besides, it's kind of a bad idea to get involved with a guy from the team my dad manages, you know?" I don't want to open up a can of worms we might not be able to close if we allow ourselves to indulge in activities we shouldn't. Kind of like the way addicts always say "Just one more hit," I think Ryan Kingston could be my drug of choice.

"I don't know that I'm going to be able to forget that night, but you're right: it's best if we keep it platonic."

That bolsters my ego a little. "Shake on it?" I hold my hand out.

Slowly he clasps my hand in his much larger one. "We keep it platonic."

"Deal."

He's still holding my hand, eyes locked on my face. Actually they're locked on my lips.

I hear a crunch and the low hum of bass, which tells me a car has pulled into the driveway. "My dad's home."

"Oh crap. I really gotta go." Kingston yanks me forward. I stumble and plaster my hands on his solid chest. I can feel his heart beating a staccato rhythm. His lips brush my cheek. "I promise I'll do my best to keep it strictly platonic."

He disappears out the back door before I can say anything else.

# CHAPTER 6

## STRIDES

*Queenie*

Things I have discovered over the course of the last few days: my dad loves paper and forms. I've also learned how to decipher the nearly illegible handwriting of nearly thirty players. I glance at Bishop Winslow's paperwork—I'm almost at the end of the list, thank baby Jesus riding a freaking unicorn—and try to figure out what the hell he wrote in response to a rather arbitrary question pertaining to the off-season workouts. I'm pretty sure it's pithy and a sexual innuendo, but I can't be sure because his handwriting is atrocious.

A knock drags my tired eyes away from the form. It's almost five, and I'm determined to finish inputting all this stuff before I leave for the day.

"Uh, hi, Queenie." Kingston is standing in the middle of the doorway, thumbs hooked into the pockets of his khakis, eyes bouncing all over the room, pausing at the open door to my dad's office and then shifting back to me.

"Hi, Kingston. Did you need to see Jake?"

"Jake?" He blinks a few times, as if he's never heard the name before. "Oh, uh, no. I don't need to . . . there's a delivery." He thumbs over his shoulder, and a guy whose head barely reaches Kingston's shoulder comes into view.

Every interaction with Kingston since the first day has been awkward, to say the least. I'd be offended, but I honestly think he doesn't know how to deal with this situation any better than I do.

The delivery guy squeezes past Kingston, who takes up the majority of the doorway with his broad shoulders, and holds out his electronic device and a stylus. "I just need you to sign here."

"Are these the tablets I ordered?" I ask as I take the stylus from him and sign my name.

"Sure are. You ordered a lot of 'em." He glances at my nameplate poised on the corner of my desk. "Queenie, is it?"

"That's right."

"Beautiful name for a beautiful woman."

"All right, well, thanks so much. I can take it from here," Kingston says loudly and then drops a huge box on my desk, very close to the delivery guy's pinkie. When the delivery guy doesn't make a move to leave, Kingston says, "Have a nice day." Following it with a fake-looking, close-lipped smile.

The delivery guy gives me a nod and Kingston the side-eye as he leaves the office.

I'd call him out on whatever that was, but I'm too excited about the delivery to care. I open my desk drawer and rummage around for a pair of scissors.

"How do you find anything in there?" Kingston leans on the box while I sift through the contents of the drawer.

"It's my miscellaneous drawer."

"It's a mess."

"Me and the drawer have a lot in common," I mutter, and I finally find what I'm looking for. "Aha!" I produce a pair of craft scissors better suited for a five-year-old, but they'll have to do. I elbow Kingston out of the way—he's still hanging off the box—and attempt to use the cut-proof scissors to break through the tape. Unfortunately it's completely ineffective, so I resort to picking at the edge. Sadly, I've been anxious lately—see the guy standing next to me, watching me fight to get into a cardboard box, for details—so I've been picking at my nails, and they're pretty much stubs.

"Can I offer my assistance?" Sitting in Kingston's palm is a utility knife.

"Why am I not the least bit surprised that you have one of those?" I nab it from his palm, then fight to get the blade out, because again, nail stubs aren't great for traction. I finally manage to get it open and cut through the tape securing the box. I open the flaps and sift through the packing peanuts, grabbing hold of one of the packages. Styrofoam peanuts litter my desk as I pull the box free and squeal with excitement. "You are going to save my eyeballs and my sanity!" I kiss the package and hug it to my chest.

Kingston's deep chuckle reminds me that I'm not alone, and that he's just witnessed me talking to and kissing an inanimate object. I glance his way, ready to give him a little sass, but the words get stuck in my throat.

Because he's full-on smiling, and it's ridiculously beautiful. Particularly because there's a tiny chip out of the corner of his front tooth, and for some reason, that slight imperfection is incredibly endearing. And sexy.

Of course, this is the very moment that a highly inconvenient memory also surfaces. One where he was wearing the same smile. Because he managed to give me not one, but three consecutive orgasms with his incredibly competent mouth.

Our gazes lock, and it feels like some kind of magnetic field prevents us from looking away. His smile fades and his tongue peeks out, skimming the imperfect tooth.

"Is everything okay out here? I thought I heard—oh, Kingston, hi." My dad breaks the spell. "What's this?" He motions to the giant box taking up more than half my desk.

"So, remember the other day, when I was asking you about the technology budget?"

"Uhhhh . . ."

"You said you had no idea and that I should ask Alex," I remind him. I also asked when he was clearly in the middle of something, on purpose.

"That sounds about right."

"Well, turns out we have a pretty sizable technology budget, and Alex has all kinds of connections because of all of his previous endorsement campaigns, so I managed to get a set of tablets for the entire team at a highly discounted price. All we have to do is tag the company in a few social media posts. Isn't that awesome?"

"Um, yes?" My dad rubs the back of his neck and glances at Kingston, as if he's going to help out here. "Why exactly do we need a set of tablets for the whole team?"

"Because you're using entirely too much paper. It's like a tree graveyard in your office, and every time we have a meeting I have to make four million copies. Also, these guys have worse penmanship than a class of preschoolers." I turn to Kingston. "Except you. Your handwriting is extremely legible."

"Thanks." He grins again, and my brain shorts out for a second.

"You're welcome," I finally whisper-breathe. "Anyway, once I get all the documents on file as PDFs, they'll be able to complete the forms via tablet, and I won't have to manually input anything, which will free up my time, save my sanity, and preserve at least one forest somewhere. See why I'm so excited?"

"This seems like a lot of work, and won't you have to teach everyone how to use them? And me? I'll have to learn how to do all that stuff." I can see that my dad's starting to panic.

"I promise it'll be simple, and I'll give you a tutorial. I can even make a video for the guys. I'll walk you through the whole process. You're working with a bunch of kinesthetic learners, and this helps make everything accessible and interactive."

"It's actually a great idea," Kingston chimes in. I'm not sure if he's trying to save my ass, or he really thinks it's a great idea, but I appreciate the support.

"I'm sure Lou-Ellen was a great assistant, and I know she was lovely, but you're still stuck in 1999, and the rest of the world is two decades ahead of you. I know it seems like a lot, but honestly, I'm about to make your life a hell of a lot easier."

"Okay." My dad blows out a breath and nods. "If you think this is going to make things easier, then I'm game, as long as it doesn't interfere with any of your other duties."

"It won't. I promise."

He looks to Kingston. "Did you need to see me?"

"Oh, no, sir. I was helping Queenie. I should head out." He thumbs over his shoulder and takes a step toward the door. "I'll see you tomorrow. At practice. Have a nice night. Bye, Queenie." He awkward waves, his face having turned bright red once again, and darts down the hall.

My dad cocks a brow. "He seems smitten with you."

I snort laugh; it's a horrible sound. "He's like a poster boy for the Boy Scouts of America. I think a Girl Scout leader would be more his type."

"Opposites attract." He shrugs, maybe trying to come across as nonchalant, but I know my dad, and I can tell he's fishing.

"Are you saying I couldn't be a Girl Scout leader?"

"You're more suited to the rebel faction, I think." He grins and I laugh.

He's not wrong. "Well, he seems like a rule follower, and you made it pretty clear that I'm off limits, so I don't think you have anything to worry about with Kingston." It's me he should be concerned about, because as much as we might be mutually off limits, there's clearly an attraction we're both fighting. Kingston seems a lot more capable of keeping himself in check than I am.

# CHAPTER 7

## DODGE AND WEAVE

*Queenie*

Over the next couple of weeks I settle into a routine. In the morning I make eggs and avocado toast for me and my dad, which we eat while we review the schedule for the day.

I write a lot of memos, arrange meetings, answer emails, and study team statistics whenever I have a little downtime. Having completed almost all the required courses for a psych degree, I've taken stats, and it's something I actually enjoy and excel at, so analyzing numbers is fun for me.

And it's so much easier now that I've moved everything over to digital. I still make my dad paper copies, but at least we're only killing a few trees and not an entire forest. He was reluctant at first, but when he realized how much more streamlined everything became, he finally relented. It's made my job so much easier, and it means I can focus on something other than endless paperwork.

Since I'm fully immersed in the world of hockey and everything that entails, I've also observed preseason training camp several times. Watching those guys in action gives me a renewed respect for how hard they push themselves physically. It explains Kingston's exceptional stamina and flexibility.

And so far we've got the awkward platonic thing down. He's always polite, always appropriate, and always red faced when I run into him.

I'd like to say I give him a wide berth as a result, but that would be untrue. In fact, I derive perverse enjoyment from watching him flounder and splutter every time we cross paths, because it's so very different from how he was that night we spent together. I can't figure out which version is authentic, or if it's both.

Today the team has on-ice practice, so I pack up my laptop and the notes for a memo I'm drafting, as well as the schedule of events for the next month. We'll be heading into exhibition games soon. I also get to watch Kingston tend goal without being obvious about it. It's a win all the way around.

The patter of little feet and the high-pitched excited voice of my favorite toddler grabs my attention. I glance over at the bench and smile as Rook smothers his son's face in sweaty kisses. Bowman's sister, Stevie, has stopped by a bunch of times over the past two weeks. She's hard to miss with her pale-blue hair. She's always been friendly and chatty with me, and she's easy to talk to.

"Daddy! No!" Kody pushes on his father's cheeks, but he's giggling.

Stevie, who also happens to be Bishop Winslow's wife—there are some interesting dynamics with these players—gives her attention to Bishop. He pulls her in for a kiss that isn't quite PG. She does the same thing Kody did to Bowman, pushing away while laughing.

"Stop mauling my sister, Winslow!" Bowman gripes.

"I'm not mauling her. I'm saying hi to my wife." Bishop smirks and winks at Stevie.

Bowman sets Kody down, and the moment the kid sees me, his eyes light up. Kody bounces up the stairs and clomp-run-hops excitedly over to me.

Kingston, who's been a silent observer thus far, glances over his shoulder, watching Kody bumble toward me. Our gazes meet briefly, and the corner of his mouth quirks up before he turns away. And like every other time we make eye contact, a flush creeps up the back of his neck and travels to the tip of his ears.

"Keenie!" Kody climbs into the chair beside mine and stands on the seat so he can hug me. He really is the cutest kid. He has his mother's dark hair but his father's eyes and the signature Bowman dimple. It's impossible not to fall completely in love with his adorableness.

"Hey, Kody, I'm so glad you're here today!"

"Aunt Evie bring me to watch Daddy practice 'cause Mommy is napping. She's tired 'cause my baby brudder is dancing all night in her tummy!" He pats his belly. "I'm a big boy now, so I don't need naps."

"Is that right?"

"Uh-huh." He nods. "Mommy says my brudder is gonna be an acto-bat. Imma play hockey like my daddy." He puffs out his little chest. "Daddy says if I want to be a hockey player I has to eat all my vege-ables, but I only like corn."

I tap my lip. "Hmm, that's tough, but your dad is right: you do need to eat vegetables if you want to grow up and be a big, strong hockey player like him." I give his biceps a squeeze.

He makes a face. "I don't like broccoli." He lowers his voice. "When no one's looking I feed it to Brutus."

"Brutus is your dog, right?"

He grins again and nods, eyes twinkling with mischief. "It makes his toots smell like rotten eggs." He giggles.

"What's going on over here?" Stevie tickles him under the arms, and he squeals. "Hey, Queenie, how're you?"

"I'm good. Looks like you're on aunt duty today."

"Sure am." She grins as Kody scales the seats so he can be closer to the ice, and then she takes the one beside mine. "He couldn't stop talking about you on the way over here. I think he believes you're actual royalty."

I snort a laugh and tuck my bag under the seat. "Maybe I'll wear a crown the next time you bring him by the arena to visit."

"Oh my God, that would be priceless."

"Lainey feeling okay?" I've also met Rook's wife a few times. She's quieter than Stevie; actually, they're basically opposites in most regards. Where Stevie is outspoken and outgoing, Lainey's more introverted and introspective. But I like them both equally.

"She's doing pretty good, but the baby's been kicking up a storm at night, so Lainey hasn't been getting the best sleep. Plus this one"—she points to Kody—"has decided that playing hockey in his bedroom at five in the morning is a good idea. Needless to say, she's tired. I don't have clients at the clinic until later this afternoon, so I figured I could bring Kody here for a couple hours, and Lainey could catch a nap."

"That was sweet of you."

Stevie shrugs. "It means I get time with my nephew, I get to heckle my brother, and I get to watch my man in his element. So pretty much all my favorite things in one place." She winks and motions to the ice, where the guys are doing drills. "So, what kind of research are you doing this morning?"

"Mostly I'm watching the players interact: seeing who relies on who, which players read their teammates best, who's fastest, who scores the most, and how it lines up with their stats. The usual."

"No wonder your dad hired you as his assistant. You know the game, don't you?"

I shrug. "I spent a lot of time in arenas when I was little, not so much as I got older." Since there were a number of years when I couldn't stand to watch the game, I avoided it. It's only now that I'm working here that I realize how much I've missed it. "But I get what makes a good player, and how sometimes switching out one player can strengthen or weaken a line."

"That definitely makes sense. When Bishop came to Seattle, they moved him from forward to defense."

"Really? Why would they do that? He and Rook are the top scorers on the team."

"He's a big guy, so they thought it would be a better fit."

"I guess I can see that." I scroll through the lineup of players. "Do they ever play Rook and Bishop on the same line?"

"Uh no, not that I've ever seen. Why do you ask?" Stevie pulls a pack of mints out of her purse and pops one in her mouth before offering them to me.

"Just curious. I get wanting to keep them separate so both lines are strong, but it would be interesting to see what putting them together would do for the team."

"I guess if they don't beat each other to death with their sticks it would be an interesting experiment."

"Is that likely to happen?" I've seen those two bickering before. They're worse than toddlers fighting over toys.

Stevie shrugs. "I'd say there's a fifty-fifty chance."

"Could be entertaining, if nothing else."

We sit in silence for a while and watch the players, noting who passes to who the most, whose form is the smoothest, and who takes the most risks, and the best shots. I find myself fixated on Kingston, although he is their main target. He's also let in a lot more goals today than his stats indicate is normal for him. Another puck slips by, through the five-hole this time, and he tosses a glove on top of the net, rubbing the back of his neck, clearly frustrated. Bishop skates over and puts a hand on his shoulder—checking in, I assume.

"I wonder what's going on with King today? He's playing like sh—poop," she says, censoring herself, although Kody isn't paying attention to us.

"He's usually a lot smoother," I agree.

"And less distracted. Do you watch them practice often?"

"Not usually, no. But it's easier to be where my dad is so I don't have to go back and forth between the office and the arena if I have pressing questions." He doesn't answer texts or emails during practice.

Stevie taps her lip. "Interesting."

I should keep my mouth shut and not ask questions, but I'm terrible at the whole impulse-control thing. "Interesting how?"

"Because he keeps looking over here, and I'm one thousand percent sure it's not me he's checking out."

I fight to keep my eyes off him and fail. She's right: he's looking at me, and yet another shot gets by him, this time because he's hugging the post.

"Oh my God, look at how red your face is! Do you have the hots for Kingston?" She says it way too loud while elbowing me in the side.

"What? No! Shhhh! Keep your voice down!" I duck my head, pretending to focus on my laptop, which would be more convincing if it weren't sitting closed on my lap.

We're close to the bench, and while there are only a couple of players making adjustments to their equipment, my dad is right there. As if I need him to overhear this conversation.

"Oh my God! You totally do! What is going on between the two of you?" She grabs my arm, eyes alight with some kind of weird excitement.

"Nothing. There is nothing going on. Can we drop this, please?"

She cocks a light-brown eyebrow. "I'm totally calling bullshit."

"Call it whatever you want, but there's a no dating players policy in effect, so there really is nothing going on between us." My face feels like it's on fire.

"Since when?"

"Since I started working for my dad."

"There's definitely a story to go with that comment."

"There are actually many, and I'm not telling any of them right now." I nod toward the bench, where my father is standing with his arms crossed.

"Okay, fine, dropping it." She smirks. "For now."

I don't have a chance to come up with another retort because the sound of more children in the arena draws our attention. We both look over our shoulders to find Violet, Alex Waters's wife, making her way down the stairs with two children in tow. I've met her once before, but she only had the two oldest boys with her that time. This time she ushers a pair of kids down the stairs. They look to be a little younger than Kody, and they're holding hands.

"All the way down, River!" Violet calls out. When River reaches the aisle we're sitting in, he tugs on his twin sister's hand, but she ducks behind him and shakes her head.

Violet pats her on the head. "It's okay, Lavender; you know Rainbow Stevie."

The auburn-haired little girl sticks her fingers in her mouth, and Violet crouches down in front of her and whispers something to her. Eventually she follows her brother down the aisle, gripping the back of his shirt.

"Lavender's shy around new people," Stevie explains.

"She's adorable."

"She is definitely that," Stevie agrees.

The little boy stops in front of Stevie. "Hi, Evie."

"Hi, River. Hi, Lavender. It's so great that you could come to see everyone play today."

Lavender peeks out from behind her brother and lifts her hand in a quick wave before she tucks herself behind him again.

"We get to go for ice cream after." He shifts his green-eyed gaze to me and holds out his tiny hand. "I'm River Waters. My daddy is the coach. This is my sister, 'ave-der. She's shy." Based on the rote way he speaks, I'm thinking this is his standard introduction. He has incredible speech for such a young kid. He steps to the side, but his sister mirrors the movement, keeping herself hidden behind him.

I shake his little hand, impressed by his firm grip. "It's great to meet you both. I'm Queenie, and my dad is the general manager. He works with your dad, and so do I."

Lavender peeks out from behind her brother, and I get a glimpse of wide, bright-blue eyes. She tugs on her brother's sleeve, and he leans in so she can whisper something to him. He frowns and shakes his head, but she tugs on his sleeve again and nods.

"Are you Queen of the 'rena?"

I chuckle at that. "Nope, but that would be a pretty fun job, I'd think."

"Why don't the two of you have a seat? Lavender, I have your coloring book right here." Violet pats the empty seat next to her.

Lavender tugs on her brother's hand. "We has to sit," he tells me and then lets his sister tug him toward their mother. They cram themselves into the same seat. River helps his sister unpack her coloring supplies and hands her the crayons one at a time, always seeming to know what color she wants next without either of them saying anything.

"They're adorable," I tell Violet.

"Thanks. Don't let Lavender fool you, though. Once she's comfortable with you, she'll talk your ear off. Isn't that right, River?"

"Yup." He nods solemnly.

Lavender gives her brother a look and then whispers something in his ear. He turns to me. "She says her voice gets lost with new friends."

"Nothing wrong with saving up your words for the people who count," Violet says. "Your grandma said I was the same way as a kid. Not sure when that changed, but it'd probably save me a lot of embarrassment if I could manage to keep my trap shut instead of the constant verbal diarrhea I spew when I'm nervous, which is about ninety-five percent of the time." Violet drops down beside Stevie and motions to the rink. "Anyway, enough about that. You two enjoying the eye candy?"

"Definitely not going to complain." Stevie grins. "Right, Queenie?"

"Right," I mutter, and I try to keep my focus off Kingston, but every time I peek over at him, he's looking right at me.

For the next twenty minutes I don't do much in the way of note taking, mental or otherwise, since I get sucked into a conversation about preseason exhibition games and who they're most worried about playing this season.

"Geez. What's up with King today?" Violet asks. "That's the third puck he's let in since I got here."

I elbow Stevie in the side, hoping she'll keep her mouth shut about her hypothesis. "He's distracted."

"Seriously. Did someone swap out his milk for Red Bull? He keeps looking over at the bench every four seconds. Did Alex give him crap or something?"

"Not sure," Stevie says with a shrug.

"Well, let's hope he's not playing like this during the season, or defense is going to have their work cut out for them," Violet mutters.

I have the urge to defend him, but that would be suspect, so, like Lavender, I keep my mouth shut.

My dad and Alex grab Kingston as the rest of the guys are getting off the ice at the end of practice. They have a very brief conversation, during which Kingston nods and kneads the back of his neck constantly, before he, too, disappears down the hall and into the locker room.

Lavender and River are busy putting the crayons back in the box.

"When I was your age I used to do the exact same thing." They both pause and look up. For the first time, I get a good look at Lavender's face. She looks a lot like Violet, but her eyes are a piercing icy-blue color. I motion to the box poised in her lap. "I always put the colors back so they made a perfect rainbow. Drove my dad batty because it took forever. He didn't understand how important it was for every crayon to be in its rightful place." I wink, and a sweet yet mischievous smile lights up her face.

Once the crayons are taken care of, Lavender and River carefully put everything into her backpack, apart from her coloring book, which she hugs to her chest.

We stop at the vending machines, and the twins get to pick out a snack, and then insert the coins and press the buttons. Lavender's expression is gleeful as she chooses a bag of rainbow candies and then watches the coil unravel. Before anyone is allowed to open their snack, they all have to use hand sanitizer.

"There's my beautiful wife and my amazing children." Alex swoops down and picks up Lavender. "Did you have fun?"

Lavender squeals and giggles when Alex smothers her little face with kisses. She loses her grip on her art book, but it's nabbed out of midair before it can hit the ground.

"Nice save, King," Violet says.

"Thank you, ma'am. I mean, Mrs. Waters. I mean, Violet." He turns to Lavender and gives her a smile that nearly liquefies my panties. "Did you drop something important, Miss Lavender?"

She nods and then buries her face in her dad's neck, but she peeks out a few seconds later and gives him a flirty smile when he holds out her coloring book.

She takes it from him, hugging it to her chest again, still wearing that huge grin.

"What do we say, Lavender?" Alex asks quietly.

A few seconds pass before she murmurs a barely audible "Tank you" in the sweetest voice I've ever heard in my life.

"Good girl," Alex says, and he kisses her on the cheek before he sets her back down. She beelines it right to her brother, and they take each other's hand. He's scowling at Kingston, which is pretty damn cute.

"Hello, Stevie." Kingston lifts his hand in an awkward wave and slowly, almost reluctantly, addresses me. "Hi, Queenie. I'm sorry you had to witness my poor performance on the ice today." He shoves his hands in his pockets as his face turns bright red.

Alex claps him on the shoulder. "It's one practice, King. Nothing to worry about. You on your way to see Jake?"

"Yes, sir," he says to his feet.

"Don't be too hard on yourself. We all have bad days," Alex reassures him.

"As long as they're not when we have a real game against another team." King nods in our direction. "Ladies, have a lovely evening." And then he hightails it down the hall toward my dad's office. Which incidentally is also where my office is.

Stevie and Violet exchange a knowing look, and Vi smirks. "I expect we'll be seeing you at our Wednesday Night Movie Club soon."

"What's Wednesday Night Movie Club?"

"It's when all the hockey wives and girlfriends get together to watch movies. Like a book club but a lot less work and a lot more eye candy."

"But I'm not a hockey wife or girlfriend."

"Yet." Violet's smirk grows wider.

"Right, okay. We'll see about that." I clap my hands together loudly, startling myself. "I have some paperwork to finish up, so I should really go!" And just like Kingston, I bust my ass down the hall.

"Might as well cancel any Wednesday night plans you have starting now!" Violet calls after me.

I push through the door to my office, shaking my head. Kingston can barely look at me without bursting into flames. Besides, there's the whole "no dating players" rule I have no intention of breaking.

It's already after five, which means technically I'm allowed to go home. But I don't want to leave until I check in with my dad and make sure there isn't anything else he wants me to take care of. His office door is closed, though, and I know better than to knock, especially since Kingston is with him.

I clean up my emails and add to my player notes while I wait. The longer it takes, the more my stomach twists. A fine bead of sweat trickles down my spine.

This is crazy. Why the hell am I so nervous? Kingston is just a guy. So I've been naked with him. Big deal. So what if just the tip has been inside me? Accidentally. Or that I've thought about him nearly constantly since that night that happened more than two months ago. Who cares if he's great with kids? Why is that thought actually making me *hotter* for him?

Emails sorted, I make sure all my documents from today are saved before I shut down my computer. I'm packing up my laptop when my dad's office door swings open. "Hey, sweetie, I didn't realize you were still here. I should've told you to head home after practice was over."

Kingston appears behind him, eyes darting around, bouncing off me like a Ping-Pong ball, just to return a second later.

"It's no problem. I had some emails to clean up and a few notes to make. Are you ready to go?"

My dad makes a face. "Uh, I actually have a few more things I need to take care of before I can call it a day."

"Oh, okay. I can wait if you'd like."

"You don't have to do that. Why don't you grab an Uber?"

"Okay. Sure."

"Great." My dad claps Kingston on the shoulder. "Remember what I said. You need to ease up on yourself, son."

"Yes, sir."

"Take it easy tonight. You're looking a little flushed." My dad disappears into his office, leaving Kingston and me alone together.

As usual he makes brief eye contact, then looks away as his face turns progressively redder. He jams his hands in his pockets and rocks back on his heels. "I can drive you home."

"You don't need to go out of your way; I can grab an Uber." I fit my laptop into my oversize purse.

"I really don't mind. Besides, Ubers aren't always the best. I'm a very safe driver."

"I bet you are." I shoulder my bag and head for the door, Kingston falling into step beside me.

"So I can drive you?" he asks as we walk down the hall toward the arena parking lot. "Friends do that for each other, don't they?"

"I guess, yeah." Two people who know each other intimately and try to avoid each other don't exactly qualify as friends, but he seems to be insistent on this, so I guess it won't hurt to let him drive me home this once.

"Great. Then it's settled. I'll give you a ride."

I bite back a snicker at his inadvertent sexual innuendo.

# CHAPTER 8

## GIRL FRIEND

*Kingston*

I lead Queenie across the parking lot to my car. I've spent the past couple of weeks feeling like an idiot for following her home that first day. Every time I see her, I get tongue-tied and I remember things I shouldn't. I figure offering her a ride home is a good way to smooth things over. I unlock my car and round the passenger side so I can open the door for her.

I wipe my sweaty palm on my pants and hold it out.

She looks at it questioningly.

"I can help you up."

"Oh, uh, thanks?" It's more question than response, as if maybe she's surprised by the offer of assistance.

She slips her fingers into my palm, which instantly causes goose bumps to travel up my arm. Heat shoots down my spine, and other, less appropriate parts of my body react in ways they should not to the brief contact as she climbs into my SUV. I wait until she's settled before I round the hood of the Volvo, reminding my body that now is not the time to get excited.

I repeat that mantra in my head as I settle into the driver's seat, set my phone in the dash charger, check all the mirrors, and turn the engine over. I also lower the windows, because my car is filled with the scent of Queenie, and while I can certainly appreciate it, it also makes it difficult for me to think.

I turn my blinker on and check both ways before I pull out of my spot and head for the arena exit.

"I guess you don't need me to tell you where I live, huh?" Queenie asks.

Heat—the kind that comes from embarrassment—works its way up the back of my neck and settles into my cheeks. "I'm sorry I did that. I just didn't know what else to do, and we needed to talk."

"I'm playing around with you, King. You don't need to apologize."

"Right. Okay. I'm still sorry, though." I turn the radio down so it's not a deterrent to conversation before I signal out of the parking lot and drive toward Queenie's house.

"It's really fine." Queenie pops the button on her cardigan and shrugs out of it. She's wearing a tank top under it. One with lace accents.

"Should I put the air on? Is it too warm in here for you?" I sound like I'm doing a repeat of puberty and my voice is halfway to changing.

"This is good." She rolls her window all the way down and rests her arm on the edge. "Do you always drive like this?"

"Like what?"

She motions to my hands. "Like you're taking a driving test."

"Nine and three are the safest places to hold the wheel. And in an accident, you're less likely to break fingers if the airbag deploys." Also, keeping both hands on the wheel means I don't give in to the urge to tuck the pink strap of her bra back under her tank.

"Good to know." She glances at the speedometer. "Careful: you're over the speed limit."

I glance down and notice that I'm driving five miles above the posted limit, so I take my foot off the gas and slow down until I'm back where I should be.

"I was kidding." Queenie crosses her legs and shifts in her seat so she's turned toward me. "Have you ever had a speeding ticket?"

"Never. I'm a very careful driver."

"I can see that."

The light we're approaching turns yellow, so I slow down instead of risking it turning red while I'm in the intersection. A horn blares from the car behind me, and the alarm on my phone goes off.

Queenie glances at the screen. "You have an alarm set for dinner?"

"I have to eat frequent meals, so it helps if I set a reminder, particularly at the beginning of the season, or when we're traveling. Otherwise it can interfere with my workout schedule, since exercise on a full stomach isn't particularly effective." I don't generally touch my phone when driving, but since we're stopped at a light, I silence the alarm.

"That makes sense. You guys must get hungry often, considering how hard you all push yourselves," Queenie replies.

"I try to eat every two to three hours."

"Or for an hour straight," she mutters.

"What was that?"

"Nothing." Her cheeks flush pink to match mine. I'm pretty sure she just referenced our night together. "If you need to stop and grab something, go ahead."

"Are you hungry? We could grab something together."

"Uh, that's nice of you to offer, but it's probably not a good idea."

"Why not?"

"Well, that's kind of like a date, isn't it?"

"Friends go for dinners, don't they? Bishop and I go for food all the time."

"Yeah, but you haven't ever wet humped Bishop, have you?" Queenie slaps her palm over her mouth. "I'm sorry. I don't know why I said that."

I grip the wheel tightly, trying not to let the memories surface. "I can take you home if that's what you prefer."

"I'm sorry, Kingston, I didn't mean to make this awkward. We can grab something to eat. As friends."

I glance over at her. "Are you sure?"

"Yeah. I'm sure. It'll probably help us get over all the awkward, right?"

"Definitely." Or at least it should. I hope. "How do you feel about a steak house?"

"I feel good about it. How do you feel about it?"

"Also good." I signal left and switch lanes, slowing down so I can make the turn, then heading away from Queenie's house and toward one of my favorite restaurants. It's nice but also casual, so it should feel less like a date.

Except they seat us in a cozy corner in the back of the restaurant, at a private table.

Our server, who is a guy in his midtwenties, tucks Queenie into the table, which is what I should have done if he hadn't gotten to it before me. "Can I get you something to drink? Would you like to look at the wine menu?"

"Oh no, that's okay," Queenie says. "I'll take a root beer, please."

"And for yourself?"

"I'll take a large milk. Two percent if you have it, please." I wait until the server leaves before I turn my attention back to Queenie, who looks like she's trying not to laugh. "What?" I swipe at my chin, worried I have something on my face.

"Milk?"

"I have a glass with every meal."

Queenie props her chin on her fist. "So did I as a kid; my dad insisted on it." She's grinning, and obviously poking fun at me. I'm used to it. The guys on the team like to razz me about it all the time.

"I have a sensitive stomach. It helps coat it before a big meal. Also, it's good for your bones; has lots of calcium, essential vitamins, and minerals; and is a good source of protein," I explain.

Queenie chuckles and bites her lip. "I'm just playing with you. I think it's cute."

"Cute?"

"Mmm, cute." She ducks her head. "You're an interesting guy, you know that?"

"Because I drink milk with every meal?"

She makes a general motion toward me. "Because you're you."

"That's not much of an explanation."

The server returns with Queenie's root beer and my glass of milk. We order our meals, and I opt for chicken and pasta with a salad so I can cover all my food groups and everything is easily digestible. Queenie orders steak, truffle fries, and a garden salad. I have to remind myself that this isn't a date, just two friends having dinner together.

Once the server leaves us alone again, I prompt her to elaborate.

"Well, you're this famous hockey goalie, except you're really low key about the whole thing."

"It's my job, that's all."

Queenie rolls her eyes. "Well, yeah, but you make seven figures a year, and a lot of your teammates are all about social media and showing off, but you're just . . . not like that at all. Plus you have this incredibly wholesome image, from the milk with every meal, to the driving the speed limit all the time, to the whole khakis and polos deal. What's that all about, by the way?"

I run a hand over my chest. "Is there something wrong with khakis and polos?"

"No, but other than a suit or goalie gear, it's the only thing I see you wear." Her gaze shifts to my chest and then back up.

"Well it's like semicasual, semiformal, isn't it?" When she cocks her head to the side, I continue. "And jeans can be uncomfortable, but khakis are always soft, and you can always dress them up or down with shoes. If I'm going to a barbecue, I can throw on a pair of tennis shoes and it's casual, but if I'm going for dinner, like tonight, I can dress them up with a pair of loafers or dress shoes." I stick my foot out so she can see my black, polished shoes. "Plus, white shirts are easy to wash. I can always put a capful of bleach in the load, and I don't have to worry about faded colors, or mixing colors."

"So it's a convenience thing?"

"Mostly, I guess. Once I accidentally put a red shirt in with my whites and everything turned pink, which I'm not opposed to, and I was in the middle of a breast cancer campaign for my cousin, so it wasn't necessarily a bad thing, but you can see how the colors can be an issue."

"Okay, so let me get this straight. You drink milk because you have a sensitive stomach and it's good for you."

"Correct," I supply.

"And you wear khakis because they're convenient and white shirts because it's easier than colors."

"Also correct."

"And you're a famous goalie."

"I'm not famous."

"You are, at least in the hockey world, and it's not something to feel bad about." Queenie taps her lip. "How many long-term serious relationships have you had?"

"What does that have to do with my wardrobe and sensitive stomach?"

"Nothing. I'm just curious and trying to figure you out. Plus, I know what you're like when you get naked, and it doesn't match the milk-drinking, khaki-wearing Boy Scout." She's smirking, and her eyes glint with mischief and maybe some memories of that night.

"That's not really what I'm like."

"That's not what you're like, period, or that's not what you're like with anyone but me?"

"That's . . . I don't . . . I'm not—" I stumble over my words, unsure how to respond, because I'm not sure the truth is something I should divulge if we're supposed to be keeping this platonic.

"Sorry, I shouldn't have asked that."

"The alcohol made me less inhibited," I blurt.

"So, lowered inhibitions are to blame?" Based on her grin, I think she's still poking fun at me.

"Yes. No. I don't know. I've only been drunk three times."

Queenie's eyes flare. "Like, ever? In your entire life?"

"Yeah. I had a bad experience as a teenager that I haven't wanted to repeat ever again."

"Did you get trashed at some hockey party in high school or something?"

"Uh, no. Let's just say my older brother wasn't a great influence." And not much has changed since I was a teenager.

"Still, sort of an extreme reaction, to never drink again."

"I drink, but usually only one, and never shots," I explain. "What about you?"

"I've made plenty of bad decisions while under the influence; unlike you, I don't seem to learn from them."

"But you said you don't usually go home with random strangers."

"Oh, I don't. That was a first for me. And just so we're clear, you were actually one of the best bad decisions I've ever had the misfortune of making." Queenie winks.

I focus on my glass, wishing this situation were less complicated, and that I'd taken her out on a date before we'd ended up in bed, naked, and then almost had sex. "I'm glad you feel that way. And I'm still sorry about . . . how overzealous I was."

"I happened to enjoy your overzealousness." Queenie blows out a breath. "Anyway, let's change the topic, since this one is probably going to get me into trouble. What's your favorite thing to do when you're not playing hockey?"

"Trouble how?"

"It's probably not a good idea to stroll down that memory lane, you know? Especially since we're working on the friend angle."

"Right. Good point. I like pretty much anything that's a physical activity."

Queenie laughs. "Well, you're good at physical activity, so that makes sense."

"What about you? What do you like to do when you're not at work?"

Queenie shrugs and focuses on cutting her steak. "I used to like to do arty things."

"Arty like what?"

"Whatever I felt like, really."

"So you're creative, then? How did you end up working as your dad's assistant?"

"The crafty stuff is a hobby. And I ended up working for my dad because his old assistant's husband had a heart attack and needed surgery, and she decided to take early retirement. I was between jobs, so I offered to help him out until I can figure what the heck I want to do with my life."

"You mean career-wise?"

Queenie points her fork at me. "Whoa, hold up, it's my turn to ask a question."

"I didn't realize we were taking turns."

"You get a question and then I get a question." She pops the bite of rare beef into her mouth and chews thoughtfully for a few seconds. "What's your favorite TV show?"

"*The Big Bang Theory.*"

Queenie snorts a laugh. "Why does that not surprise me in the least?"

"My turn. What's your dream job?"

"For a while I wanted to be a therapist."

"But not anymore?"

She wags a finger at me. "My turn."

"You didn't even answer the question, though."

"Sure I did. I said I wanted to be a therapist."

"For a while, which implies past tense."

"It's not a realistic goal, hence the whole dream-job thing. I'd ask what yours is, but I think you're already doing it, aren't you?"

"I am. Why isn't becoming a therapist a realistic goal?"

"I don't think I'd be good at helping people."

"Why not?"

"Because I don't have it together, so I can't very well help anyone else if I don't even have my own life sorted out."

"How can you say that? You have a job that you're good at."

"I'm working for my dad. I don't think it really counts." She waves her fork around in the air. "Anyway, this was supposed to be like a fun twenty questions, and you're making it all serious. What's your favorite dessert?"

"Vanilla anything."

She chuckles and shakes her head.

"What's wrong with vanilla?"

"Nothing."

"Then why are you laughing at me?"

"It's just ironic, that's all."

"What's your favorite dessert?"

71

"It depends on the day."

We end up ordering the chocolate lava cake with ice cream for dessert so I get my vanilla ice cream and Queenie gets her chocolate fix. And as much as I remind myself that this is a platonic thing, my body and my brain aren't synced up. At all. Because all I can think of is how good Queenie's mouth would taste if I kissed her right now.

◆ ◆ ◆

"I had a lot of fun tonight. Thanks for dinner," Queenie says when I pull into her driveway.

"It was my pleasure, and me, too, about having fun. Maybe we can do it again soon?"

"Sure. I'd like that."

"Next time it could be a real date."

Her smile turns rueful and my stomach sinks. "I really like you, Kingston—"

"It sounds like there's a *but* coming." I try to make it sound like a joke, but it falls flat.

"You're a great guy, and a lot of fun, but I can't date you." Now she looks apologetic. "Not because I don't want to, but my dad only laid down one rule when I took the job as his assistant, and that was not to date any of the players."

"But maybe if we talked to him—"

"He did me a huge favor by giving me this job. I lost my apartment because I couldn't afford it, and between the night I met you and him giving me the job, I got canned at two other restaurants, which, honestly, isn't a surprise, because I really, really suck at waiting tables. I don't want to put him in a weird spot or disappoint him. I just . . . can't. I'm sorry, Kingston, but we can still hang out if you want, as friends?" She chews her bottom lip, looking hopeful.

"Sure, yeah. We can hang out as friends." It's honorable that she wants to abide by the rule Jake laid down, even if it's inconvenient for me.

"Thanks for understanding." She leans over the center console and presses her lips to my cheek. I fight with myself not to turn my head. Thankfully my restraint wins out over my hormones.

"Oops." She makes a cringey face and rubs at my cheek, presumably because she left lipstick behind. "See you tomorrow, King. Drive safe." She winks and then she's out the door.

I guess being friends is better than nothing. For now.

# CHAPTER 9

## TERRITORIAL

*Queenie*

I expect Kingston to lose interest when I tell him dating is off the table. So I'm surprised when the exact opposite happens.

For the third day in a row he pops his head into my office. "You waiting for your dad?"

I glance at his closed door. "He got a call and he said it might be a while. You offering to be my Uber driver?"

"I'd be happy to drive you home, but I need to make a stop on the way, if that's okay with you."

"Sure, I don't mind." I send a message to my dad to let him know I'm leaving for the day, pack up my stuff, and fall into step beside Kingston. "How was practice today?"

"Really good. You know Alex has been testing Rook and Bishop on the same line, like you suggested, and they actually play really well together." He holds the door open for me, and we cross the parking lot to his car. He parks in the same spot every day, at the far end of the lot.

"That's great. I'll have to make a point of coming to practice later this week."

"You should. It's interesting to watch, and it means some of the guys on the third line are getting more play, which is only going to help our game as a team."

"That makes me so happy!" I mean it too. I'm glad I was able to point out something of value to my dad, and that it's helping the team.

As usual, Kingston opens the passenger door and holds out his hand to help me up. I could easily manage without the assistance, but I like the contact—probably more than I should. I enjoy spending time with Kingston, even though it's supposed to be just as friends and most of the time my thoughts are well beyond the platonic zone.

Once I'm seated, he rounds the hood and takes his spot behind the wheel. Kingston checks the rearview mirror, makes a minor adjustment to the right-side mirror, and tests the blinkers to make sure they're working.

By now I'm used to his excessive caution: signaling before he even leaves the parking spot, braking as soon as the light turns yellow (even though he has more than enough time to pass through the intersection before it turns red), driving exactly the speed limit, if not a couple of miles an hour under it. He's worse than a ninety-year-old, and I kind of love it.

"So what's this stop you have to make?" I ask as he makes a left out of the lot instead of a right.

"You'll see." He gives me the Kingston version of a smirk, which is really just a cute, slightly devious smile.

"Well, that's kind of cryptic. Am I supposed to guess?"

"You can go ahead and try if you want."

"Are we going to the SPCA to pet cute puppies that need a home?"

"No, but I could arrange that if it's something you'd want to do. I actually had an endorsement for the SPCA last year, and I try to go once a month to their adoption days: sign autographs and that kind of thing."

"Why are you so perfect?" It makes it hard to stick to the whole "we can just be friends" rule when he tells me things like this.

"I'm not even close to perfect."

"I've yet to find a flaw that isn't endearing." I tap my lip. "Are we going to a seniors' retirement village, where all the little old ladies will pat your butt and you'll smile and pretend it's not happening?"

"Uh, no, and I seriously doubt little old ladies would do things like that."

"If I was a senior and you showed up at my retirement village, I'd totally pat your butt." I hold up a finger. "Let's pretend I didn't say that."

"You're actually welcome to pat my butt anytime you want, but I don't know that it would bode well for the platonic rule." He winks, and I laugh.

I'm glad we both seem to be getting over the whole semihookup. Or at least we're comfortable enough with each other that we can joke about it.

Ten minutes later he pulls into the parking lot of what looks like a bar, at least at first glance. "What is this place?"

A smile breaks across Kingston's face that's somewhere between excitement and mischief. "You ready to have some fun?" His tongue peeks out and slides over the chip in his front tooth.

I hold up a hand. "Okay, that right there has to stop."

His smile drops and his eyes dart around. "What has to stop?"

"What you're doing. Or what you just did. The being all cute and sexy and saying things that can be interpreted with innuendo."

He frowns. Even his frowns are sexy. This whole platonic thing is rough. "There wasn't any innuendo."

"You don't think so?"

"I asked if you were ready to have some fun."

"You think so?" I adjust my pose and uncross my legs. I run my palms down my dress-pant-covered thighs and part them slightly. Yes, I'm overdoing it, but I'm also proving a point. I drag my tongue along my top lip, then bite the bottom one before I put on my best phone-sex voice. "Are you ready to have some fun, Kingston?"

He strobe blinks at me a bunch of times. His voice is two full octaves lower than usual. "I didn't say it like that."

"Maybe not, but the impact was the same as if you had. Let's get out of this car before the pheromones take over." I open my door and jump out before we make any informed bad choices.

Kingston is much slower to get out of the car. He makes a covert adjustment in his pants, and his cheeks are red, which makes me feel better about my own hidden response to the in-car flirting.

Regardless, he holds the door open and ushers me into the bar, but he keeps his fingertips pressed against the dip in my spine. Initially we enter a bar, but beyond that . . .

"Uh, Kingston, are those people throwing *axes*?"

"They sure are." He settles a palm on my hip and pulls me into his side.

I don't understand the sudden touchy-feely business until some bearded hipster dude with a tattoo sleeve approaches us. "Kingston! I'm glad you made it!" His eyes flare just a touch when he notices me. "And you brought a friend, I see."

"Ronan, this is Queenie. Queenie, this is Ronan. He runs this place."

Ronan laughs. "King and Queenie? That's epic."

"We're just friends," I explain.

Kingston's fingers flex on my waist. "I'll take a half pint of the house lager. Queenie, what would you like?"

"Whoa, wait a second. He'll have a pint of milk, and I'll have a root beer." I poke Kingston in the chest. "Alcohol and ax throwing do not go together."

"Just friends, huh?" Ronan snickers. "Stall four is reserved for you. Boot up and you're good to go." Ronan saunters off.

"Ax throwing?"

"It's fun."

I take his face between my palms and turn his head from side to side. "Who are you, and what have you done with my Boy Scout?"

Kingston bends down, face inches from mine. "I am your Boy Scout, Queenie. Just because I wear polos and khakis and drink milk instead of beer most of the time doesn't mean I don't know how to have fun."

"I'm fully aware of your ability to have fun," I whisper—or moan; I'm not sure which is more likely, all considered.

Kingston's gaze darkens, and he strokes a finger gently from my temple to my chin. "Don't bait me, Queenie. Guilt is not an emotion I enjoy experiencing." He steps back but then links his pinkie with mine and tugs me toward the ax-throwing stalls.

I can totally handle myself in this situation. Kingston is just a guy throwing an ax.

Except he's *not* just a guy throwing an ax. He's the milk-drinking, door-opening, extra-polite Boy Scout *friend* who is all of a sudden grabbing pairs of steel-toed boots. "What size are your feet?" he asks.

"Five." It comes out all breathy.

He glances down and nudges my toe with his. "Really? Wow, you have tiny feet."

He hands me a pair of hot-pink boots, and I drop down on the bench.

Instead of sitting down beside me, Kingston pulls up one of the short stools and positions himself in front of me. And then he proceeds to remove my heels and tuck my feet into the pair of pink-and-black work boots.

My lady parts are ridiculously excited about the physical contact. Especially when his long, warm, thick fingers wrap around the back of my calf. It should be completely innocuous, but it feels like it's not. Because of the look on his face, and the way his touch affects my entire body. I'm lucky that Kingston is such a rule follower and won't be the one to break the platonic rule.

I convince myself I need to make it through the next hour, and everything will be fine.

Until he pulls his polo over his head.

And hangs it carefully over the bench.

He's not shirtless. It's Kingston. The only time he's shirtless is when he's ready to get down and dirty.

So, so politely dirty.

Instead he's wearing a thin white tee. The kind where I can see the outline of his abs, and his tiny little man nipples. Which I've touched . . . with more than my fingers. I would like to be able to make sound, well-thought-out decisions right now, but the white shirt, the transparency, and the damn axes make it tough.

I can't decide if this is the best thing ever or a form of torture. Or both.

Because I've never thrown an ax before, Kingston gives me a lesson. I'd like to say I listen raptly to what he's saying, but that would be untrue. Mostly I keep trying to swallow down the drool pooling in my mouth, which is probably matched by another part of my body that's making my panties damp with excitement.

The muscles in his back and arms flex as he takes aim and then releases the ax, hitting the bull's-eye on the first try. He wears the sexiest, most self-satisfied grin as he saunters over to our table, takes a swig of milk, and wipes his mouth with the back of his hand.

"Your turn." He hands me a much lighter and smaller ax.

I try to mimic his stance, but my lack of attention to detail must show.

"Hold on. Let me help." He moves in to stand behind me and nudges my feet farther apart with the toe of his boot. The entire front of his body presses against the back of mine, and his arms encircle me. "Keep your arms straight and bend at the elbow." I follow his instructions as he makes minute adjustments to my stance, shifting my hips so I'm facing the target straight on. "That's it, good girl. Bend your knees a little."

I do, which means my butt pushes against him, and we both still. "Kingston?" It comes out way breathy.

"Yes?"

"I can feel you poking me in the back. It's not very platonic of you."

He chuckles. "Some parts of me are less considerate than others."

"I have a deep appreciation for your inconsiderate parts." And now it sounds like I'm on the verge of an orgasm.

Kingston exhales a long, slow breath, squeezes my hip, and steps back, severing the connection. My first attempt is crap, and I barely hit the board, but my next shot is better. We alternate back and forth, and the touchiness ramps up to nearly intolerable levels.

Kingston is in the middle of a throw when his phone starts ringing from the back pocket of his khakis. "That's momster. Can you answer it for me, please?"

"Uh, sure?" I slip my fingers into his back pocket, aware I'm semi-touching his butt. It's a video call, which I'm unprepared for, but I answer it anyway. "Hey! Hi, Hanna! Kingston's in the middle of throwing an ax, so he asked me to answer for him."

Her eyebrows pull down and bounce up. "Throwing an—oh! Ax throwing? You must be Queenie."

"Um, yeah. I am." She seems unfazed by the activity, and the fact that I answered the phone, but I'm sure my own confusion is obvious.

She smirks, and I can see the family resemblance in their smile and their eyes. "Ryan may have mentioned you before."

"Is that so?"

A loud thud startles me. I glance up to see the ax embedded in the wall rather than the target. "Hey, Hanna, we're a little busy here right now!" Kingston calls out.

Hanna ignores him, eyes lighting up. "So King took you ax throwing, huh?"

"He did. So far he's beating me, but it's my first time. He just screwed up a throw pretty bad, though, so I might recover some points."

"It was one bad throw." He appears over my shoulder. "Hey, momster, you mind if I call you back later?"

Her grin widens. "How cute are the two of you together?"

Kingston plucks the phone from my hand. "Bye, Hanna."

"I love you, Ry-Ry."

Kingston closes his eyes and shakes his head. "I love you too, momster. *Bye.*" He cracks a lid, his eyeball focused on me.

"Ry-Ry?"

"She's the only person who calls me that, and she only does it to get under my skin."

"I think it's sweet that you have that kind of relationship with her."

"We've always been tight."

"That's quite obvious." I'm almost jealous of his relationship with his sister-mom. I don't have any siblings, or a mom I'd even want to be that close with, especially since all she's ever done is make me feel like I'm not good enough. "I can't believe you told her about me."

Kingston shrugs, cheeks still pink. "We've been hanging out a lot lately, and I don't keep much from her." He picks up my ax and hands it to me.

I step up to the line on the floor. "How much have you told her?"

"We're close but not *that* close." Kingston settles his hands on my hips, and I feel his breath on my cheek when he bends down and whispers, "I'd like her to keep believing I'm a Boy Scout, even if you and I know that isn't always true."

# CHAPTER 10
## WINS AND LOSSES

*Kingston*

The first exhibition game of the season is in LA, so we're about to board the team plane.

"King, can I have a word?" Jake claps me on the shoulder and pulls me aside.

"Yeah, sure, of course. What's up?" I motion for Bishop to go on ahead of me and hook my thumbs into my pockets. Jake looks stressed, which in turn makes me stressed.

"You've been spending a lot of time with Queenie lately."

"Yes, sir, as friends, sir."

"Yeah, I know. She's been pretty adamant about that part." He blows out a breath. "She's a bit of a restless soul."

"We can all be that way."

"Mmm." He nods. "She can also be quite impulsive."

"I'm not sure I follow." Sure, there have been a few times since we've started spending time together when the tension between us tested our resolve. But as far as impulsivity, I feel as though it's been more me than Queenie getting close to the line.

Jake chews on his bottom lip, as if he's debating something. "I have a favor to ask of you."

"Of course. What can I do?"

"I'm sure Queenie's told you she'll be traveling with the team."

"Uh, yes, she's mentioned that."

"Can I ask you to keep an eye on her for me? I don't want to smother her, and I know she's an adult, but some of your teammates are smooth talkers . . ." He lets it hang there.

"I understand, sir."

He pats me on the back, his smile holding relief. "Thanks, King. I knew I could count on you to watch out for my baby girl."

I would feel so much better about this request if I hadn't already been naked with his baby girl, but I'm more than happy to keep the rest of my teammates away from her.

Our brief conversation means Jake and I are last to board the plane.

Queenie's at the front of the plane, sitting in the aisle seat, laptop open and typing away. In the row beside her are Alex and Rook, who are deep in conversation. Queenie glances up from her laptop as we board and gives me a small smile, then moves the messenger bag from the seat beside her. I recognize it as Jake's. I spot Bishop at the back of the plane, so I make my way down the aisle toward him.

"You can take the window seat if you want," I tell Bishop when he makes a move to get out of his seat to let me in.

He makes a face. "You hate the aisle seat."

"I don't mind. I'll take the window on the way back."

"Suit yourself." He slides over. We're on the opposite side of the plane from Queenie, which means I have a pretty decent view when she leans on her armrest.

Bishop pulls a newspaper out of his bag, and I scroll through the movies. Sort of. I'm half paying attention to the movies and half paying attention to Queenie when I get an elbow in the side. "Ow! What was that for?"

"Dude. Stop being so obvious."

"What are you talking about?"

Bishop leans over so he can see past the seat in front of us. "Really, King?"

"I'm looking for a movie." I tap the screen in front of me.

"No, man, you're not. Maybe that's what you want me to think you're doing, but the only way you could be *less* conspicuous is if you went up to the front of the plane and sat in her damn lap. Stop staring. It's borderline creepy."

"I'm not staring."

"Yeah, man, you are. You've been doing it a lot, not to mention driving her home and hanging out with her," he says quietly. "What the hell is going on between the two of you?"

"There's nothing going on. We're just friends."

He gives me a look. "Why are you lying to me?"

"Can you drop it for now?" I glance to my left, where our teammates are sitting and potentially listening to our conversation.

He pokes at his cheek with his tongue. "You're spilling it later. But you need to check yourself, King, before people other than me start to notice, if they haven't already."

"Right. Yeah." I keep my eyes glued to the screen for the rest of the flight. Mostly.

Several hours later we arrive at the hotel. Bishop and I always room together, so we wait with the rest of the team for the elevators and head up to our respective floors. I lose track of Queenie along the way, partly because I'm paranoid that Bishop is right, especially since Jake just finished asking me to watch out for her.

When we get up to the room, I do what I always do: unzip my suitcase and find my portable steamer. When I turn around to retrieve the hangers from the closet, Bishop is standing in front of it with his arms crossed.

"Can I get in there?"

"Not until you spill it. What the hell is going on with you and Queenie?"

I open my mouth to speak, and he raises a hand. "And do not say, 'Nothing.' We've known each other for years, and I have never seen you tail a woman like you do her. Even Stevie has noticed, and she usually couldn't give less of a shit about stuff like that."

I rub the back of my neck. "Okay, okay. But this has to stay between us."

"I'm antisocial as fuck, King. Pretty sure you don't need to worry about me running my mouth to anyone apart from my cat and maybe Stevie, but she's a vault."

I nod and blow out a breath. "So you remember when I found out that Hanna is actually my biological mom?"

"Yeah, of course. You were appropriately freaked out, and then you did what you always do: you got over it in five minutes and moved on."

"Yeah, well, that's not quite what happened."

"Right. You said you went to a bar. There's no shame in getting drunk once in a while, King. No one is going to hold it against you, except maybe you." He uncrosses his arms and leans against the wall.

"I didn't get drunk by myself."

"Also not a crime."

"And I brought a woman home with me."

"As long as that woman was a coherent and willing participant in whatever you got up to—which I'm assuming she was, because you're you—that also isn't something you should beat yourself up about. I'm not getting what this has to do with Queenie."

"She's the woman I brought home. But she left before I woke up the next morning, and I didn't see her again until the first team meeting of the season."

85

Bishop blinks, and blinks again. "Holy shit. Are you telling me you had a one-night stand with the GM's daughter?"

"No. I mean . . . sort of? We agreed that night that we were just going to have fun and forget that our lives were kind of messed up. I would have given her my number, but I didn't have a chance. And we didn't have sex. Not really, anyway."

"How do you *not really* have sex? You either do or you don't, King. There's no actual in-between."

"There was some wet humping."

His eyebrows lift. "Wet humping?"

"Like dry humping but without clothes." I lace my hands behind my head and pace some more. "I sort of slipped for a second."

"Slipped?"

"In. I slipped inside. But just the head." This is more sharing than I've ever done before. But it's Bishop. He's good at keeping his mouth shut, because I'm one of the only people he actually willingly speaks to on a regular basis.

"Wow. I haven't played just the tip since high school."

"It's not a joke, Ship. And we weren't playing just the tip. We were both under the influence and not making the best choices, and we got carried away, but we didn't have *actual* sex."

"I can't believe you're just telling me this now."

"It isn't personal. I don't talk about this kind of thing."

He waves the comment away. "Yeah, yeah. I know, just . . . wow. I can't believe you've been hanging on to that for this long. So what's going on with you now? Clearly not nothing, since you've been spending time with her."

"I told her I wanted to date her, but Jake made it clear he doesn't want her getting involved with the players, so like I said, we're keeping it platonic."

He blows out a breath. "And you think it's gonna stay that way?"

"Unless Jake changes his mind, it'll have to. Besides, he asked me today to keep an eye on her."

"Why would he ask you to do that?"

"Because we've been spending time together, and he trusts me, I guess."

Bishop snorts. "Looks like that trust is misplaced, huh?"

I run my hand down my face. "If I'd known who she was, I never would've brought her home with me. I don't even do that in the first place. I'm trying to keep a level head here, but it sure hasn't been easy."

"Because you feel guilty?"

"Sort of. Yeah. No. I don't know."

"That's a yes." Bishop crosses the room and flops down on a chair. "You haven't done anything wrong."

"I brought a random woman home with me while we were both under the influence of alcohol. It could've gone incredibly wrong."

Bishop gives me a look. "King, you're the most conscientious person I know. Your moral compass is always pointed due north. I'm sure you asked about four hundred thousand times if she was okay with what was happening, and based on how you two can't seem to stay away from each other, I'm guessing she sure as hell wouldn't mind if it kept happening."

"But it can't."

"But you would like it to."

"What I want is irrelevant, since Jake has already laid the rules down."

Bishop drops his head back, rolling his eyes at the ceiling. "Oh, come the fuck on, King. You're a problem solver. Solve the fucking problem."

I throw my hands up in the air. Annoyed. "The only solution is to stay away from her, and I can't."

Bishop snorts. "Get permission to date her."

"But—"

He holds up a hand. "I know what Jake said, but you're like the poster boy for freaking wholesome. If there's anyone he'd be okay with his daughter dating, it's you."

"Not if he knew what happened between us already." Or all the very wrong things I'd like to do with and to his daughter.

Bishop smirks. "As long as you don't confess all your sins to him, I think you'll be fine, King."

"Yeah, right." That's easy for him to say. In all the years Jessica and I were together, I never wanted her the way I want Queenie. For a while I wondered if it was in part because Queenie's supposed to be forbidden or because we have insane chemistry. But no matter how much time I spend with her, I still have to constantly remind myself to stay in check.

The conversation comes to an abrupt end when my alarm goes off, signaling that we have ice time. It means I'll have to wait until later to unpack, which I don't love, but I don't really have a choice. Queenie doesn't come to the arena with us. She also isn't around afterward when we hit the restaurant for dinner.

When we get back, Bishop heads up to the room so he can call Stevie, and I hang out with some of the other guys on the team so he can have a little privacy. Jake and Alex disappeared together after ice time, and Queenie is still nowhere to be seen.

I'm usually in bed by ten unless we have a late game, and I always get a solid eight hours of sleep, especially the night before a game, so when I get the all clear from Bishop, I head up to our room.

As I arrive at our floor, the elevator directly across from me opens, and Queenie steps into the hall. She's wearing a pair of flip-flops, yoga pants, and a fitted shirt, layered with a zip-up hoodie. Her hair is pulled up in a ponytail, she's laden down with several bags, and she's holding a takeout cup.

"Hey, I haven't seen you since we got off the plane."

"I had to run some errands." She tries to brush past me but loses her grip on her key card.

I bend to pick it up, and when I try to hand it back, I notice that her eyes are red. "Are you okay?"

"I'm fine. Just clumsy."

And snippy apparently. "Can I help you carry anything to your room? I didn't realize you were on this floor too." Although maybe that was planned, since I'm supposed to be watching out for her and all, per my conversation with Jake.

"I'm fine. I can manage, but thanks." Her voice cracks at the end, and she drops her head on a long exhale. "Please, Kingston. I can't deal with you right now."

"Deal with me? I'm offering to help because you look like you're carrying more than you can handle," I say softly, trying to figure out why she's so intent on brushing me off, especially when it's clear she's upset.

Her eyes fall closed and her chin trembles. "I'm sorry. It's been a day; don't take it personally." Then she turns and heads down the hall, stopping at the door across from mine.

I tap the key card against the sensor, and when the green light appears, I turn the handle and follow Queenie into her room.

Despite her having been here for only a handful of hours, it still manages to look like a tornado has been through it, much like her place in Seattle. Her suitcase lies open in the middle of the bed, the contents vomited all over the comforter. I spot the bras right away. Specifically the pink lace one. That I've taken off her body.

She drops the bags she's holding on the floor and sets the takeout cup on the dresser, keeping her back to me. "Thanks for helping. I know it's late and you have a big day tomorrow."

Her shoulders curl forward and her body shakes like she's trying and failing to repress emotion. I've seen a lot of tears over the years for a variety of reasons: jerk boyfriends, failed tests, the death of a grandparent, and, in my momster's case, every single important and monumental milestone I've ever met. I'm not afraid of tears.

"Hey." I rest a palm gently on her shoulder.

She tries to shrug me off. "Please. You don't need to see this."

"Queenie." I gently urge her to turn around. When she finally does, I pull her against me and wrap my arms around her, dropping my head so I can breathe her in.

"What're you doing?" she mumbles against my chest.

"Hugging you."

"Why?"

"Because it seems like you could use one."

Eventually she relaxes against me, and her arms encircle my waist, linking at the small of my back. She shudders through an exhale.

"What happened today?"

"Nothing. I'm fine."

"You can talk to me." I take her chin gently between my thumb and finger and tip her head up. I've never seen her this upset—or upset at all, really, apart from the night we first met, and even then she was more cynical than emotional. "Tell me what happened."

Tears track down her cheeks, so I brush them away. "Please don't."

"Don't what?"

She turns her head away. "Don't be nice. Don't be sweet."

"Hey." This time I'm not as gentle when I tip her head back. "Look at me."

Her eyes flutter open and meet mine somewhat reluctantly.

"Why won't you talk to me?" I ask.

"Because it makes me wish things were different." There's so much vulnerability in both the statement and her eyes that it makes me hesitate, but Queenie is guarded and strong and closed off all at the same time, and the only way to get in is to force my way through the walls she's built to keep people out.

"What things? I'm right here. Just let me in. Tell me what's going on so I can help."

She seems despondent, frustrated, afraid. "My mom called."

90

"I take it that's a bad thing." I know her mom bailed on her when she was a kid, and that their relationship has never been positive.

"We don't speak often." She bows her head. "She lives in LA. She knows the team is here, and she knows I'm working for my dad. She was trying to find out what hotel we're staying at so she could drop by, even though I haven't seen her in years. I told her I was too busy and so is my dad, which she didn't like."

"Did she get angry?"

Queenie lifts a shoulder. "It's less about anger than it is about her being vindictive."

"How so?"

Queenie sighs and her eyes drop, her focus on my chest. "She likes to tell me that I'm the reason she and my dad never worked out. That if I wasn't so needy, he would've had the career and the life he deserved, and so would she, but I got in the way."

"That's a horrible thing to say."

"In her mind it's true. And maybe in some ways she's right. I am the reason they're not together. By the time my mom figured out she was pregnant, it was too late to terminate. She'd wanted to give me up for adoption, but my dad convinced her that they could do it together. She couldn't handle being a mom, though. I guess she felt trapped, like she was missing out on all the fun of being nineteen, so when it got too real for her, she bailed on both of us."

Queenie fidgets with my sleeve, shoulders slumped, eyes still on my chest.

"It's just . . . a really toxic relationship, which is why I try to avoid her. But she called from a number I didn't recognize, and I got sucked into the conversation with her. She gets into my head, and then it's a big spiral. I should've hung up as soon as I realized it was her, but I didn't, so I went out and bought a crap load of junk food because it's good fodder for wallowing in doubt and self-loathing."

"I'm sorry you had to deal with that."

"This is what happens every time I talk to her. I keep hoping one day it's going to be different, and it never is. What's the definition of insanity? Doing the same thing over and over and expecting a different result?" She blows out a breath and pats me on the chest. "And now you know how much of a mess I really am."

"You're not a mess, Queenie."

"I'm my dad's personal assistant, and I live in his pool house. When he was my age, he was raising a four-year-old on his own."

I tuck her hair behind her ear. "That's like comparing apples to oranges."

"I'm surrounded by highly driven, insanely successful people every day. Tell me you wouldn't feel like an underachiever."

"You can't measure yourself against your father, or any of the guys on the team. I get that it's hard not to, especially when you have someone who's supposed to be supportive and encouraging telling you to do the exact opposite. You just have to focus on what's going to make you happy."

"The things that make me happy aren't exactly lucrative."

"Money might make life cushier, but it doesn't equal happiness, Queenie."

"I don't want to be anyone's burden." She bangs her head against my chest a couple of times. "I'm sorry. I'm a downer tonight. This is not something you need to be dealing with, especially when you have the first exhibition game tomorrow."

If I were less invested, I would take the out, but I want this woman and all the issues that potentially come with getting involved with the GM's daughter. I cup her face between my hands. "I wish you could see yourself through my eyes, Queenie. Then you might have some idea as to how incredible you really are."

Our gazes lock and hold. For some reason I'm reminded of a lesson from my eleventh-grade English class, when we studied Shakespeare and the characters talked about humors, and my teacher likened physical chemistry to laser beams shooting out of people's eyes.

And the whole thing suddenly makes sense. Because every time Queenie and I connect, it's like there's energy passing between us, the kind that keeps drawing us together, making it impossible not to give in to it. Which is exactly what I find myself doing. "There's a reason I can't stay away from you, even if it would be easier for both of us." I dip down and press my lips to hers.

"It's probably my mad blow job skills."

"That's just a bonus." I take advantage of the fact that her mouth is open by stroking inside.

I'm honestly too tired to keep fighting against the pull, so instead of staying inside the lines we've drawn for ourselves, I tromp all over them. Like every other time we've had our tongues in each other's mouths, it escalates quickly.

"I really tried to keep it platonic." I kiss along the side of her neck, finding that sensitive spot behind her ear and grazing it with my teeth.

"I know. We were doing okay for a while. The ax throwing was almost a tipping point for me." She pulls my shirt free from the back of my pants and runs her warm palm up my back.

"God, I love your hands on me." I bite her earlobe, then start working my way across the edge of her jaw. "Why was the ax throwing almost a tipping point?"

Queenie angles her head to the side, giving me more access to her neck. "You looking so proper, throwing an ax like it was your job, wound me up. Your hard-on against my spine. All the touching."

I pull back so I can look at her. "Do you want me to stop?"

"No. Definitely don't stop. And if I'm being one hundred percent honest, I'd also love it if your face lips ended up making out with my vagina lips."

I close my eyes, because seeing her expression and hearing those words does nothing to help my self-control. "Wait. I think we need to figure this out first, before we get carried away."

Queenie blows out a breath. "Figure what out?"

"What's happening between us."

"I think it's pretty obvious. I was sad; you consoled me. We have chemistry and we're acting on it."

"It's more than that, though."

Queenie rolls her eyes. "You must really enjoy blue balls, King. Can't we be spontaneous and hump on each other without all the psychoanalyzing? Let's get carried away now, and we can talk after." She drags her nails along my abs.

"I want to date you," I groan.

This time she's the one who pulls back. "We've already been over this and why that can't happen right now."

"I want to take you out for dinner and go to the movies and hang out with you."

"We already do that, apart from the movies. We throw axes instead."

"But I don't get to kiss you good night. Or sleep next to you. I don't want you to be a secret I have to keep."

"I guess you'll need to convince my dad it's okay for me to date you, then." She tugs on the back of my neck. "Let's finish this conversation after we fool around."

I let her bring our mouths back together, and for a while I get lost in a long, slow kiss. Somehow we end up on the bed, and my shirt gets tossed on the floor. Once the clothes start coming off, things go from hot to frantic, and any thought I had about talking this out disappears.

Just like the time she came to my place, we end up naked, with Queenie straddling my face while she takes me in her mouth. I have no recollection of oral sex ever being this amazing—either the giving or the receiving—but I could literally spend hours in this exact position, or any variation that allows for mutual gratification.

Unfortunately, it starts to become difficult to concentrate after a while because my chest, face, and stomach are getting itchy. I refocus on the feel of her mouth, the vibration of her moans against my erection every time I lick her just the right way, how soft she is on my tongue, and how good she tastes. As distracting as the annoying itch is, I finally warn her I'm going to come soon. She almost knees me in the head as she shifts around.

"Hey, I'm not done with you!" I try to catch her ankle before she can get too far, but all of a sudden I have an excellent view of what she's doing to me. I groan at the sight of her stretched out between my thighs, fingers wrapped around the base of my erection, lips covering the head, cheeks hollowed out as she sucks. "You are depravedly stunning like this."

She pops off for a second, tongue circling the ridge, hand moving up and down. "Do you like it when my mouth is full of your cock, Kingston?" Her lips cover the head again and slide back down.

"You have no idea." I prop myself up on one elbow so I can skim the place where her bottom lip meets the base of my shaft with my thumb, and then along her throat when I feel the head bump the back. I try to remain civilized and respectful, but it's a challenge when she says things like that and follows it up with deep throating my entire erection. "I want inside all of you like this."

# CHAPTER 11

## THAT SEEMS RASH

*Queenie*

I don't think Kingston realizes that his constant commentary is an absolute turn-on. And it's not like he ever says anything really and truly dirty. It's more that he just keeps talking and offering praise in the form of mostly PG statements.

I hum around his erection, determined to actually take all of him, because listening to him lose it is becoming one of my favorite things. His fingertips drag along the soft, sensitive place under my chin, and he grunts his approval.

"I can't hold off anymore, Queenie," he warns.

I press my thumb against the spot under his balls, and his fingers slide into my hair, curling to grip the strands as he finally lets go. His expression reflects both hunger and satisfaction.

I've always been a fan of oral: obviously receiving is amazing with someone who knows what they're doing. But I find that with Kingston I love the giving, maybe because he gets so into it, and he likes to give while he gets. I've always assumed it would be too much of a distraction, but I'm finding I don't mind having to split my focus at all.

When he's spent, he flops back on the mattress with a sigh. "Your mouth is glorious, Queenie."

"So is yours." I stretch out beside him. His hair is an absolute mess from my hands having been in it while we were kissing, his face is flushed, and he's breathing heavily. "You wanna check to see if you have condoms in your room before you get hard again?"

He side-eyes me. "Uh . . . are you serious?"

"I get the shot, but I figure you'd want to be extra safe like the Boy Scout you are. You'll get hard in, like, five minutes; might as well be prepared for all possible scenarios, don't you think?"

He rubs at his bottom lip and exhales a long breath. "Uh, I'd like to talk to your dad first."

"Why? It's not like you're going to ask him for permission to have sex with me."

"Well, no, but I'd at least like to get his consent to date you." He runs his palm down his chest and back up.

"Oh. Right." I guess he's taking me seriously about convincing my dad it's okay for me to get involved with him. "But I don't see what that has to do with us having sex."

"I'd like to take you out for dinner first."

"What if we order room service?"

"I mean, I'd like to take you on a proper date, where I pick you up at your house and bring you flowers and chocolate. Then I'll take you out for a nice dinner."

"It's kinda late to do that tonight, don't you think?" I glance at the clock on the nightstand. It's already ten. It's way too late for a dinner date.

A grin tips up the corner of his mouth, and he scratches his neck. "It is."

"So . . . does that mean you don't want to have sex with me tonight?" He's already getting hard again. I poke his semisoft penis and frown. I'm not sure if it's the lighting or what, but it looks a little red . . . and bumpy.

"No. I mean, yes, of course. I want to be inside you more than I want my next breath." He skims my cheek with his fingertips. "But I want to do things in the right order, and so far it's all been very backward. Let me put the effort in, Queenie. I want to show you you're worth it."

"When you put it that way . . ." I prop myself up on an elbow, ready to barter for a round of wet Slip 'N Slide, but I'm distracted by the blotchy red patches that have appeared on his chest and stomach. "Uh, is this normal?"

He glances at my hand, which is right by his now mostly erect, hot-pink peen. "We're talking about sex, and you're naked, and all I can smell and taste is you, so yeah, getting hard is normal."

"No, I mean this." I poke one of the raised red welts below his navel and follow the visual trail that extends all the way up his chest, to his nipples, over his neck, and to his mouth. I can actually see it growing progressively worse with each passing second. "Are you having an allergic reaction? Oh my God, are you allergic to *me*?"

"What? Oh hell!" King sits up in a rush and runs a hand from his pecs to his peen.

"Do you have any allergies?"

"Just strawberries. I get hives if I eat them or touch them."

We both look over at the takeout cup sitting on the desk on the other side of the room. I slap a hand over my mouth. "Oh God, I just had a strawberry milkshake. What should I do?"

"I need an antihistamine. And some cortisone cream and possibly some EMLA cream." King grimaces as he rolls off the bed and gets a good look at his dick. It's sizable on a good day, but right now it's swelling and bumpy and very much the wrong color.

"I don't know if I have any antihistamines, or any of that other stuff."

"I have some in my room. The antihistamines anyway. The sooner I take it, the less severe the reaction will be. And I need to shower." He yanks his boxers on and hops around as he tries to put his pants on.

"I'm so sorry."

"It's not your fault. I should've asked about the milkshake. I was too caught up in making out to really think about it."

"There's a CVS down the street. I can always run out if you don't have all the things you need." I hurry to put on my clothes.

"The team doctor always has stuff on hand."

"Right. Okay. That makes sense." His face is getting progressively worse. His normally full lips are puffy, like he's had collagen injections or something, and half his neck is covered in red welts. "It's not anaphylactic, is it?"

"No. Just the hives. At least that's what happened the last time I had a reaction."

"When was that?"

"I think I was a teenager." King pulls his polo over his head, forgoes his socks and shoes, and crosses over to the door.

"Is it possible for an allergy to worsen over time?"

"Maybe?"

I don't bother with a bra, pulling my shirt over my head as I follow on his heels. It's not like I can do anything constructive, but with the amount of swelling around his face and mouth, I sure as hell won't be leaving him alone.

Kingston throws open the door but doesn't rush across the hall like I expect him to, so I slam into his back with an oof. "What are you waiting for? We need to get this under control before your di—"

"Oh, hi, sir!" he almost shouts.

"King? What're you doing in my daughter's room at this hour? And what happened to your face?"

Shit. Of course my dad has to pick this exact moment to drop by. I slip past Kingston, and my nipples brush his arm, causing them to peak more than they already are, especially when the blast of air-conditioning hits me in the hall. I cross my arms to cover them. "He's having an allergic reaction. He needs an antihistamine."

"A reaction to what?"

"I'm allergic to strawberries, sir."

"Shit. That's right. What did you eat that had strawberries in it?"

"I didn't eat anything, sir. Queenie had a strawberry shake."

His brow furrows. "Jesus. This is from a shake?"

Leave it to Kingston to be far too honest for his or my own good. "Can you ask questions later, Dad? I think we need to get King something for the swelling before it becomes an issue."

"Right. Yeah. Let me call the team medic." My dad pulls out his phone, clicks a couple of buttons, and brings it to his ear, then motions for us to follow him.

Neither of us is wearing shoes. "Let me grab my purse in case I need to run to the CVS for anything." I duck behind King, slip on my flip-flops, grab my bag and his dress shoes, and meet them down the hall by the elevators. I pass King his shoes, because there really isn't another option.

"We just have to go down a couple of floors. You doing okay there, King? That's a pretty nasty reaction to a milkshake." My dad frowns as Kingston slips his feet into his shoes. They're loafers, which I'd usually make fun of, but for some reason they work on King.

The crease in my dad's brow deepens as he inspects King's face more closely. His usually neat hair is a mess. Because my hands were in it. And there's a somewhat decent chance that we smell a lot like sex.

The elevator dings, and my dad turns his suspicious gaze on me. "I've got it from here, honey. You can go back to your room."

"But—"

"It's all right. It's late and you should get some rest. Thanks for your help, Queenie. I'll see you tomorrow." King gives me a slightly strained smile and follows my dad into the elevator.

I sincerely hope King is alive come morning.

# CHAPTER 12

## PLEASE DON'T CASTRATE ME

*Kingston*

My swallow is audible as the elevator doors slide shut. Jake leans against the rail and crosses his arms.

I can smell Queenie on me: not only a faint hint of her perfume but also, and far more pungently, her *special* scent, completely unique to her, because it's still all over my face. I glance at my reflection, getting a good look at my swollen lips and chin and my unruly hair. I quickly try to tame it but then realize Jake is watching me, so I clasp my hands in front of me.

"Sir, I—"

The elevator dings and the doors open. A couple in their midthirties gets on, preventing me from saying anything else. I honestly don't know what I'm going to tell him. Obviously I'd planned to talk to Jake about my relationship with Queenie, but I hadn't anticipated doing it while having an allergic reaction caused by making it to third base with her.

We get off at the next stop, and I silently follow Jake to the medic's room. Bill is already waiting for us, his bag of supplies laid out on the coffee table.

He makes a face as soon as he sees me. "Oh, man, that's one hell of a reaction. Are those hives? Aren't they itchy?"

"Yes and yes," I say with a nod. The worst of the itching is below the belt. I'm actually nervous about what things might look like down there at the moment, considering how uncomfortable I am.

Bill ushers us inside, motions for me to take a seat on the couch, and begins by inspecting my face and looking inside my mouth. "Okay, no swelling of the tongue, so that's a positive. It's not anaphylactic, but I think we should probably have you retested, since this seems to be a pretty intense reaction." He holds my chin and shifts my head from side to side. "So this is from strawberries, huh? What'd you do, smear it all over your face? It's all down your neck too." He pulls at the collar of my shirt. "How far down does it go, King?"

"I, uh . . . it's not . . . it doesn't go too far," I stammer, and then I glance over at Jake, who legitimately looks like he's going to murder me.

He pushes off the edge of the dresser. "I'm going to let you two manage this. King, I'd like you to stop by my room before you head back to your own. I'm right next to Queenie, across the hall from you."

"Yes, sir."

"You sure you don't want to wait? I'm going to give him a shot and some cream and he'll be good to go."

"I'm sure." Jake nods stiffly and leaves.

"He's in a mood," Bill mutters once the door slams shut.

"I'm sure he's just tired."

Bill makes a sound and stabs me in the arm with a needle. Then he gives me some anti-itch and cortisone cream to help settle the hives and the swelling. "I'll get you set up with a new set of allergy tests when we get back to Seattle and make sure we don't need to be carrying around an EpiPen for you, just in case."

"Okay, thanks, sir." I push up off the couch and run a hand through my hair. I try to smooth it out a little more as I head for the door.

"And next time, tell whoever you're getting friendly with not to eat strawberries beforehand. It'll save you a lot of discomfort."

"I wasn't—"

Bill raises his hand to stop me. It's not as if I can complete that sentence without outright lying. "Get some rest and stay out of trouble's way, King."

I have messages from Queenie waiting for me as I get into the elevator and head back up to my floor. She wants to know how I am and requests that I message as soon as I'm done. I put a hold on that, since I need to talk to her dad before I do anything else.

I decide it's a good idea to stop in my room first and quickly wash off the strawberry residue and the smell of Queenie before I visit Jake in his room. I have my key card poised over the sensor when the door across the hall flies open. He wasn't lying about being next to Queenie, and he looks less than impressed.

"Aren't you forgetting something?" Jake leans against the doorjamb.

"I'm supposed to wash my face and put some of this cream on, but it can wait." I desperately want to calm the itch and the discomfort, but based on how unhappy Jake looks, I think it would be a better idea to just bite the bullet. Hopefully not literally. I slip the cream into my pants pocket and take a step in Jake's direction.

He moves aside and allows me into his room. I notice the adjoining room door. The low tones of music come from the other side. Where Queenie probably is right now.

The door slams shut behind me. I wonder if this is how reluctant MMA fighters feel when they get into the ring with a superior opponent.

Jake crosses the room and retrieves a bottle of scotch from the fridge. He removes the cap and pours himself a glass but doesn't offer me one. He takes a hefty gulp. Then he stares at the wall for a long time before he finally looks my way. "I asked you to watch out for Queenie."

"Yes, sir, you did."

"I trusted you with her welfare."

"Yes, sir, you did." I want to scratch my stomach so badly right now.

He takes another massive gulp of his scotch, and I grimace at the memory of that flavor. I really don't like scotch. "It looks like that trust was misplaced."

"On the contrary, I don't believe it was."

His eyes narrow in suspicion. "I'm not an idiot. I know what the hell was going on. Look at yourself." He flings a hand out. "You're a disheveled mess. You know how many times I've seen you anything but put together? Never. Until now. I know my daughter, and I am very well aware of the effect she can have on people. It was a mistake to bring her on as my assistant." He paces the room. "I should've known better."

"With all due respect, I disagree. Queenie is an exceptional woman, and she's doing a fantastic job as your assistant. Even though this job isn't something she's necessarily passionate about, she goes above and beyond at every opportunity. She's done everything she can to prove that you made the right decision, sir, and she would be devastated if she knew you felt this way." I glance toward the adjoining door. Music is still playing on the other side, muffled but there.

Jake runs a hand down his face. "That's not what I meant. I know she's doing a fantastic job. She's impulsive and doesn't always consider the ramifications of her decisions. That's all—"

"I would like to date her," I blurt.

Jake's eyes widen. "I'm sorry, what?"

"With your permission, of course."

"You want to date Queenie?"

"Yes, sir." I can't quite figure out his tone or his expression. "I've had a chance to spend time with her, and I care about her. I would like her to be my girlfriend. I planned to ask your permission tomorrow, but then this happened." I motion to my face, which is probably not a great idea, so I jam my hand back in my pants pocket.

"Does she know this? That you want to date her?"

"Yes, sir, she does."

"And what does Queenie have to say about that?"

"She's in agreement, if I'm able to convince you to allow it. She was the one who insisted we remain platonic, because she didn't want to disappoint you. What happened this evening was my fault. I had intended to speak with you first, but—"

He raises a hand to stop me, which is good, because I'm not sure there's a good way to complete that statement. "You can stop with the 'sir' and just call me Jake."

"Of course, Jake. I apologize."

"I wish this whole nice-guy thing you have going on was a load of bullshit."

"I'm sorry?" I don't understand why he would want his daughter to date someone who wasn't good to her or nice.

"It would be easier to trade your ass for this if I didn't like you, Kingston." He sighs and rubs his chin. "You realize she's a handful." I don't think he means it in a negative way—more of a warning not to get involved on a whim.

"Nothing I can't handle, sir . . . I mean Jake. And I happen to like that about her."

He gives me the side-eye. "Yeah, your face tells me that."

This conversation would be a lot easier if I weren't covered in hives. "That's not how I meant it—"

He waves the comment away with a roll of his eyes. "You don't need to explain yourself." He drains the rest of his glass. "You have my permission to date Queenie."

"I do?" I'm surprised, considering the state I'm in and how unimpressed Jake is with me at the moment.

"Yeah. I'm not sure there's a point in saying no anyway." He runs a hand through his hair. "If there was anyone on the team I'd be okay with Queenie dating, it's you."

"Thank you, Jake. I promise to treat her with the care and respect she deserves."

He pins me with a hard look. "You do not share a room when we're at away games."

"Of course not." Especially if her room adjoins his. I appreciate that Queenie is expressive in bed, and I would prefer not to stifle that.

"And this shit better not happen again." He motions to my face.

"I understand. I'm sorry. It was purely by accident. I haven't had an allergic reaction in a long time."

He heaves a sigh. "It's late. You have an early morning."

"Yes, sir. Thank you for understanding." I head for the door.

"Go to bed, King. And stay out of my daughter's tonight."

"I wouldn't—"

He holds up a hand. "Remember that when she's trying to persuade you otherwise."

"I told you, sir, I can hold my own."

"That's what you think. Now get out of here and get some sleep."

I leave Jake's room and cross the hall to mine and Bishop's. I'm not looking forward to explaining this whole situation to him, mostly because I expect that he'll derive an unprecedented amount of joy from the awkwardness.

I have my key card in my hand when the door across the hall opens and Queenie pokes her head out. "Psst."

I glance at her father's closed door and whisper, "Hey."

"What was that about?" She tips her head in the direction of her dad's door, which is when it opens and Jake appears.

"Don't make me tape your doors closed like I did when I chaperoned that high school trip to Washington."

"Oh my God, Dad. I'm checking to see if King is okay."

"King is fine."

"I'm fine." Jake and I echo each other.

"Can we have a minute, please?" She gives Jake a look.

I stay silent because I don't want to rock the boat.

He sighs. "One minute. King needs his rest, and I need to not have a fucking heart attack tonight." He disappears back into his room, the door closing heavily behind him.

Keeping her door propped open with her foot, Queenie steps out into the hall, grabs the front of my shirt, and yanks me toward her room.

"What're you doing?"

"This isn't high school. We're not talking in the hall." She pulls me into her room and closes the door. "Your face looks a little better."

"The medic gave me a shot of antihistamine. It should be mostly gone tomorrow."

"Okay. That's good. What happened in there?" She inclines her head toward the wall abutting her dad's room.

"I asked for permission to date you."

"You did?" She seems surprised. "What did he say?"

"He wasn't happy about the situation he found us in, but he seems okay with it."

"That's because he thinks you're a squeaky clean Boy Scout." She smiles coyly. "He doesn't realize that you like to destroy panties and tongue fuck my pussy."

"Shh! What if he's listening?"

"He should know better." She runs a hand down my chest. "How's everything south of the navel?"

"I have cream I need to put on all the affected areas after I shower."

She cups me through my pants. "Too bad I can't help with that."

"Queenie, please." I cover her hand with mine.

"Is it uncomfortable?"

I nod. My intention is to remove her hand and gently remind her that it isn't a good time to be touching me like this, but she rubs over the ridge with her thumb, and it's both soothing and stimulating.

"You're sharing a room with Bishop, right?"

"I am."

"You could shower and sneak back over here after, then I could take care of putting the cream on all the affected areas."

We both jump at the sound of a fist pounding on the adjoining door. "Your minute is up!" Jake shouts from the other side.

Queenie rolls her eyes and opens her mouth. I know she's going to give him sass, because she's Queenie and she can't help herself, so I clamp my hand over her mouth before she can say something that will cause us more problems. "I'm on my way out."

Queenie narrows her eyes at me, clearly unimpressed, and bites my palm. I drop it. "We're not fifteen years old. We're adults."

"I have a game tomorrow, and he's your father. It doesn't matter how much he likes me, or if he thinks I'm a Boy Scout; he also knows I was alone in here with you and that things he'd rather not know about were happening. I also promised him I would stay out of your room at night."

"You what?"

"We can talk more about it tomorrow. I'm not really in a position to bargain." I motion to my face. "Have you brushed your teeth since I left?"

"Yeah, why?"

"Did you drink any more of that milkshake?"

"No, I threw it out."

"Good." I wrap one arm around her waist and bend to kiss her. My plan is to keep it chaste, because my lips are still swollen and half my face is covered in welts, but she sucks my bottom lip and strokes inside with her tongue.

"You still taste like me," she murmurs.

"I need to leave." I disengage from the kiss, aware that if I don't go, Jake may actually castrate me, or have me traded, or decide I'm not allowed to date Queenie.

She doesn't put up a fight as I fumble for the door and extricate myself from her hold on me. "See you tomorrow, King," she says loudly, likely for her dad's benefit.

I blow out a breath once her door closes, leaving me in the hall, alone. I slide my wallet out of my back pocket, find my key card, and hold it over the sensor, waiting until I get the green light before I turn the handle and put yet another barrier between me and Queenie. My phone is already buzzing with messages, and I can guarantee they're from her. There is no way I'm sneaking over there after I shower. That's a surefire way to screw things right up. Besides, I don't think it's a good idea to engage in any activities that might lead to friction below the waist. It could aggravate the hives.

Bishop is lying on the double bed closest to the bathroom, flipping channels. "Dude, where the fuck have you been? I was ready to send out a search party." He glances up from the TV, and his eyes go wide. "And what the hell happened to your face?"

"I was with the medic. I had an allergic reaction."

"Jesus. Are you okay? What the hell did you react to? You look like plastic surgery gone wrong."

"Strawberries, and I'm okay. Just itchy and uncomfortable."

"You're so careful about that. How in the world did that even happen?"

"It's a long story. I need to shower. I'll be out in a bit." I cross the room and lock myself in the bathroom. I hope if I take long enough, he'll pass out and I won't have to answer any questions.

I turn on the shower, pull my shirt over my head, and then fold it neatly, setting it on the vanity. I caught a glimpse of myself in the elevator and in the mirror in Bill's room, but I haven't seen my face up close. I've definitely seen better days, and my chest and nipples and stomach are covered in a series of very telling red welts.

I unzip my pants and cringe when I get a look at the damage down there. My penis is an angry red color and is mottled with hives. It's definitely not pretty. I strip out of the rest of my clothes and get in the shower, adjusting the temperature so it's not too hot and doesn't make the situation worse. I'm extra careful and gentle as I wash my face, neck, chest, and junk with mild soap, and no facecloth because it's too abrasive.

Once I'm sure I've removed all traces of Queenie's saliva, I pat myself dry and realize in my haste to escape Bishop's questions, I didn't bring anything with me to change into. I consider, briefly, putting my dirty clothes back on, but it might exacerbate the allergy issue, so I decide against it. I slather the cream all over the affected areas and wait a few minutes for it to soak in before I leave the bathroom.

I wrap a towel around my waist and cross my fingers that Bishop has passed out. Obviously, luck is not on my side tonight, because he's still very much awake and alert when I open the bathroom door.

His brows pull together. "What the fuck? Did you do a penguin slide through a field of strawberries? How the hell does that happen? How far down does that go?" He motions to my chest, his eyes narrowing as he follows the trail to where it's cut off by my towel.

"It's complicated." Logistically I can't keep this from Bishop, but I also don't want to provide details, because that would be unfair to Queenie. I toss my phone on the bed as I cross over to the closet. My dirty clothes go into a plastic bag, so they don't contaminate anything else, before I pull a T-shirt from a hanger.

"Calculus is complicated. How you ended up with a rash like this must have a pretty simple explanation." He pokes at his cheek with his tongue.

"I ran into Queenie."

Bishop bolts up in bed. "Hold the fuck on. Were you messing around with *Queenie?*"

"You know I'm not comfortable sharing those kinds of details." Just because I shared more than I meant to earlier doesn't mean I'm going to do it again. I move to the dresser and retrieve a pair of boxer shorts. I feel like loose is probably better, and hopefully the combination of the antihistamine and the cream will calm things down below the waist; otherwise, wearing a cup tomorrow is going to be incredibly uncomfortable.

"Dude, Jake is going to shit his fucking pants if he finds out about this."

"He already knows."

Bishop's eyes look like they're going to pop out of his head. "He knows his daughter blew you?"

"Wait, what? No. He knows we're dating." I shake my head. "I mean, I asked him for permission to date her, like you said. He has no idea about . . . what happened. Well, I mean, I guess he knows we were kissing, but nothing beyond that. How do you know that she . . ." I motion below my waist.

Bishop rolls his eyes. "King, bro, come the fuck on. There's a very clear trail from your mouth all the way down. It doesn't take a genius to know someone got on her knees for you. Obviously Jake didn't see how far it goes."

"No. Just my face."

"Well, keep it that way if you want your dick to stay attached to your body."

# CHAPTER 13
## EVERYTHING IS ALMOST PERFECT

*Queenie*

The next morning I'm up early, aware after last night that I need to be on the ball. My dad definitely doesn't seem as upset as he could be, possibly because Kingston presents himself as an absolute golden boy, which is true, apart from when he's naked and looking to exchange orgasms.

Sadly, Kingston did not sneak across to my room to let me help him with the cream situation. Which is probably for the best, since my dad is a light sleeper. Also, getting Kingston all worked up when his penis is covered in hives isn't very nice.

The morning is busy for the team, so I don't see Kingston apart from in passing. I'm not 100 percent on protocol in this situation, so I figure it's best to let him take the lead. Which is exactly what he does, just before they hit the locker room to change for the exhibition game.

I'm standing beside my dad, looking over the schedule for the next week, when I breathe in the familiar scent of my *boyfriend*. I glance up to find him standing a few feet away, looking nervous, cheeks pink, face mostly back to normal. His lips have returned to their full, plush state but not like he got in a fight with a plastic surgeon.

He hooks his thumbs in his pockets. "Hi, Jake. Hi, Queenie."

"You looked good out there during practice. You game ready?"

"Yes, sir. Thank you, sir." He turns his attention to me. It looks like he's chewing the inside of his lip. "Um . . . will I see you after the game?"

"Yeah, I don't really have anywhere to go other than my hotel room or the pool." Could this be any more awkward, with my father standing next to us, watching us do some approximation of the dating ritual?

I glance at my dad, hoping he'll take the hint and give us a few seconds of privacy or whatever, but he just stands there, either oblivious or totally aware that he's making this whole thing a million times more uncomfortable than it needs to be.

"Great. Okay. I'll find you after the game." Kingston nods several times in a row until it looks like he's imitating a bobble head.

"Sure. Good luck on the ice."

"Thanks." He leans down and kisses me on the cheek. When he steps back, his face is on fire. "You look lovely, by the way." He nods to my dad and then rushes to catch up with the last of the guys heading for the locker room.

"Thanks for making that super awkward, *Jake*."

He arches a brow. "Now you know how I felt last night."

"Touché." Not much else I can say to that.

By the end of the first period, Seattle is up 2–0. Kingston skates over to the bench and pulls his helmet off. He's a big guy at the best of times, but add all the gear and he's mammoth. He's also sweaty, which should be disgusting, but for some reason I find the fact that his hair is soaked and messy kind of hot. Maybe because I'm aware it's related to his incredible stamina.

"Nice work out there in net," my dad praises.

"Thanks. Defense is working hard to make my job easy." He lifts the bottom of his jersey, using it to wipe away the sweat dripping down his face.

On any other day this would be totally fine. But it exposes a strip of bare stomach and with it the residual rash, leading the eye down to where it disappears into his uniform. My dad glances at his stomach, his lips turning down in a frown. I want to tell Kingston to drop his shirt, but I can't. Bishop, however, smacks him in the arm. King gives him a *What the heck?* look. There's a lot of eye widening and silent conversation happening.

My dad's expression says everything words can't. It's obvious where that trail leads and what was going on in my room last night. He mutters something about going to prison for murder, turns around, and walks away.

Later, when we're leaving the arena with the team for a postgame dinner—Seattle won 5–1—my dad falls into step beside me and mutters, "We're setting some ground rules, FYI."

I side-eye him. "I'm twenty-four."

"I'm aware. I'm also aware that as nice as Kingston is, he's male with hormones, and you're female with hormones. He needs to be rested for games, and you need to keep in mind that when we're away with the team, you're a member of the staff and you need to conduct yourself in a professional manner."

"We're not going to make out in public."

"I know that." He rubs the space between his eyes. "I'm just saying, you can't keep my goaltender up all hours of the night."

I bite my tongue and look away, because I'm finally clued in to what he's trying to say without saying it outright. "Right. Got it. So no sleepover parties when we're traveling with the team." I pat his arm. "Don't worry, Dad. I won't give you a reason to murder him."

"Thanks. He's kind of important to the team."

◆ ◆ ◆

I expect there to be more of a reaction from his teammates to Kingston and me dating. The only real difference is that any of the guys who used to be flirty no longer are.

Another interesting thing I've learned about Kingston is that he's not the kind of guy who, once given the green light, jumps right on the sexy times. In fact, ever since he had that conversation with my dad about dating me, he's slowed things right the hell down.

So far we've been on four dates: he's taken me out twice for dinner and once to the movies, and once we went on a double date with Stevie and Bishop. We went ax throwing again. Stevie is a lot of fun to hang out with, and she has killer aim.

Unfortunately, despite all the dates and the drives home, there haven't been any sleepovers. Or anything beyond second base. No blow jobs, no invitations to sit on his face, not even a hand down my pants. Even the nipple contact has been sort of accidental and just a muted brush of thumb over several layers of fabric and padded bra.

It's kind of sweet. It's also really fucking annoying.

"Any plans tonight?" my dad asks as he puts the car in gear and heads home.

"Kingston wants to take me out for dinner." I feel a little guilty that my dad's been on his own for dinners a lot more lately. "I pulled a casserole out of the freezer for you, or you can have leftovers from last night."

"You didn't have to do that. I can handle making my own dinner."

"Yeah, but you'll order takeout, or make something unhealthy. This way I know you're not clogging your arteries when I'm not here to monitor you."

"I'm in my forties, not my eighties; you don't need to worry about my arteries." He pulls into the driveway and shifts the car into park. "Tomorrow morning I have a meeting, so you don't need to be in until closer to eleven."

"I don't remember seeing anything on the schedule. Did I miss something? Do you need me to pull anything for it?"

He slips the keys out of the ignition and opens the door. "You don't need to worry about anything. It's contract negotiations, and I can't really talk about it yet."

"Is everything okay?"

"Everything's fine. It's a private meeting, and you've been working so hard, I figured you wouldn't mind sleeping in."

We're usually out of the house by seven and home sometime after five. I don't mind getting up early, but sleeping in midweek would be amazing. And Seattle doesn't have a game tomorrow night, only practice, which means Kingston doesn't need to be in bed early.

He's not much of a nighthawk, always dropping me off at home by nine forty-five so he can get to bed by ten thirty, which is apparently late for him. He's an interesting guy with some funny quirks, but I like them. And him.

"You don't have to tell me twice." I kiss him on the cheek. "Thanks, Dad. We'll have a movie night next week. You can even pick the movie."

"It's a date." He smiles, but it looks wistful. "Have fun tonight with King, and be safe."

"Kingston's quite literally the king of safe. He drives like he's taking the learner's permit test every time."

"I know. If there was ever a guy who might stand a chance at deserving you, it's him."

"You have blinders on when it comes to me, Dad, and I love you for it." My phone buzzes in my pocket, the tone telling me it's my *boyfriend* messaging me.

"I love you back, kiddo." My heart squeezes when he turns toward the house and his smile turns sad in the reflection in the windows.

He really needs a girlfriend.

I pull my phone out of my purse and check my messages. Kingston usually favors nice restaurants. The kind where I get to dress up and look pretty, and he wears a tie and jacket. Usually he's a polo and khakis guy, but I find the whole suit jacket and tie thing works well for him. Pretty much every single state of dress works for him, actually.

However, tonight I would like to take control of this date. The regular season has already started. Kingston is a saint at away games. He never tries to sneak into my room late at night to fool around, out of respect for my dad and his presence next door, and because he takes his job seriously. And I'm fully on board with this, because I also respect my dad and his role, and the fact that Kingston needs to be rested before a game.

But I'm tired of only getting to second base, like I'm in high school all over again. I want sexually explosive Kingston to come out and play. I figure in order to make that happen, I need to push a few of his buttons and break his ironclad resolve.

So as soon as I'm in the door, I head for the bathroom and strip down so I can take care of business. While I get my personal grooming supplies out, I call Kingston.

"Why aren't I looking at your beautiful face right now?"

"Because I'm getting ready for you, and I'd prefer it if you didn't see my predate face."

"You're effortlessly stunning, Queenie, inside and out."

My stomach does that fluttery thing, and I grin at the compliment. "Well, you're going to be looking at me for hours tonight, so I'm trying to maintain an air of elusiveness."

"I'm counting down the minutes." If those words came out of anyone's mouth other than Kingston's, it would sound like a line, but when he says things like that, I believe he's being genuine. "I made reservations for seven thirty at a place not far from you, but I can definitely move it up if you want me to come get you sooner."

I check the time. If I'm quick about getting ready, I'll have plenty of time to thwart his plan. "Seven thirty is perfect. Since it's close to me, you'll be here around ten past?"

"Oh, yeah, sure, okay. Ten past seven works." I love that he sounds disappointed.

"Great. See you then. Can't wait!" I make a kiss sound and wait for him to say bye before I hang up.

Twenty minutes later I'm freshly showered, groomed, and dressed for the occasion. The Uber ride takes less than twenty minutes, which is good, because King is always on time, if not early, so I arrive on his doorstep just before six forty, which is plenty of time to circumvent his picking me up.

In the short weeks since we started dating, I haven't been back to Kingston's house again. Mostly he picks me up at my place, but he always stops in to talk to my dad first, which often leads to long conversations about hockey-related stuff. It's sweet, but it also means that Kingston has been cockblocking us ever since he officially asked me to be his girlfriend.

I'm about done with that.

I've hit the top stair on the porch when his door swings open. He lives in a big house in a nice neighborhood. In fact, a lot of his teammates live around here, based on the addresses we have on file. The front porch is decorated with pretty plants, two chairs, and a small table. I have a feeling they're more for decoration than use; this isn't the kind of neighborhood where people hang out on their front porch and drink coffee in the morning.

"Hey. I thought I was supposed to pick you up."

"I was ready sooner than I expected to be, so I figured I'd come to you." I brush by him before he can make a move to step outside. "And I'm not really feeling the whole going out for dinner thing, so I think it would be best if you cancel the reservation, and we can have a night in instead."

"You mean here?" He jams his hands in his pockets, and his eyes dart around nervously.

"Yes, here. Let's order takeout. I don't have to be at work until eleven tomorrow and your practice isn't until noon. Let's stay up late and watch a movie and cuddle on your couch." Naked. I glance around the foyer. Like Kingston, it's very tidy and well maintained.

The last time I was here, I was too busy making out with King to pay attention to my surroundings, and in the morning I was rushing to make a quiet exit.

I kick off my shoes and head down the hall. There are a couple of interesting pieces of art on his walls. Not stock pictures bought from some home-decor store but real art, possibly from someone local. I like that idea.

I keep going, though, determined now that I'm here and in his space once again. When I reach the living room, I run my hand along the back of the leather sectional couch. Memories from that night—new ones I'd forgotten until now—surface.

We'd kissed our way down the hall and bumped into the couch, and I'd ended up sitting on the back of it, my legs wrapped around King's waist. I shrug out of my jacket, toss it over the arm, and hop up onto the back of it now, exactly as I'd been then.

Kingston's hands are still shoved in his pockets, and he rocks back on his heels. "You're sure you don't want to go out for dinner? It's a nice place. I haven't taken you there before, and it's a favorite of mine." His throat bobs with another nervous swallow, and his gaze stays fixed on my legs as I cross them.

"Why don't you want to be alone with me?"

He rubs the back of his neck. "It's not that I don't want to be alone with you."

"But . . ."

His tongue peeks out to wet his bottom lip. "I'm trying to date you."

"We've been out four times in the past two weeks, and that's with your insane schedule and all the travel. We also see each other pretty much daily. I think that all qualifies as dating, and it still doesn't explain why you look like a caged rabbit right now."

"I want to be a good boyfriend."

"You are a good boyfriend." He's a great boyfriend. The best I've ever had. Almost too good to be true, really.

He looks at his feet, and the tips of his ears go red. "I'm trying to keep myself in check when I'm with you, but it's hard when we're alone."

"Why would you want to keep yourself in check?"

He blows out a breath. "I want to show you that I appreciate more than your body."

"I think you've covered that base pretty well with the whole asking my dad permission to date me, taking me out for dinner multiple times, and spending money on me without expecting a blow job at the end of the night."

"Can we not talk about that?"

"About what?"

He motions to his crotch. Up until now I haven't paid attention to it, but I sure am now. Kingston is hard. Rock hard, if I had to guess, considering I can see the outline of the ridge at the head, pushing up against his khakis.

"It doesn't look like you want me to stop talking about it."

"I'm struggling right now, and you're not making it any easier, Queenie." He's almost . . . snippy. Which is new.

I can see it in the tic of his jaw and the way his fingers twitch at his sides. He's right on the edge, and I intend to push him over so I can experience his glorious free fall.

"Tell me what you're struggling with." I crook a finger, beckoning him. "Maybe I can help."

He shifts his weight from foot to foot, shuffles forward a step, and mumbles, "Control."

I bite the inside of my cheek to keep from smiling too widely. It really is commendable how hard he's trying to behave. I'm not sure exactly why he feels compelled to stay stalled out at second base for so long, but I'm pretty sure I can fix that problem.

I slide a single finger up my thigh, bunching the material.

Kingston follows the movement. When I'm an inch away from revealing the color of my underwear, I pause. "Why do you feel like you need to stay in control?"

He licks his lips, his hot gaze shifting up to mine. "Because the last time you were here I ruined your panties."

"I didn't mind. And I wore cheap ones tonight, just in case." I take the opportunity for what it is and lift my dress over my head, tossing it on the floor. My bra and panties are lace and satin from the bargain bin, because I am very much hoping for a repeat of last time. "It's okay if you want to lose control with me, King. I definitely want to lose control with you."

He exhales a shaky breath, and his gaze moves over me in a hungry sweep. The smolder in his eyes sparks and flames. He crosses the room in four long strides and comes to an abrupt halt in front of me. His hands curl into fists, flexing and releasing as a low groan bubbles up from his chest. Still fighting to keep his leash on.

I uncross my legs and hook my foot around the back of his knee, tugging him closer.

His threads of control pull tight, threatening to snap.

He moves into the empty space between my thighs, and his hand shoots out, sliding into the hair at the nape of my neck to anchor there. His other hand runs up my bare thigh to cup my ass, fingertips digging in hard as I wrap my legs around his waist. I moan when his erection presses up against my stomach.

He tips my head back, lips only a breath away from mine, eyes dark with need and lust. His tongue peeks out to touch the imperfection in his front tooth. "You are entirely too much of a temptation to resist."

"So stop resisting."

I expect him to give in and kiss me, but instead he drops his head and drags the tip of his nose along the column of my throat, lips following until he pauses at my ear. "You may need to set some parameters for me, my queen, so I know how out of control I'm allowed to get here."

I shiver in anticipation at his low warning tone and this new endearment. "No parameters."

He pulls back, lips temptingly close. "None?"

I bite the edge of his jaw, enjoying the slight sting and tug at the base of my skull when his fingers tighten in my hair. "I've been waiting for months to get back into your bedroom." I arch up and nibble his bottom lip. "Lock the Boy Scout in the closet and let yourself off your leash, King."

# CHAPTER 14

## UNRESTRAINED

*Kingston*

I very rarely lose control.

Actually, that's untrue.

Pre-Queenie I very rarely lost control. Now it seems every time I'm alone with her, the word becomes an elusive, untenable concept. Especially when we're unclothed. Which is part of the reason I've avoided bringing her back to my place after our dates. Or spending any time with her in either of our hotel rooms at away games. I'm trying to be respectful of my girlfriend and our situation.

But tonight I planned to bring her back here. *After* I picked her up, brought her flowers and chocolate—those are sitting on my kitchen counter—and took her out for a nice dinner.

Because I haven't done more than kiss her in the past two weeks. I haven't touched her, tasted her, made her come. And it's literally all I can think about when I'm not on the ice.

I haven't been this hormonally driven since I was a teenager. And back then I used hockey to work out the frustration. It's become an ineffective strategy where Queenie is concerned.

In hindsight, the two-week wooing period in which I deprived Queenie and myself of any kind of gratification was probably not my smartest move. And now she's given me explicit permission to loosen my reins.

Queenie's fingertips drift down my cheek. Even that innocuous contact sends a shot of heat down my spine and makes my erection twitch behind my fly. A tiny moan leaves Queenie's lips, pulling me out of my head.

"I'm taking you to bed." It's more growl than words.

A shiver runs through her, and she clasps her hands behind my neck as I hoist her up. "That's all I'm asking for," she murmurs in my ear, nipping at the lobe.

"I think you're asking for a lot more than a make-out session and a snuggle." I squeeze her lush bottom as I carry her down the hall.

"An orgasm would be incredibly welcome." Her lips part against the side of my neck, and her wet, warm tongue sweeps out, teeth pressing gently into the skin.

I shoulder the door open and carry her over to the bed, laying her out on the freshly washed sheets. "Just one?" I ask as I climb up after her.

Queenie yanks my shirt free from my pants and rises up on her knees, palms flattening against my stomach, pushing my shirt up. I pull it over my head and toss it on the floor while Queenie goes to work on my belt. "Last time I was here I lost track, so if you can make me so incoherent I forget how to count, that would be perfect."

"I should be able to manage that." I slide a hand into the hair at the nape of her neck, fingers twisting in the satin strands and gripping gently. I tip her head back and brush my lips from the base of her throat to her chin, biting softly before I angle her head to the side and cover her mouth with mine. I groan when she eases her hand inside my boxer briefs and her soft, warm palm encases my erection.

I mirror her actions, skimming a nipple with a fingertip and gliding lower, slipping into her satin and lace panties. I stroke slick, swollen skin and murmur against her lips, "You're already wet for me."

"That shouldn't be a surprise," Queenie chuckles breathily and whimpers when I circle her entrance.

"Mmm, it was more of an observation than anything." I ease a single finger inside her, and she moans. I curl forward, finding the spot that makes her grip on my erection tighten and her rhythm falter. When I slip my hand out from between her thighs, she sucks in a breath and breaks the kiss.

"What're you doing? Don't stop," she whines.

It's my turn to laugh. "Don't worry, my queen, you'll get what you want." My fingers are still twined in her hair. I drag my sex-wet finger across her bottom lip, then suck it between mine. "You taste like you're ready to come," I whisper.

"Please, King." She squeezes my erection.

I brush the tip of my nose against hers and ease my hand back into her panties. "Are you? Ready to come?" This time I push two fingers inside and feel the slight pulse as I brush her clit with my thumb. "I think maybe you are."

I watch her face as I move my fingers inside her, enthralled by the sweet moans and whimpers that grow louder and lower with every curl and pump. She releases my erection so she can grip both of my shoulders, nails digging in as she rolls her hips. "Please tell me your mouth is next."

"As soon as you come you can ride my tongue," I assure her.

Apparently that's the right thing to say, because she clenches around my fingers, body shaking with her first orgasm. I don't even let her ride it out. Instead, I yank her panties down her legs—I don't destroy them, though—and, like the last time we were in my bed, I stretch out and move her to straddle my face so I can bring her to orgasm again with my mouth while she takes me in hers. When she's come twice more, I lay her out so her head rests on the pillows and kneel between her parted thighs. Her hair is wild and tangled, lips swollen, cheeks flushed. Her eyes are glassy and soft.

I use the head of my erection to tease her wet, swollen sex. "Tell me what you want." I know what I'd like to happen now, but I want to make sure we're on the same page.

"More of you." She stretches out her legs and rests her heels on my shoulders. "All of you."

I kiss her left ankle and drag the head down, nudging at her entrance. "Do you want me to fill you up?"

She moans and fists the sheets, toes curling. "Please, yes, God."

I shift her leg so I can reach the nightstand drawer.

"What're you doing?"

I pause. "I should get a condom?" I don't know why it comes out as a question. It's definitely what I should do. It's the safest, smartest option.

"I get the shot. Every three months. I'm safe." She bites her lip, uncertain. "You can pull out if you're worried."

"I'll make a mess of you."

"I don't mind. We can take a shower together after." She gives me a coy smile. "You can clean me up after you get me all dirty."

I laugh and shake my head. "You really are perfect for me, you know that?"

"You'd be perfect for me if you'd stop teasing me and just fuck me already."

She nudges the back of my neck with her toe, and I let her pull me down on top of her until her knees hit her chest. I adjust her legs so they're wrapped around my waist and brush my lips along her jaw. Rolling my hips, I slip low again. I don't push in, though, instead savoring her soft moans and the tremble in her limbs.

"Make me yours." She drags her fingertips down my cheek. "It's all I want, just to be yours."

I curve my palm around the back of her neck and push inside on a low groan that she echoes. She arches, chin tipping back, eyes rolling up, and I shudder at the feel of her clenching around me.

"God, Queenie, are you coming already?"

Her nails dig into my arms and her lids flutter open, her hazy gaze meeting mine. "Is that what you want?"

Heat slams through my veins, and the urge to just . . . *take* becomes painfully acute. "Yes."

"Tell me," she murmurs.

"I want you to come while I'm inside you." I suck her bottom lip and roll my hips again. "I want to covet every single one of your orgasms, and when I'm done with you there won't be any question as to whether you're mine."

"Was there ever really a question in the first place?"

"Not for me, no."

She strokes the edge of my jaw, a hint of vulnerability in her eyes. "And are you mine?"

I sweep my thumb along the side of her neck. "All yours."

"Good." She pulls my mouth down to hers, smiling against my lips. "Now fuck me like I know you want to."

I ease my hips back, pulling out all the way to the ridge before sinking back in. The first few strokes are slow, but with every moan and whimpered plea from Queenie to go *harder, faster, give her more, make her come again, goddammit*, the final threads of control threaten to snap.

"I'm not made of glass. Stop worrying that you're going to break me." She slaps my ass.

I push up on one arm and give her a look, sweat dripping from my temple to the pillow beside her, dangerously close to her cheek. I lean to the side, still trying to maintain some kind of rhythm as I wipe my forehead on the sheets, then shift so I can see her face again. "Jeez, Queenie, how much harder do you want me to go?"

"Why? You getting tired? Need to get on your back and let me do the work for a while?" She arches a challenging brow. "I'm more than happy to bounce around on your cock like you're my personal pogo stick if you need a break."

"Are you questioning my stamina?"

"Maybe we should do a couple of shots. You were a lot less restrained last time," she goads.

"Last time I wasn't inside you." I punctuate the statement with a heavy thrust.

Queenie groans and slaps my ass a second time. "Again."

So I do. And it gets me another ass slap.

"Stop slapping my ass."

"Or what?" She does it again.

I give my head a slow shake. "Remember that you asked for it."

Her eyes light up with something like triumph and then confusion as I push up, sit back on my heels, and pull out.

"What—"

I grab her ankles and flip her onto her stomach. She shrieks and then gasps when I grip her wrists and stretch out on top of her, raising our hands over her head. My erection slides along the crack of her ass, and I adjust my position until I'm nudging against her entrance again. I brush my lips over her cheek. "Is this okay?"

"Yes. More than okay." Her voice vibrates with excitement. "This is what I've been waiting for."

I press my lips to her temple. "Tell me if it's too much."

"It won't be."

I ease in and Queenie lifts her hips, pushing her butt up with a groan. And I give in, letting need and desire take over as I drive into her. I release her wrists, afraid I'm cutting off the circulation. She reaches back, fingers twining in my hair, twisting her head, seeking my mouth. I tuck one hand under her chin, tipping her head up and back so I can kiss her while I . . . basically pound her into the mattress.

There's not a lot of finesse on my part. The headboard slams into the wall, a piece of art hits the floor, but I keep moving over her, groaning as she clenches around me, ridiculously pleased that she's coming again, because it means I can let go.

The orgasm hijacks my body, slamming into me like a punch in the spine. I bite her shoulder, my erection kicking inside of her as I come. It isn't until I collapse on top of her and she grunts out a "You're really fucking heavy, King" that I push up on my dangerously shaky arms and roll off of her.

I wipe my sweaty face on the pillow. "Crap, sorry." I brush her wild hair out of her face. It's a knotted, tangled mess, and that would be 100 percent my fault. I skim the bite mark on her shoulder and cringe. "Are you okay?"

She props her chin on her fist and grins. "I'm great. How are you?" She reaches out and runs the fingers of her free hand through my damp hair.

"I'm . . . are you sure you're okay? I went at you pretty hard."

"I'm positively positive. I'm actually fantastic times a thousand. Also, I asked you to go hard." She bites her lip, eyes searching my face. "I can handle a good dicking, King, especially since the only thing you've done in the past two weeks is dry hump me for a few seconds when you kiss me good night and graze my nipple through layers of fabric. I think we both needed that, don't you?"

I laugh. "Yeah, I guess we did." I slide an arm under her back and pull her closer so she's sprawled out over my chest.

I brush her hair away from her face, but she's just as sweaty as me so it sticks to her cheek, and it takes me a couple of tries before I manage to tuck it behind her ear.

"I think we need a shower," I say.

"Probably, but it might be a good idea to get in sex round two before we do that, since I assume we're going to get sweaty again."

"You want a round two?"

She arches a brow. "Don't you?"

"Well, yeah, of course, but—"

"But nothing, then. This time I get to ride you." She braces her hands on my pecs and straddles my hips. "And if I forgot to mention it, I'm staying over again, but this time I won't do a runner in the morning."

# CHAPTER 15
## MORNING AFTER

*Kingston*

I crack a lid and glance to the right. Beside me is an empty pillow with a head dent. My disappointment at Queenie's absence in my bed is short lived as I breathe in the smell of sex and . . . bacon?

I throw off the covers and sit up with a groan. Foreign muscle aches make moving more difficult than usual. Being a professional athlete means I'm in pretty damn good shape, but it's been a while since I've had sex.

*So much sex.*

And definitely *not* the hair-pulling, neck-biting, thrust until the headboard dents the drywall and art falls on the floor kind of sex I had last night.

Banging and clanging comes from my kitchen and . . . singing? I smile and push off the mattress, fighting another groan at the ache in my thighs and my glutes.

I grab a pair of boxers from my dresser and leave the room—bed still unmade and last night's clothes scattered all over the floor. It's not how I typically operate, but this morning isn't typical, so the tidying up can wait. Until after I find my girlfriend, who, judging by the smell, is making breakfast. I don't know why it surprises me, maybe because I've assumed she'd be more of a sugary cereal and Pop-Tarts kind of woman.

My kitchen is a mess. Spoons, bowls, and measuring cups litter the counter, along with flour and discarded eggshells. Several cutting boards and knives are stacked by the sink. My first thought is that this is going to take forever to clean up. My second thought is that I'm glad my cleaner will be here tomorrow to take care of what I can't today. Including the pile of sheets and towels heaped in my closet. We ended up changing them more than once, and showering twice.

But any worries I have about the mess disappear as soon as I spot Queenie amid the chaos. She's wearing an apron that my family gave me as a joke. It has a buff male body on it, which is odd, with the way her chest accentuates the pecs. She's holding one of my mixing bowls—I don't use them very often, but the guy who comes in to prepare my meals every week is always grateful for my stocked kitchen. I have my mother and momster to thank for that.

Queenie looks up from the open book on the counter and starts when she sees me. "Did I wake you? I was kind of hoping to surprise you." She stops stirring whatever is in the bowl and sets it on the counter. "I thought we deserved a really great breakfast, but I know you like to follow the recommended eating plan so I made some high-protein, slow-release pancakes with oats, and then I figured that was kind of boring so I made some with shredded coconut, pineapple, and macadamia nuts, and I also made banana-pecan ones because they're still healthy. I considered adding chocolate chips, but I wasn't sure if you'd eat any of them, so I held off. Oh, and I made bacon, because it's delicious, and if you're going to cheat on your meal plan, you should always cheat with bacon."

I open my mouth to speak, but all the words get lost as soon as Queenie turns her back to me. And I find out that the apron she's wearing is the only article of clothing adorning her amazing body. A bow frames the center of her back, the ties dangling tauntingly over the swell of her perfectly bare bottom.

Queenie looks over her shoulder, her expression expectant. When I don't answer right away, she tips her head to the side. "Kingston?"

"I'm sorry, what was the question?" I ask her butt.

"Would you like some of the turkey bacon in your fridge? It has a Post-it on it that says 'Friday,' and I wasn't sure if that meant it's for Friday or if it goes bad by Friday, which would mean it should get eaten sooner rather than later."

"I'm good with whatever bacon you've already made." I move in behind her, slip my finger under the tie along her waist, and pull the bow. "How much time do we have until breakfast is ready?"

Thirty minutes, an orgasm each, and some almost-burned bacon later, we're sitting at my breakfast bar eating pancakes I would literally kill for, bacon, and a fresh-fruit platter.

"Move in with me," I blurt. I blame it on the banana-pecan pancakes.

Queenie pauses with a strip of bacon halfway to her mouth—she's eaten six. "You should probably wait until you've seen me have a real meltdown before you start throwing out invitations to move into your pad. I mean, I know I give a mean blow job and I make delicious pancakes, but you should be sure you can handle all of this before you decide you want to share a bed with me every night." She motions to her now T-shirt clad body. It's one of mine, and it almost reaches her knees, and the sleeves hang past her elbows. "Especially since I'm a cover hog."

She's obviously trying to let me off the hook for saying something so asinine. There is no way I'd ask a woman to move in with me after two weeks of dating, at least until Queenie. She's a tornado, and half the time I don't know what to do with her, but I still want to get caught up in her vortex.

"I'm pretty confident I can handle anything you throw at me."

She props her cheek on her fist and gives me a soft smile. "We'll have to wait and see if that's true, won't we?" She slides off her stool, gathering her empty plate. "Are you done, or do you want to see if you can polish off the rest of this?" She motions to the half-finished fruit platter, dish of pancakes, and few remaining strips of bacon.

I pat my stomach. I could definitely keep going until everything is gone, but it'll make me lethargic at practice later. "I think I'm good for now."

"You can save it for breakfast tomorrow." Queenie grabs our plates and carries them over to the sink.

While Queenie tackles the dishes, I put away the leftovers. She doesn't rinse the plates before she puts them in the dishwasher, and there doesn't seem to be any kind of rhyme or reason to how she loads it.

"What's up? You look like you're about to have a coronary." Queenie jams the mixing bowl in between the plates.

"Nothing. Everything's good."

She stops what she's doing and props a fist on her hip. "Do you need to rearrange this?"

"No. It's fine." I grab the dishcloth and run it under the hot water so I can wipe down the counters.

She grabs the rag from me. "You're going to switch everything around when I'm not looking."

"I'm not—"

She fights a grin. "Just do it. You know you want to."

I give in, because she's right. I unload the dishwasher completely, rinse everything off, and reorganize it so all the dishes will get clean. Queenie absently wipes the same spot over and over on the counter, watching me with an entertained smirk.

I raise a brow. "What's with that look?"

"Your quest for order entertains me." When I close the dishwasher, she dangles the rag from her fingers. "Wanna show me how to wipe down counters properly now? Just so I know for future reference."

She grabs my hand and places it on top of hers, then turns to face the counter. I stand behind her, and she lifts things out of the way as I smooth the cloth along the surface. Wiping counters down has never been an activity I would consider sexy . . . until now.

I stop paying attention to what I'm doing about halfway through, because her butt is rubbing up on my erection. She pulls her chestnut hair over her shoulder and exposes her neck, so I lean down and kiss the creamy, sweet expanse. It turns into another orgasm exchange before I finally finish cleaning up the kitchen and put everything back where it belongs while Queenie sits on the counter, laughing at me.

"Do you want kids?" she asks when I finish rinsing out the cloth and setting it to dry on the edge of the sink.

"What?" If I were drinking something, I probably would've choked on the word.

"Kids, do you want them? And I'm not asking because I suddenly want to have your babies. I'm sure they'd be pretty and all, but we're not even at the let's move in together stage, let alone the let's plan a family stage."

I smile at her explanation and the pink tint to her cheeks. "Um, yeah, I want kids, eventually. Do you?"

"I think so, yeah. I'd just like to have my own life figured out before I go adding someone else's welfare to the list of things I need to manage." She picks at a loose thread on my shirt. "You do realize that kids are balls of chaos, right?"

"Well, yeah, sure I do." I've spent enough time around my coach's and teammates' kids to know that they make constant messes. But that's why I have a cleaner.

"It means you'll have to give up all the nitpicky order and organization."

"Maybe they'll all like order and organization too."

She laughs and jumps off the counter. "Maybe."

My phone chimes from the breakfast island. "That's Hanna. We usually video chat every other morning to check in."

"I'll go get ready for work and give you some privacy."

"You don't have to do that. I'm sure she'd love to say hi."

"I should probably be wearing something other than your T-shirt for momster conversations, though, don't you think?"

I look over her outfit. "Hmm. You make a good point."

She rises up on her toes and kisses the edge of my jaw. "You talk to your momster, and I'll get ready for work. I can say hi another time when I look less like I've been fucked six ways from Sunday." She pats me on the cheek and leaves me alone with my phone and my third erection since I woke up this morning.

I'm falling in love with her chaos.

Fifteen minutes and one brief and slightly embarrassing video chat later—Hanna called me out on my messed-up hair, and my stammered responses told her more than she needed to know—I find Queenie standing in the hallway outside my bedroom. Her bag is slung over her shoulder, and she's wearing a pair of black dress pants and a very pretty gauzy top that's both professional and sexy.

I wonder how long I have to wait before I tell her she should leave clothes here for future sleepovers.

"You have really cool art." She motions to the piece hanging from the wall. "Where did you get this?"

I move in behind her and wrap my arm around her waist. "Hanna's the artist in the family. She calls it a hobby, but she's incredibly talented. Has her work in a bunch of cafés in our hometown that feature local artists. Anyway, almost every painting I have is one of hers."

Queenie turns her head and rubs her cheek on my biceps. "She has great vision. The colors are stunning."

"She does. She's a financial consultant, but she really loves this, so she teaches classes on the side." I've been looking for a way to bring this up without being too obvious. "You paint, too, don't you?"

She tips her chin up, her confusion evident. "How do you know that?"

"You have an easel at your place." I noticed it the first time I was at her house, and once I peeked under a covered canvas while she was getting ready for a date. She also talked about being arty that first time we went for dinner, but she didn't elaborate at all. It makes me think it's something she doesn't like to talk about.

"Oh, right. I used to do it a lot when I was in college, but not so much anymore." She ducks out from under my arm. "You should get ready so we can head to the arena."

I want to push, but I also don't want to admit I've snooped, so I leave it alone. For now.

# CHAPTER 16

## THE CALM BEFORE THE STORM

*Queenie*

My morning is awesome. I've had more orgasms in the past twelve hours than I've probably had in an entire month collectively. I'm quite literally in the best mood ever.

And I have the most amazing boyfriend in the world. Who asked me to move in with him. I'm sure it was an accident—a knee-jerk reaction to awesome pancakes and morning BJs—but still, it's a great start to what is going to be a fabulous day.

Kingston and I part ways when we reach the arena so he can train with the team and I can get to work. I check my phone on the way down the hall. I have messages from Stevie about getting together for another double date and a girls' night when I have time.

I love that I've made such great connections with the women here. And that they've accepted me so openly as part of their circle. As challenging as it can be, I'm lucky that I get to travel with the team, because it means I don't have to miss Kingston. On the flip side, it also means that I miss out on the girl time. Although I don't plan to have this job forever, so eventually I'll be in the same position as the rest of the hockey wives and girlfriends—if Kingston and I last, anyway.

I'm aware I'm a lot to handle. And while he seems pretty enamored with me, that could easily change. He's the calm and I'm the storm.

My dad's office door is still closed, which means he's either on the phone or still in a meeting. I'm not sure exactly what the meeting is about, but I know he was pretty worked up about it last night.

I settle in at my desk, prioritize all the things I need to accomplish today, and start on my emails. I scan all the necessary documents and tab them in the appropriate places. The tablets have proven to be a success. At the last meeting I snapped a few great candid photos and posted them to the team's social media accounts, which made the company very happy. I've tried to streamline everything, and it's been a pretty easy transition for everyone. This job may not be the one I want to do for the rest of my life, but I'm determined to make sure I'm effective while I'm doing it.

I've just finished uploading the most recent paperwork file when Violet pops her head in the door. "Hey, Queenie, have you seen Alex? He's not in his office."

"Sorry, not since I got here, and that was about forty-five minutes ago. My dad's in a meeting, though, so maybe he's involved in that?" I thumb over my shoulder to the closed door.

A little head of wavy auburn hair pops out from behind her legs, and huge blue eyes register recognition.

"Hey, Lavender!"

She ducks behind her mother's legs.

"You remember Queenie, don't you, Lavender?"

She looks up at her mother and gives her a serious nod. Then she turns that beautiful blue gaze back on me, and a huge smile lights up her face. She lifts her hand in a wave. "Hi, Keenie."

Violet's eyes flare, and she blinks a bunch of times before she strokes her daughter's hair and beams down at her. "Good job, sweetheart. Maybe after we're done here I should take you for ice cream. Would you like that?"

Lavender nods vigorously, her smile growing even wider.

Based on Violet's reaction and my previous interaction with Lavender, I'm taking it that it's a big deal for her to have actually said hello to me and used my name.

Violet checks her phone. "They've been in that meeting since eight thirty this morning. I hope this works out, or it's going to be a lot of headaches and hours spent negotiating for no reason."

I lower my voice. "Do you know what's going on?"

"Only that they're trying to negotiate a contract, but there's some huge NDA attached to the deal, so he can't even say who they're negotiating the deal for."

"It must be a pretty high-profile player."

"Has to be; otherwise he wouldn't be so tight lipped about it. Anyway, I was dropping by to see if the deal was done, because I'm nosy and I want to know all the secrets, but Lavender has a doctor's appointment, so I guess it's going to have to wait." She reaches for Lavender's hand, but she's no longer standing beside her.

Instead she's next to me. She tugs on my sleeve and holds out a piece of artwork.

"Did you draw this?"

She nods. "For you," she whispers.

"You drew this for me?" I take it from her when she nods.

While it looks very much like the art of a child, it's clear that Lavender has an incredible eye for the use of color, which is cool to see, since she's so young.

"Good remembering, Lavender. She's been holding on to that for weeks now, asking when she can see you."

"Well, I love it. Thank you very much, Lavender. And the next time you stop by, we'll have to draw something together. Sound good?"

She ducks her head with a smile and rushes back to the safety of her mother's side. Violet and Lavender head out, and I find a place to tack up my new art. When I was a teenager, I used to go to an art camp in the summer for a couple of weeks. My favorite part was always working with the younger kids. When I started my college degree, I'd wanted to do something with art and children. At least until I lost my confidence and dropped out.

I'm about to get back to work when laughter comes from behind my dad's office door. A few seconds later he steps out, followed by Alex. They're smiling widely, which I'm taking to mean that whatever they were negotiating went well.

"Queenie, honey, it's great that you're here. I want to introduce you to the newest member of our team, and then you can help me get his paperwork together."

"Of course, I'd be happy to." I push away from my desk, preparing to greet the unnamed player. As far as I know, it's uncommon for a trade to happen once the season has already started, but he and Alex seem pretty pleased.

A man appears, and my dad claps him on the shoulder. "Queenie, this is Corey Slater."

I have to fight to keep my smile from turning into a grimace.

I know Corey.

Not because he's an NHL player and is always in the media for some bullshit or other, but because he's my ex.

# CHAPTER 17

## THE STORM IS A DOUCHE

*Queenie*

This isn't happening.

Not today. Not when I'm rocking a seriously sweet postsex high. Or was.

Because now a horrible blast from my past is here, ruining everything.

Corey Slater is a giant dick.

His man unit is anything but, however.

He's the reason I stopped watching hockey for a good six years. Especially when he first made the NHL and played for my favorite team. Even now I tend to avoid the games when I know his team is playing. But I can't do that anymore. Because he plays for Seattle.

For half a second I consider pretending I don't know Corey, but I realize it's probably not a great idea.

Especially with the way he's smirking.

Corey tips his chin up. "Hey, Queenie."

"Hello, Corey. It's been a long time."

My dad looks between us, head whipping back and forth a few times. Sort of like a cat following a digital mouse on an iPad screen. "You two know each other?"

"We went to college together a long time ago. My first year." I sound like a robot, but I'm sort of freaking out.

I never thought I'd have to see Corey up close again. Sure, I knew that I'd see him eventually during the season at a game, but he was supposed to be playing for Philly, so I'd only have to see his last name scrawled across his jersey. Not his stupid, smug face every single damn day. Minus my rare days off.

And there's no way I'll be able to keep this from Kingston. I realize that it doesn't look great. Not at all.

"So you're working for your dad now, huh?" Corey asks.

To most people it might seem like he's trying to make polite conversation. But I know better. He's judging me. Because I'm still relying on my daddy to help me survive and he makes millions of dollars a year to shoot a piece of rubber across a slab of ice.

I realize it's a lot harder than that oversimplification, but again, I'm not excited about seeing him. It means I'm mentally lashing out, because I can't actually lash out at all. I have to be professional.

"It's a temporary position. My father's previous assistant had to take early retirement and I was asked to help out, and since I know hockey, it seemed like a good fit."

"You definitely know the ins and outs of hockey players," Corey says, nodding solemnly.

That might sound like a compliment, but really he's insulting me and insinuating that I'm a stick chaser. And now that I'm working for my dad and dating a member of the team, that's exactly how it looks.

"Corey needs to complete some paperwork, and it would be great if you could show him around the arena." My dad usually gives directives with authority, but right now he seems uncertain.

I turn my fake smile on him. "Of course. I'll need to set up a tablet for him, but if you want the forms completed today, I can see if you have paper copies in your office."

It's my way of getting my dad alone for a minute so I can explain and, hopefully, set his mind at ease. Although I'll be adjusting the amount of information I intend to share, because he sure as hell doesn't need to know all the details. I'll give him the bare-bones story and hope like hell Corey is on the same page when it comes to leaving the past where it should stay: buried under a pile of red plastic cups in a college frat house.

I brush past Corey into my dad's office. He tells Corey to make himself comfortable and follows behind me. My whole body is vibrating with anxious energy, and I'm sweating. I take a deep breath as I turn to face my dad.

"What's the history between you two?" He thumbs over his shoulder at the closed door.

I have to work hard not to fidget like I usually do when I'm nervous, which I very much am right now. I busy myself by opening his filing cabinet so I can look for the paper copies I made of all the initial paperwork. "It's nothing to worry about. We dated briefly my first year of college."

My dad crosses his arms. "How briefly, and which college?"

I've been to a few over the years. "Just a couple of months. During my undergrad, when I was taking art and psych." I transferred closer to home the second semester because I'd said I was homesick. He doesn't know that Corey was the real reason for the switch. "It's not a big deal, and it was a long time ago. It'll be fine. I'm just surprised, since I had no idea he was even a trade option."

He runs his hand through his hair, lips pursed and his eyes narrowed, as if he's trying to see inside my brain and find out what's really going on. "I would've told you if I hadn't been bound by an NDA."

I wave the comment away and pull a bunch of forms, checking to make sure there are extra copies before I close the filing cabinet. If I'd known about this in advance, I would have had the tablet already set up for him. "It's fine. It'll be fine." I'm not entirely sure that's true. It depends a lot on whether Corey can keep his trap shut. It's not something he's been notoriously good at over the years.

He's an absolute pain in the ass on the ice, always pushing the opposition's buttons and generally being a douchebag. He was the same off the ice, and I'm not sure much has changed. But he's one of the best players in the league, so he gets away with a lot of shit.

I don't even want to know how much money they must have offered to get him to come to Seattle. I also don't want to think about how this will change the team dynamic. I can't see Bishop liking this guy or keeping his mouth shut if he happens to pull out his douche card, which is highly likely.

"You're sure you're okay to show him around?"

"Of course. It's my job." I flash what I hope is a seminormal smile.

"That's not what I mean. I don't want to make you uncomfortable."

"It was six years ago, Dad. Besides, doesn't he have a pregnant fiancée or something?" I accidentally stumbled on an article a month ago on some hockey site or other. There was a picture of him and some woman in a supertight dress showing off her baby belly and her giant rock.

"He does, yes."

"So he's moved on, and so have I." I shuffle all the papers into a file folder and print Corey's name across the top, internally cringing as I remember how I used to make the *O* into a heart. But then, at eighteen one does cheesy things like that. "We shouldn't keep the superstar waiting longer than necessary." I close the folder and tuck it under my arm, then think better of it, since I'm sweaty.

My dad seems reluctant to let me leave the office. "We'll talk more about this on the way home."

"Sure. Sounds good." It actually sounds the exact opposite of good, but I'm not going to tell him that.

Corey's lounging in one of the waiting room chairs, long legs stretched out and crossed over each other, phone in his hand, smarmy smirk firmly in place. I'm sure he's going through one of his social media accounts, looking at all the comments from the women who want to hump him and the would-be hockey stars who want to be him.

"All set, Corey. Would you prefer paperwork first or a tour of the facilities?" My face feels stiff with how fake my smile is.

He clicks away on his phone for an inappropriately long time while my dad and I stand there, waiting for him to acknowledge us and respond. Finally he shuts down his phone and slips it in his pocket. "I'll take the private tour first." While the words themselves aren't inappropriate, his tone is slick and slimy.

I'm pretty sure I hear my dad's teeth grind together beside me. Or maybe they're mine.

"Great. We'll be back in a bit." I do an about-face and head for the hallway, not checking to see if he's following. "I'll show you the gym first, and then you can tour the locker room and the rink."

After several long seconds of silence, I finally give in and glance over my shoulder. Corey's phone is back out and he's thumb typing away, shambling along like he has all the time in the world and I'm absolutely irrelevant.

Which I suppose I sort of am and honestly probably always have been. *You're just a warm hole to fill, like the rest of them.* Those were the words he once used, while drunk, after I caught him cheating on me. In the bed we shared. With some puck bunny he'd met by the keg in the living room of the frat house we were shacking up in.

Obviously my taste in men wasn't great at eighteen. And truthfully, until Kingston my poor taste was an unfortunate trend that extended throughout college. It's sad, really, considering I have such a great father, and logistically I should have been able to make better choices when it came to men and dating. I'll blame low self-esteem and insecurity for all the less-than-stellar boyfriends. And possibly flat keg beer.

I don't bother to slow down or look over my shoulder again to see how far behind he's fallen until I reach the gym. Unfortunately, it's empty, since the team has long since finished its preskate workout.

"I remember when you used to come by the college gym to see if I was working out." He's right behind me. So close that I can feel his breath on my temple.

I open the door forcefully and elbow him in the side, smiling at his oof. Letting go of the door so he has to catch it or risk getting his fingers caught between it and the jamb, I step inside and create some space between us.

"First of all, you don't get to stroll down memory lane with me. Ever."

"Come on, Queenie, we had some good times."

"I can probably count all of them on one hand. And that time I found you banging a bunny in our bed pretty much cancels out every single damn one of them."

"I was drunk."

"As if that's an excuse."

"I thought she was you." He says this while picking his nail.

I hate him so much. "She was blonde and I am not. The only way she resembled me even remotely was because she had boobs and a warm hole."

Corey sneers. "Still the same bitchy attitude you had back in college. And you wonder why you couldn't keep anyone entertained for longer than a few months."

I grit my teeth, aware that he's needling me on purpose and that if I have an outburst of any kind I'll be giving him exactly what he wants—a reaction. It will also make me look unprofessional. I have to see his jerk face on a regular basis, so if I feed into this now, it's just going to make it infinitely more difficult in the future.

"Although if I remember correctly, you could do a few things with that mouth that were worth hanging around for."

I spin to face him and give him my widest, most syrupy smile. "I think we need to set some ground rules."

He leans against the closed door. I know it's meant to make me feel like I'm trapped, but I know all the exits out of here, while he does not. Still, it's annoying that he believes he can use these kinds of tactics to intimidate me. "I'm engaged, in case you didn't know, and she's preggers, so you and every other bunny are off limits. For now, anyway."

God, he's disgusting. And worse than he was when I first started dating him all those years ago. I hold up a finger. "One, I'm not a bunny."

"That's not what I hear."

"Ex-fucking-cuse me?"

"Rumor has it you're chasing guys on the team."

"Well, rumor has it wrong. Secondly, even if you were the last man on earth and the entire welfare of our species hinged on me sleeping with you, I would gladly forfeit my own life and that of the entire living, breathing universe to avoid ever having your hands or any other part of you on my body."

"That's not how you felt in college."

"It took about six weeks for me to develop a strong aversion to you, since your misogynistic asshole side didn't come out until we were living under the same roof. You need to keep your mouth shut about what happened between us."

"You mean when we—"

I hold a hand up in his face. It's annoying how high I have to reach because he's so tall and I'm not. "Do not finish that statement. Ever. You will take it to the grave with you, and so will I."

"Or what?" He sneers, body bowing forward so he can get up in my space.

I try to take a step back, but there's a piece of workout equipment behind me, so there is quite literally nowhere for me to go. It's rather unfortunate, because Corey must've eaten something spicy and garlicky recently, and he's breathing it right in my face.

I motion between us. "Does your pregnant fiancée know what happened?"

Confusion mars his expression. For as skilled as Corey is on the ice, he's sort of an anomaly in the hockey world, since he's not all that smart. Usually these guys have the brains to match the brawn, and Corey definitely doesn't. "No."

I wait for him to process the information. It takes three long, stinky garlicky breaths before he finally clues in. And then the aggressive dick I knew and learned to loathe back in college rears his ugly head. He moves in even closer and barricades me against the machine. "Is this your attempt at a threat, Queenie? Look at you, still running home to Daddy when things don't work out for you. Just like you did back in college. I mean, how pathetic can you be?"

# CHAPTER 18

## BACK OFF MY GIRL

*Kingston*

Today has been amazing. I had a great workout and an excellent practice. One of the best of the season so far, and I'm attributing that to Queenie. And amazing sex. I'm definitely looking forward to more of that.

I whistle as I head for her office, hoping I can convince her to stay at my place again tonight. We have a game tomorrow afternoon, and normally I'd avoid the possible sleep disturbance, but considering how beneficial it seems to have been today, I feel like a repeat would only be helpful.

The sound of people arguing causes me to pause as I pass the gym. I hesitate to get involved, concerned I'm intruding on something I shouldn't be, until I catch sight of Queenie, chin tipped up in defiance while some huge guy gets right in her face.

I have a low tolerance for any kind of behavior that threatens the fairer sex. Not because I believe women can't fend for themselves but because men generally have the physical advantage, and this is especially true when it comes to Queenie. She's petite.

I can't tell who has her cornered, but there is absolutely no way I'll allow this to continue. Even if it's Jake. Especially if it's Jake.

I yank open the door as the guy grabs for her wrist and she tries to duck out of the way, except he has her pinned up against a piece of equipment. "Hey, buddy, you need to back off. Now." I don't recognize my voice, which seems to be more growl than actual words.

The man encroaching on Queenie's personal space turns around, his expression reflecting irritation. I recognize him, I realize. He's Corey Slater, forward for Philly, and one of the most difficult players in the entire league. He has more game suspensions than any other player. Even more than Lance Romero in his rookie years, and that's saying something. But he's also leading in goals, so while he has a reputation for being a general pain in the ass, he's one of the top players in the league.

A smug smile turns up the corner of his mouth as he looks me over. "This is a private conversation, *buddy*, so maybe you need to mind your own fucking business." He turns back to Queenie, dismissing me.

Anger like I've never felt before makes my spine hot and my fingers curl into fists. I step into the gym and let the door close behind me. "Queenie happens to be my girlfriend, so the fact that you're putting your hands on her and using your size to physically intimidate her makes this one hundred percent my fucking business."

Queenie's eyes flare in surprise, and Corey chuckles.

"So it is true. How's your daddy feel about that?" He shakes his head and glances over his shoulder. "Get out while you can, man. She's not worth the trouble."

I take pride in the fact that I've never been in a fight on the ice, or ever, really. Even when I was a teenager and hormones made tempers flare, I was always able to keep it together and avoid reacting without thinking.

But the way Queenie's face has crumpled and her shoulders have curled in, like she's physically trying to protect herself from his words, and the actual words themselves, cause a spike of rage to short out my entire center of reason. I also realize, based on that one statement, and the way he's invading her space, that Corey and Queenie know each other, possibly in ways I don't want to consider too closely.

I grab his shoulder, which finally puts his attention on me. "Do not disrespect Queenie. Not ever."

His smug sneer pulls higher, distorting his face. "What're you gonna do about it?"

I edge my way between him and Queenie, creating a barricade. "Do *not* push me, Slater."

He has the audacity to laugh. "Look at you, getting all righteous and defensive over some chick. I didn't think you actually had any balls, Kingston."

I fist his shirt. In the back of my head I recognize violence isn't going to help. If anything at all, it's going to make the entire situation worse, but I can't seem to stop myself. "First of all, Queenie is not *some chick*. She is my goddamn girlfriend, and if you talk to her or about her like that again I will not hesitate to put you in your place. Secondly, who the hell do you think you are, coming in here, talking to her like that?"

"First of all, I'm her *ex-boyfriend*, so Queenie and I go way back, don't we?" He glances over my shoulder, his smirk growing. "Secondly, I'm your new teammate, so it might be a good idea to reconsider putting me in my place, unless you want to end up watching games from the bench."

"What?" I don't know which one of those pieces of information I find more shocking.

"God, you're such an antagonistic dick, Corey." Queenie puts her hand over mine and tries to pry my fingers loose from his shirt. "Let him go, King. He's actually not worth the time or energy it would take to kick his annoying ass." She squeezes my biceps gently.

I let go of Corey's shirt, more because Queenie is touching me than anything else. Corey and I take a step away from each other. He's still smirking, but there's uncertainty lurking there now where there wasn't before. I pull Queenie into my side and wrap a protective arm around her.

"I think you can probably manage the rest of the tour on your own." Queenie holds out the folder of paperwork, but Corey just stands there. She sighs, and I have to assume she's rolling her eyes. Queenie tosses the folder at his feet, and half the papers scatter across the floor. "You should have this back on my desk by tomorrow morning, and before you make me chase you down for it, be aware that they won't actually let you on the ice if everything isn't signed." She pats my hand, which is resting on her shoulder. "Let's go, King."

I follow her out of the gym and across the hall, into one of the empty conference rooms. She closes the door behind me and turns the lock.

"Can you tell—"

I don't have a chance to finish my question because Queenie grabs me by the front of the shirt and yanks my mouth down to hers.

I'm confused and a little stunned as her tongue pushes past my lips. I indulge the kiss for a few sweet strokes of tongue before I gently take her by the shoulders and disengage. "What're you doing?"

"Kissing you." She wraps her hand around the back of my neck and tries to reattach her lips to mine.

I cup her face between my palms and plant a single chaste kiss on her very tempting lips. "While I very much enjoy your mouth, I think we need to talk about what happened back there. Particularly the part about you having dated Corey Slater. I feel like I need more information about that since apparently he's now my teammate, which is another thing we need to discuss."

Queenie sighs and just sort of . . . wilts, like an unwatered flower.

I drop my hands, and she takes a couple of steps away from me as if she needs the space, which I don't like, or understand. She addresses the last part first.

"Apparently there was an NDA or something, because my dad didn't so much as hint at it, so I'm as shocked as you are about him being on the team. And we dated my first year of college, when I was eighteen years old and too stupid to realize he was a huge dickhead. It lasted all of two months."

"Oh."

"Yeah, oh." She links her hands behind her head and stares up at the ceiling, blinking quickly.

"Why was he in your face like that?"

"Because he's a bully and a jerk with no personal boundaries." Her lids flutter closed and two tears slip out of the corners, tracking a path down her cheeks.

"Hey, hey. Don't cry. It's going to be okay. He won't be a problem for you. I won't let him."

"You've seen how he is on the ice, though. It's how he is all the time. Always needling, always belittling people."

"Is that what he was doing to you?"

She shakes her head and steps into me, wrapping her arms around my waist. "I just didn't expect to see him. I mean, I knew eventually he'd be at a game, but I never thought he'd be playing *for* Seattle."

"I don't understand why Jake would bring him to Seattle in the first place," I say, more to myself than to her.

She pulls away and runs her hand over my chest, smoothing out the wrinkles in my polo. "He didn't know we dated. Like I said, I was young and stupid, and the relationship was pretty much over before it began. I never expected to be working for my dad. All the more reason to figure out what I want to do with my life so I can stop causing him problems."

"Hey." I tuck a finger under her chin and gently tip it up. "You're not allowed to do that."

"Be honest?"

"Berate yourself to me. Not everyone has it figured out from the start, Queenie. Sometimes we need to take a few detours before we find the path that's right for us."

"Yeah, well, I've taken a lot of detours, and I still haven't stumbled on the right path."

"Are you sure about that? You crossed my path, and it feels pretty right to me." I tuck her hair behind her ear and skim her cheek as more tears fall. I don't understand them the way I want to.

She gives me a tremulous smile. "It's more like my cyclone crossed your path and you got sucked into it."

"I love your cyclone." I dip down and press a soft kiss to her lips. "I want you to stay over at my place again tonight."

"You have a game tomorrow."

"I'll be responsible and make sure we're in bed at a reasonable time."

"I don't want to mess with your game."

"You won't. I had the best practice ever today. I was nearly flawless."

"I have to finish up some paperwork and manage emails still."

"That's okay, I can wait."

"We'll have to stop at my place to get me a change of clothes."

"I don't mind at all." It's quite perfect, actually, because tonight I'd like to take her out for dinner, and I'd also like her to bring a few extra outfits to leave at my place.

"Okay. I'll stay over again."

I hang around the office until she's finished with emails and paperwork, partly to make sure she's really okay the way she says she is, and also because I refuse to leave her alone on the off chance Corey should come back. I want to say something to Jake about Corey, but it's not my place to interfere, and I feel as though there's more to this than Queenie's letting on.

I'm aware pushing her tonight isn't the best option, though. At least not without softening her up first. She's too on edge, and storms get out of control when there are too many variables affecting them.

So instead I treat her exactly as she deserves to be: like she's my queen.

Jake has to stay late—I'm assuming because of the trade, especially with the official season underway, and this will mean shifting around lines and players to accommodate Slater. So when we get to Queenie's, I follow her into her bedroom and stretch out on her double bed while she packs her overnight bag. I have to bend my knees and rest my feet against the wrought iron frame to make myself fit.

Her room is ultrafeminine, painted a soft, buttery yellow, her quilt a patternless pale green, the accent pillows also pastel.

"You look ridiculous on this bed, FYI." She tickles the bottom of my foot as she crosses over to the dresser for the third time.

I yank it out of reach and rub the spot.

She pokes at her cheek with her tongue, expression suddenly full of mischief. "Are you ticklish?"

"No. You just surprised me." It's a lie, but not a harmful one.

"I don't believe you." She tosses a lacy mint-green bra on the comforter. I bet it looks amazing against her tanned skin.

She grabs for my foot again, but my reflexes are far better than hers. I gather both of her wrists in one hand and pull her onto the bed. After stretching her arms up over her head, I roll over on top of her and prop myself up on my forearm. "Is this okay?"

"You on top of me is always okay." The words vibrate with excitement.

"I'm glad you feel that way." I brush my lips over hers and pull back. "Are *you* ticklish?"

Her eyes flare with understanding, throat bobbing thickly. "Not really," she lies.

"Are you sure about that?" I drag a single finger down the inside of her forearm to her elbow, smiling as goose bumps rise along her skin.

"King," she half warns, half moans.

I kiss the sensitive spot at the bend in her elbow. "Yes, my queen?" She shivers, and I lift my gaze to hers as I continue to trail my finger along the inside of her bicep until I reach her underarm.

She shrieks and wriggles. So I do it again until she's begging me to stop the tickle torture while laugh-crying. The mood shifts and I release her hands, but instead of grabbing on to my hair or curling her fingers around the nape of my neck, she stays exactly as she is, panting, eyes suddenly soft.

"Why do you want to be with me?" She hooks her fingers around one of the decorative wrought iron curls behind her head.

"Because you're you. What other reason would there be?"

She smiles, but sadness shifts behind her eyes, and I want to understand what's put that emotion there. Today hasn't been easy for her, and I have a feeling her past with Corey is more complicated than she's letting on. Instead of asking questions, I kiss her. Our tongues tangle, and still her fingers stay curled around the bedframe.

It isn't until I whisper in her ear that I want to feel her touch that she finally lets go. We undress each other between kisses and caresses. This time when I enter her, I don't lose control. I show her without words that she's worth whatever trouble she seems to think she's going to bring my way. I'd rather have her chaos than stay stuck in the calm, where everything is lackluster.

An orgasm later, bracketed by two for Queenie, she's stretched out beside me, long hair cascading over my shoulder and arm, hand splayed out on my chest, leg hooked over mine.

I'm currently wondering how long I have to reasonably wait to tell her how I feel about her. It's probably too soon. And Queenie seems a little gun shy about feelings, so it's better to hold off awhile longer. I'd ask Bishop, because he's my best friend, but he's also generally clueless about relationships and how to manage them, let alone the emotional component. I can talk to Hanna, though. She always has objective, thoughtful advice.

I look around for a clock, wondering exactly how long we've been at it, and I notice the artwork hanging on the wall across from her bed. I'm not sure how I missed it before, other than my attention being fully on Queenie while she sifted through her underwear drawer and made painfully difficult decisions about which pairs she should leave at my house. I obviously gave her some input.

I point to the art. "Who painted that?" I'm fishing. The style alone tells me it has to be her creation.

"It's something I did in college." She waves a dismissive hand toward it. "It's old, and not very good."

"Untrue. It's stunning, just like its creator."

She snorts and pats my chest, then pushes up and tries to roll away.

"Hey, where are you going?"

"We should get dressed if we're still going out for dinner; otherwise we'll get guilted into staying here and barbecuing with my dad." I realize she's changing the subject on purpose, but she also has a point. I would definitely prefer that he doesn't come knocking on her door when we're both naked and lying in her bed. It's one thing for him to have the inkling that we're sleeping together; it's another thing to have it shoved in his face—the rash was bad enough. Maybe even worse.

I clear my throat, because the image of how I ended up with that rash is still stimulating despite the unfortunate effects. "Would you rather stay here?"

"If it was another night, sure, but after today . . . I know he has a pile of questions he probably wants to ask, and I'm not really interested in answering them."

It sounds like that statement is meant for me just as much as it is for her dad.

"Okay. Let's get dressed so I can spoil you with food, embarrass you with public displays of affection, and then stay up irresponsibly late making you come."

"Should I wear panties I don't mind parting with, then?" She plucks a pair from her dresser and dangles them from her finger. Based on the complete lack of fabric, I'm guessing it's a thong.

"That was an accident." I sit up and throw my legs over the edge of the bed.

She turns away from the dresser and drops the scrap of fabric on the wrinkled comforter. Queenie nudges my knees apart with one of her own. She's still naked and so am I, which means it's hard to focus on anything but the bare expanse of skin in front of me. I tip my head up so I'm not staring at her nipples.

She bites her lip and runs her fingers through my hair, smoothing it out, running her nail along the part. "You know it's okay to want someone so much that you can't wait to get them naked, right? Everything about that night was entirely consensual, including my ruined panties. And they were made out of cheap, flimsy material, so you can stop feeling bad about this insane chemistry we share."

I trace the contour of her hips, following it to the dip in her waist. "It's never been like this before. I feel—"

"Hungry all the time. Insatiable." She trails her fingers down the side of my neck and over my shoulders.

"Exactly." I could forgo food, stay in bed for days with Queenie, forget every single obligation there is, including my job, if it meant being able to appease my appetite for her.

"It's nice to be wanted." She bends, and I think it's to kiss me, but her lips skim my cheek and brush my ear. "Maybe I'll skip the panties altogether. Then you don't have to feel bad and I don't have to risk losing another pair."

She snatches up the panties from the comforter and tosses them in her overnight bag. It's a distraction, a way to end a conversation that makes her feel . . . uncomfortable? Vulnerable, maybe? But I'm not sure that's it. Not after everything that's happened today.

Every time I think I've made some progress, I run into another wall. But I'm nothing if not patient. I'll get inside more than just her body. Eventually I'll work my way inside her fortress of a heart too.

# CHAPTER 19

## THE EDGE OF THE SWORD

*Queenie*

I fully expect my dad to stage a massive inquisition about Corey and my previous relationship with him. But for whatever reason, that never happens. Possibly because he's too busy putting out fires with his new asshole superstar. He and Alex have been in a meeting with Corey's agent for the past hour and a half, and, based on the number of times I've heard raised voices, it's not going well.

It's amazing how much one person can change the entire dynamic of the team. Corey is the same entitled, self-indulgent, egotistical jerk he was six years ago. In the short time since he's come to Seattle, he's had altercations with several players—on his own team.

Despite Corey's unpleasant reappearance in my life, and the dissension he creates for the team, things between Kingston and me are amazing. When we're in Seattle, I spend most nights at his place. I have an overnight bag already in his car for tonight.

Kingston is a big fan of what he calls "little surprises." Pretty much every time I end up at his house, there's something new in his closet for me, which now has a rack that's slowly amassing outfits in my size. He's even started to fill a drawer with cute pajamas and pretty lacy bra and underwear sets—some expensive and some not. He says it's so I don't have to worry about packing an overnight bag all the time, and if I forget something, I'll have the essentials at his place. It makes logical sense, and I love his thoughtfulness, but sometimes I wonder if I truly deserve all this, him included.

I give my head a shake and focus on work. As I wrap up replying to emails, Violet pops her head in the office. While she's always a bit of a verbal whirlwind, she's also generally very put together. Today that doesn't seem to be the case.

"Oh, thank God you're here. Have you seen Alex? He's not in his office."

"He's been in a meeting for"—I check the time on my computer screen and cringe—"a couple of hours now. I'm not sure when he's supposed to be done."

"Is it important? Do you think we can interrupt?" Two little figures appear behind her: Lavender and River. Today they're not holding hands, though. Instead, River is clutching one of those plastic beach pails to his chest. His little shoulders cave in, and he makes a sound that's a combination of a groan and a sob before he wretches. Lavender pats him on the back, and Violet turns her head and tries to suppress a gag.

"Oh God, is River okay?"

"I think he has the flu."

I grab a handful of tissues and round my desk. After leading him over to one of the chairs, I get him to sit down while Lavender clambers into the one beside him. I wipe his clammy face and brush his damp hair away from his forehead.

"Thank you for doing that. I have a hard time with—" She motions toward her face and the bucket River is holding.

"It's fine. So does my dad. Whenever I was sick as a kid, I had to keep him away from me so he wouldn't react by tossing his cookies too."

"I can totally relate to that." Violet blows out a breath. "I have an appointment with his doctor in half an hour, but I was hoping I could leave Lavender with Alex, because I'd really like to avoid her getting it too. Or being in a doctor's office with a bunch of other sick people." Violet pats her daughter on the top of her head but keeps her gaze averted from the contents of the beach pail.

"Lavender can hang out with me until he's finished his meeting, if that works for you."

Violet drops down into a crouch so she's at eye level with Lavender. "Do you think you'd be okay to stay with Queenie for a while? Just until Daddy is out of his meeting?"

Lavender looks from her mom to me and back again, little lips pursed in a line.

"Did you bring your coloring stuff? We could draw together while you wait for your daddy," I offer.

Lavender considers that for a few seconds before she finally nods.

"Awesome. Looks like you're good to take River to the doctor and get him all fixed up," I tell Violet.

"Thank you so much. I really appreciate this."

"It's no trouble at all."

Violet kisses Lavender on the forehead. "I shouldn't be too long: an hour and a half or so tops. And I'll call or text with updates so you don't worry too much," she tells Lavender.

"What about Robbie and Maverick? Are they here too?"

"They're in school until four, and then Robbie has his Botany Club and Maverick has hockey practice, so we're all set there." She guides poor River out of the office, murmuring reassurances.

I turn to Lavender, whose attention is focused on the empty doorway. Her hands are in her lap, and she's wringing them nervously. "We should probably wash our hands, shouldn't we?"

She drags her gaze away from the doorway and nods once. After slipping off the chair, she follows me to the bathroom. She's too small to reach the sink, so with her permission I lift her up onto the vanity and turn on the taps. She runs her hands under the water, and I pump soap into them. "We'll wash them really well so you don't get what River has, okay?"

She nods again and rubs her hands together, and I start singing "Happy Birthday."

She tips her head, and a slight smile curves one corner of her mouth.

I pause to tell her, "My dad always sang 'Happy Birthday' twice when we washed our hands; then we'd know all the germs were gone. Do your parents do that?"

She shakes her head.

"Want me to keep singing?"

At her nod, I start over, thinking it doesn't hurt for us to wash our hands longer, considering how ill her poor brother seems to be. Once we're all done, we dry our hands with paper towels. Back in my office, I clear a spot on my desk for her and grab some paper from the printer while Lavender unpacks her knapsack.

I pull up a chair beside mine, and Lavender sits on her knees, shimmying forward until she can reach the desk and her crayons. She picks up a piece of blank paper and very carefully lines up the corners, her tongue poking out as she tries to get one side to line up and then the other. But her little hands make it impossible.

"Do you want to make a card for your brother?"

She nods.

"Can I show you a trick?"

Another nod.

"You hold the corners for me, okay?" I wait until her little fingers are pressed on each corner; then I pinch the center on both ends, helping her flatten it out. For the next half hour we sit side by side, quietly coloring. Every once in a while Lavender peeks over at my paper to see what I'm drawing.

Crayons aren't the best medium for fine art, but I follow the contours of her face, sketching lines with a pencil first before I start filling them in with color. When Lavender is done with the card for her brother—she spells River without any vowels, although she's barely four—she starts another picture while I continue working on mine.

Lavender tugs on my sleeve to get my attention.

"What's up, kiddo?"

She points to the two crayons I've been using to shade in the area around the nose and then the picture itself. "How do that?"

She's pretty shy around people she doesn't know, but maybe since we've met a bunch of times, she's getting more comfortable around me. "You mean the shading?"

"Yes. The sading." She points at her own picture. This one has a big sun in the sky. "I want here."

"Want me to show you how?"

We bend over her picture together, and I lightly run the yellow crayon around the edge of the sun, filling in the middle. Lavender hands me the orange crayon when I set down the yellow one and slips it back in the package.

She doesn't have the manual dexterity yet to be able to manage it, but I can already see her eye for color in the way she sets up her pictures.

"Do you ever use paint instead of crayons?"

Her lips pucker and her fingers flex, lids fluttering rapidly. She exhales a loud breath and says softly, "At home. It's too messy for here."

"Mmm. Good point. But maybe we can find a time to paint together, when it's okay to be messy. Would you like that?"

A huge smile breaks across her face, and she claps her hands. "Oh, yes!"

"I'd like that too."

We go back to working on her drawing, heads bent together over her paper while we shade in her sun, then give it a silly face.

And that's exactly how King finds us when he stops by, likely wanting to discuss our dinner plans for tonight. His eyes flare with surprise, and a wide grin makes his gorgeous face even more stunning. "Miss Lavender, what a wonderful surprise."

She ducks her head and gives him a shy smile, peeking up at him from under her lashes as she waves.

"What are you two up to?" He tucks his thumbs into the pockets of his khakis and rocks back on his heels.

"Creating masterpieces, of course." I hold up the card she made for her brother, where Lavender re-created a version of a puking emoji sitting in a sunny field, but instead of throw up, it's a rainbow coming out of his mouth.

"That is definitely a masterpiece. We should call the Louvre and tell them we have the next Picasso on our hands."

"I totally agree."

Lavender blushes some more and snuggles into my arm.

The door to my dad's office opens, and a man I've seen once before, when Corey was first brought to the team, steps out. I have to assume he's Corey's agent. I seriously hope he gets a decent cut of his salary for dealing with so much bullshit. Alex and my dad follow behind him. They all look a little worse for wear, and agitated. The men shake hands, and Corey's agent nods at us, then rushes out like his ass is on fire.

Alex runs a hand down his face and sighs. "Well, that's three fuc—" He stops just before he completes the curse, his gaze landing on his daughter, whose eyes are as wide as saucers, and a hint of a naughty smile flirts at the corners of her mouth. I'm sure she's heard bad words before, since Violet often forgets to censor herself.

"Lavender? Hey, sweetheart, I didn't realize you were here." Alex gives me a look that's halfway between questioning and apologetic.

Lavender hops off her chair and rushes over to her dad. He scoops her up and plants loud kisses all over her face. She giggles and then snuggles right into his neck.

I bet every pair of underwear I own that Kingston would be exactly the same kind of dad. And that thought makes my lady parts excited. Which is crazy, because I'm only twenty-four and I'm in no way ready for kids. We haven't even dropped the L bomb on each other.

"Is everything okay? Where's Vi?"

I stop staring at Kingston and address Alex. "River isn't feeling well, so Violet took him to the doctor. She was hoping she could leave Lavender with you, but since you were in a meeting, I volunteered to hang out with my favorite budding artist."

"Is River okay?"

"Violet thinks he might have the flu." I look at my phone to check how long she's been gone. "I have messages from her. Hold on." I pull them up and scan them quickly. "Yup, it's the flu. She's going to take him home and get the nanny to come over to watch him so she can come back and get Lavender."

"When did Violet drop her off?" He adjusts his hold on Lavender so she can effectively wrap her arms around his neck without choking him.

"Maybe a little more than an hour ago."

He rubs the space between his eyes and then kisses his little girl's cheek. "Jake, I might need to run Lavender home. I don't want Vi to have to leave River with the nanny if he's sick."

"Or we could take her," Kingston offers. "Queenie and I, I mean. I don't need to be on the ice for a couple of hours."

Alex looks conflicted. "Lavender, would it be okay with you if Queenie and Kingston took you home?"

She rubs the space between her dad's eyes and then leans in, whispering something in his ear.

"I'm okay, honey. It's just work stuff and nothing you need to worry about."

She places her hand on his cheek and says quietly, but audibly, "Okay. I go with Keenie and King."

He blinks a bunch of times, clearly taken aback that she's answered without whispering in his ear, which is pretty typical, from what I've witnessed. "Okay. That's great." He kisses her on the cheek and sets her down.

Together she and I put away all her art supplies. It takes far less time with me helping than it does when it's her brother.

"Oh, this is for you. Do you want to put it in your sketch pad?" I pass her the crayon portrait.

Alex leans in so he can have a look. "You drew this? I didn't know you were an artist."

I wave off the comment. "It's just a crayon doodle."

"That makes it even more amazing. You know, if you get tired of working for this guy, you can teach Lavender art classes." He thumbs over his shoulder at my dad.

I laugh at that. "I'm not sure that's a great way to earn a living, but I'm always happy to spend time with Lavender."

Once she's all packed up, we head out to the parking lot, and Alex hands over his car keys, which is easier than moving the car seat into Kingston's SUV.

"You want me to drive your car?" Kingston stares at the keys like they're acid-soaked zombie piranhas.

"You're the safest driver I know. Much safer than my wife, but don't ever tell her I said that. You either," he says to Lavender.

She gives him a coy little smile but makes the zipped-lips sign and lets him buckle her into her car seat. Kingston and I get in the car, and he turns the engine over. It's another two minutes of seat and mirror adjustments before Kingston is ready to leave the parking spot. I turn the radio on, and a familiar song comes on. I glance in the rearview mirror and smile as Lavender shimmies in her seat. "You know this song?"

She nods.

"Want me to turn up the volume?" Kingston isn't a huge fan of loud music in the car, because he worries he won't be able to hear emergency vehicles, but turning it up a little louder can't hurt.

She gives me a thumbs-up, little head bobbing to "Fireflies" by Owl City. When we get to the chorus, I sing along. I can carry a tune most of the time, and it's a catchy song. What I don't expect at all, and apparently neither does Kingston, is for Lavender to start singing too. Not only can she draw but she has an incredible little set of lungs on her. I find her absolutely fascinating.

When we arrive at Alex and Vi's house, we get to see the real Lavender. The one who speaks above a whisper. In full sentences. Lavender insists that Kingston and I see her bedroom and her art room. Violet puts the kibosh on the bedroom, since her brother is currently sleeping and they share a room, but I get to see where she obviously spends a lot of time. The room has great light and a balcony. The floors are covered in some kind of easy-to-clean vinyl, but the walls are what grab my attention. One wall boasts chalkboard paint, and the rest are covered in poster paper that turns the majority of the room into a massive changeable canvas.

"This is so cool!" I walk the perimeter, taking in the splatter-paint designs, the crayon drawings, and the chalk pictures.

"It's her favorite place to be," Violet says. "Isn't it, Lavender?"

"Yup. I love coloring. And painting. 'Specially with my hands!" She grins up at us and rocks back on her heels.

Kingston has to get back to the arena, but I promise to come back and have an afternoon of finger painting soon.

Once we're back in the car, I turn the music down and settle into the passenger seat. "Well, that was . . . something else, wasn't it?"

"I've never heard her talk like that. It's like she's a totally different person when she's at home."

"It must be about her comfort level." I kick off my shoes and cross my legs. "I wonder if they're doing art therapy with her, and that's why they have that room set up. It's supposed to be great for helping with anxiety."

Kingston shifts his foot from the gas to the brake when the light turns yellow, even though he totally could have gone through it. The person behind him obviously doesn't appreciate it, since they honk at him. Instead of flipping them the bird, he waves.

But his hand doesn't return to the wheel. Instead it slides along the back of my seat between my neck and the headrest. His thumb smooths down my nape. "Can I ask you something without you getting defensive or changing the subject?"

If it has to do with Corey, the answer to that will be no. "I guess it depends on what it's about."

He smiles, like he expected as much. "You said you had most of an art degree. Why didn't you finish?"

This is definitely one of those questions I don't want to answer. "Because I wasn't good enough to make a career out of it." And I'm too emotionally messed up to effectively be an art therapist; my mom made sure of that.

The light turns green, but the arm stays slung across the back of my seat. "Who told you that?"

"What does it matter? It's the truth. I'm mediocre at best. I'll never be in galleries, so it's a waste of money." The words taste like cardboard as I spit them out. Words that felt a lot like knives when they were given to me.

Kingston stays silent as he makes a right into the arena parking lot, and as usual, he takes a spot near the back. I hit the release on my seat belt, wanting to escape him and this conversation.

"Hey." His warm, calloused fingers wrap around my wrist, and he lifts it to his lips, kissing each of my knuckles. "You're anything but mediocre, Queenie. You're magnificent, and whoever told you that you're not talented is malicious and jealous."

He's not wrong. "My mother is the one who told me that." And she is most definitely both of those things.

His eyes fall closed, and his cheek tics with his slow exhale. When his lids flip open, his gaze holds sadness and anger. "I want you to listen to me, Queenie. You are not mediocre. You are amazing and the world is at your fingertips. The sooner you realize that, the easier it will be for you to shine like you're supposed to."

"Please don't say things like that to me," I whisper.

"Why not? Especially when it's the truth." He unbuckles his seat belt. "You should be proud of yourself, Queenie. I know I am. You were amazing with Lavender today. You make me want things I've only thought about in the abstract until now."

"What does that mean?"

"I don't know that you're ready for what that means yet." He drags his fingers down my cheek. "But you should seriously reconsider finishing that art degree. Success and worth don't need to be based on something as arbitrary as whether or not you have pieces in a gallery. It can definitely be part of your dream and your journey, but I'd hate for you to walk away from something you're so obviously passionate about because you've allowed one person's misguided jealousy to form your entire opinion of yourself."

"Where did you even come from?"

"Tennessee."

"Ha ha, that's not what I—"

He presses his lips to mine. "I see you, Queenie. Don't let anyone tell you that you're not worthy."

I slide my hand around the back of his neck and deepen the kiss instead of responding with words. Because as much as I want to believe him, there's a heaviness that weighs on me. One I thought I'd buried six years ago when I walked away from Corey and ran where it was safest: home. And the only person who's never turned his back on me: my dad. Even he doesn't know how very bad some of my mistakes have been. If he did, he might turn his back too. So why wouldn't Kingston?

# CHAPTER 20
## THE FALL OF HAPPINESS

*Queenie*

The thing about happiness is that it isn't meant to last. Life is a roller coaster: slow climbs to the top, a brief balance in euphoria, and then a steep drop that leaves you screaming and gasping for breath.

This isn't a metaphor for an orgasm, either, although it could be, because they fall under the same principle.

Over the next few days I skip blindly through that state of suspended euphoria, ignoring the niggling worries and doubts that nip at my heels and threaten my bubble of bliss. I wear Kingston's words like battle armor, protecting me from the fears and self-doubts that no amount of therapy—another thing my dad has footed the bill for—could ever seem to cure.

I should know better than to rely on any one single thing to make me happy. Especially not a single person. But I feel like I've finally found *my person*. The one who won't try to tame my chaos but will let me live in it and help me balance my impulsiveness with stability. He's yin and I'm yang. He's sugar and I'm salt.

It's a game day, so the team will be at the arena soon to get ready. I have a few more emails and memos to tackle, and then I can enjoy the game from the comfort of the box with Lainey, Stevie, Violet, and some of the other girls. I love watching Kingston tend goal. He's so focused and intense. Just like he is in bed.

Once I'm done with the emails, I switch to my personal account and click on the new email from the University of Seattle. After the conversation with Kingston in his car the other day, I pulled out my college transcripts and reviewed all the courses and programs I'd taken over the years. I dropped out with one semester left to go for my art and psych degree. Then I tried a couple of other programs, but neither of them was a good fit.

So maybe it's time to go back and finish what I started and see if maybe my mother is wrong—that even if my art isn't gallery worthy, it's still worth something. That I can do something that will give my dad, and me, a reason to be proud of myself for once.

I respond to the email from the local college confirming the appointment for next week with their admissions team, then head down the hall to the copy room to make duplicates of a few important documents. I kick the stopper in front of the jamb so the door doesn't close on me. It's wonky and doesn't like to stay open without some help.

I'm waiting on the last document when the door behind me closes with a soft click. I assume it's Kingston, because he always finds me before he suits up. "Looking to add the copy room to your pregame make-out session list?" My smile dissolves when I turn around and find not Kingston but Corey. "What the hell do you want?"

He leans against the closed door, blocking the only way out of the room, which now feels infinitely smaller with his huge body taking up space in here. He's dressed in a suit, reminding me of the first time we met, back when he was playing varsity-level hockey. How stupid I'd been to fall for his charming smile and smooth lines back then.

He crosses his arms. "We need to talk."

"No. We don't." I grab the last of the copies and slip them into the file folder. Tipping my chin up, I face him with confidence I don't feel, and that niggling feeling starts to spread, churning in my stomach and seeping into my limbs. "Move, please. You have a game to get ready for, and my dad needs to see me." I try to push past him, but he's like a brick wall.

"No, he doesn't. He's already in the arena, and we have shit to discuss." He eyes me with contempt.

"You can't lock me in here with you and force me to listen to whatever bullshit you feel like slinging in my direction, Corey."

"Looks like I've already done that, so your best bet is to shut your fucking mouth and listen for once. You've caused me more than enough headaches, and I'm sick and tired of your 'I'm so entitled because my daddy is a big shot' whiny bitch attitude."

My stomach twists uncomfortably with anxiety, and my cheeks heat with anger and embarrassment. "What the hell are you even talking about?"

"My girlfriend tried to apply for a marriage license this morning, and you know what happened?"

"She saw something shiny in a window and it distracted her?" His girlfriend, Sissy, comes to all the home games, and she's forever dressed in sequins. It makes her baby belly look like a disco ball. Which is probably the point.

Corey's lip twitches. "Always such a fucking smart-ass, aren't you? She couldn't get one."

"Because she's not capable of filling out the required paperwork?"

"Do you think you're funny, Queenie? You think it's some kind of joke that you're forever fucking up my life?"

"I've had nothing to do with you for six damn years, and I would be more than happy to never have anything to do with you again. You know what? I'm done with this conversation. It's not my fault your girlfriend doesn't know how to fill out applications." I try to elbow him out of the way, but he won't move. "Let me out."

"We're not done here." He holds up a hand to keep me at bay. "My girlfriend can fill out applications just fine. *You* are the reason she couldn't apply for the license."

"What? That doesn't even make sense."

"It does, though. Because *we're* still fucking married." He motions between us aggressively.

That horrible churning in my stomach ramps up. "That's impossible. There must be some mistake. I filed the papers."

"Well, you fucked up somewhere along the way, like you always do. They never went through, and now she's losing her goddamn mind, and it's your fucking fault."

"How the hell is this *my* fault? I did my part. In fact I did everything! I got the paperwork; I tabbed every page you damn well needed to sign. I stood there while some bunny hoovered your damn neck and flipped the pages *for you* so *you* wouldn't fuck it up. I even handed you half the damn money in person. All you had to do was pay the fucking fee!"

Corey's brow furrows and then he sneers, leaning in so his face is close to mine. "If you hadn't gone running home to Daddy when shit didn't work out the way you wanted, we could've gone right to the courthouse and taken care of things, so don't try to turn this around and make it my fault."

"Is that supposed to make any damn sense? Did you or didn't you pay the filing fee?"

"It was a long time ago. How the hell am I supposed to remember?"

"Jesus Christ, Corey. Do you take responsibility for anything in your asshole privileged life?"

"My life is privileged? Fuck you, little Miss 'I'm the Queen of My Fucking Castle.' It wasn't like you couldn't afford to pay the entire thing, with your dad sitting all high up in the NHL administration ranks."

"It wasn't like I could ask him for money to pay for a *divorce*! I was eighteen!" I don't know why I'm engaging in this argument with him. It's pointless. Corey is the master at deflecting blame.

He rolls his eyes. "God, you're still so fucking pathetic. You want to know the real reason I married you in the first place? Other than the fact that I wanted to pop that precious fucking cherry you were so intent on holding on to. You weren't even that great in bed. Pretty fucking boring, actually."

"I'm done listening to this! Let me out of here." I try to get around him to open the door, but it's useless. Corey is bigger and stronger than I am by a lot. He's not going to let me go until he's finished tearing me down.

"You're done when I tell you you're done. Your dad had connections, and he could get me what I wanted a lot easier than waiting for the scouts to pick me up. That's the only reason I kept you around as long as I did. It's the only reason I let you talk me into marrying you. And then I realized what a clingy, needy nightmare you were. I mean, is it really a surprise that I went looking elsewhere to get what I needed? Plus, I was twenty. Like I was going to spend my best years on one lame pussy."

"You're a pig."

"I'm honest. It's not my problem you never liked to hear the truth. I wonder how your Boy Scout is going to feel when he finds out he's been fucking *my wife* all this time."

"I wouldn't be your anything if you'd paid the filing fee!" Panic makes it feel like I'm being choked. "You can't tell Kingston."

"I guess you better fix it if you don't want him to find out, then. Don't you think he deserves to know what kind of flake you really are, hiding behind your daddy and his success, leeching off his fucking players like you're special, when you're not? Even your name is a goddamn joke. The only thing royal about you is how much of a pain you are in everyone's ass." He opens the door, finally. I don't try to push past him, though, aware he's not quite done taunting me by the way his smile curves even higher. "It must suck to be surrounded by awesomeness all the time and be so damn average. Fix the problem, Queenie, unless you want everyone to know what a fuckup you really are."

He steps out into the hall and pauses, looking over his shoulder, that same awful sneer in place. "And you were never anything to me, Queenie. You were a means to an end. And a mistake, since I got where I wanted to be without you to drag me down. Seems to be the story of your useless life, doesn't it? You're everyone's mistake."

# CHAPTER 21
## CRASH AND BURN

*Kingston*

My phone buzzes with messages from my family, wishing me good luck tonight, and my buoyant mood only increases the closer I get to Queenie's office. I need to suit up for the game, but first I want to stop and tell my girlfriend the good news and steal a few kisses.

Corey comes around the corner as I reach Queenie's office. He's dressed in his suit—he's always name and brand dropping, like people are actually impressed by what he wears. We all know what his salary is. He's a big earner, but he's no Rook Bowman. He smirks and starts whistling a funeral march as he heads in the opposite direction I am, toward the locker room.

I don't like that he was down here, where he could potentially run into Queenie without me around to make sure he keeps his distance. I stop by her office, but she's not there, which amps up the anxious feeling that's making my shoulders tight.

Jake's office door is open, so I pop my head in there, too, but it's empty. I decide to check the copy room, on alert because Corey came from that direction. I round the corner just as Queenie does, scaring the crap out of her and causing her stack of papers to flutter across the floor.

"Shit!" She presses one hand against her chest and the other against mine. "You scared the hell out of me."

I run my palms down her arms. "I'm sorry. I just wanted to see you before the game, and I passed Slater in the hall. He was coming from this direction, and I wanted to make sure you were okay. Did you run into him too?"

"What?" Her eyes lift to mine briefly and then dart down as she crouches to pick up the scattered papers. "Oh, no. I didn't run into Corey."

I help her gather up the pages and notice the tremble in her hands. "Are you sure you're okay? Your hands are shaking."

She exhales an unsteady breath. "I'm fine. You just scared me, that's all. I was in a bit of a rush, wanting to get to the arena so I can meet up with the girls."

"Why don't we walk down together?"

"Okay. Sure. That would be great." Her smile is still tremulous, but I did scare the heck out of her, so it's understandable.

We drop off the stack of papers on her desk, which is always a disorganized mess, but she seems to know where things are. She shuts down her computer and grabs her purse, rummaging around in it for her jersey—the one I bought for her a few days ago—with my name and number on the back.

She pulls it over her head, and I take it upon myself to smooth out her hair. Of course, the innocuous contact always makes me want to touch more of her. I follow her into the hall. She fumbles with her keys, so I take them from her and help lock up. We speed walk through the building to where it connects to the arena, fingers threaded together.

"Hey, I have some news."

"I need to talk to you about something," she says at the same time. Her cheeks are flushed, no longer pale, but something still seems to be off.

"Is everything okay?"

"Yeah. Everything is fine. Good. It can wait until later, after the game. What's your news?"

"You're sure you don't want to talk about it now?"

She bumps her shoulder against my bicep. "I'm sure. Tell me what's going on. You seem excited."

"My family usually makes a trip out here to see me play at least once a season, and Hanna's birthday is coming up so I thought it would be great for them to visit around then. You know, since this one will be kind of different now that my relationship with her has changed some." I tap my access card on the sensor and open the door for Queenie. Silence gives way to the sound of hockey fans in the distance, and my excitement ramps up.

She squeezes my hand. "I think that's a great idea. When's her birthday again? I know you told me, but I'm terrible with dates."

"In a couple of weeks. My family usually stays at my place, so it can be hectic, and often it's for, like, a week or more, but it'll be a great time for you to meet everyone."

"Meet everyone? Like your entire family? All at once?" Queenie's voice is pitchy again.

"Don't worry." I squeeze her hand this time. "They're going to love you, Queenie, just like I do."

She comes to an abrupt halt about ten feet from the locker room. "What did you say?"

"They're going to love you." At first I don't understand why her eyes are so wide, until it dawns on me what I've inadvertently said. I take her free hand in mine and give her a chagrined smile. "I'm sorry. That wasn't how I meant to tell you that."

"Or maybe you're trying to distract me by throwing me a curveball." She smiles uncertainly.

"No curveballs or distractions. I love you, Queenie. I want you to meet my family so they can fall in love with you too."

She blinks a few times, and her eyes go glassy. "King, I—" She shakes her head and has to clear her throat.

I duck down, getting in close, because security is only a few feet away and I don't want them listening in on our private conversation. I also don't want to put her on the spot, even though I'd like to hear those words from her too. "It's okay if you're not ready to say it back."

"It's not . . . that's not it." She strokes my cheek with her knuckles. "I just haven't heard those words in a long time . . . from anyone other than my dad, I mean." She shakes her head. "I love you too."

"King! Man, you're gonna see Queenie in like four hours. Get your fucking ass in the locker room and get your gear on unless you wanna watch the game from the bench and give Van Horten a shot to hone his skills in net. He's been dying to show your ass up all season," Bishop yells from all of five feet away.

I shoot him a glare. "Are you serious right now?"

"Well, it's true. You'll see Queenie after the game, and Van wants to hump your net more than you want to hump your girl. No disrespect meant, Queenie." Bishop gives me a knowing smile.

Queenie ducks her head and chuckles. "Go do your job. We can talk about . . . everything else later." She pushes up on her toes and tips her head back.

I bend to kiss her and whisper "I love you" against her lips.

"I love you, too. Now go."

She pats me on the butt as I pass her, and I nearly flip Bishop off with the way he's smirking. I manage to control my fingers, unlike my mouth and the things that come out of it with Queenie. I glance over my shoulder before I disappear into the locker room. Queenie's already rushing down the hall, fingers at her lips.

I don't let the ribbing from the guys get to me as I suit up for the game.

"You're a little late, eh, King? We thought we were gonna have to bring in the reserve," Slater says as he adjusts his laces.

"Just lost track of time." There's no way I'll let him dampen my good mood.

He hasn't been a positive addition to the team. His linemates are always on edge, never knowing what kind of garbage he's going to pull when he's on the ice. He's guaranteed to get at least one penalty a game.

"I hope you didn't waste all your game energy on some used pussy."

I'm halfway dressed in my gear, but no shin guards or chest pads, so I still have the benefit of mobility. Before I can even consider how bad an idea it is, I'm off the bench. I grab the front of his jersey and haul him up so we're eye to eye. "I already warned you once, Slater: do not disrespect Queenie, or we'll be having more than words," I hiss.

He throws his head back and laughs. "Do you even know how to throw a punch?"

"You looking to find out?"

"Jesus, King, back the fuck down, unless you want to sit this game out. This jock-rot fuckstick isn't worth the bench time." Bishop grabs me by the back of the neck and tries to loosen my grip on Corey's jersey with the other hand.

"He's disrespecting Queenie."

"He disrespects his own mother every goddamn day just by existing. Still not worth damaging your hands over."

He has a point. I can't do my job if I break my hands. And if I get a suspension, I could end up on the bench, or, worse, I could be told I can't even travel with the team. I've seen it happen before. Then I wouldn't be able to keep an eye on Queenie. I don't like that thought—not at all. It's the only reason I let go.

"Such a fucking Boy Scout, huh, King? Never like to get your hands dirty, do you? Except now you are, and you don't even fucking know it."

"What are you talking about?"

"Just remember: she was mine before she was yours. You're welcome for breaking her in." He winks, still smirking.

"You son of a bitch." I lunge for him but end up in a choke hold before I can do something really stupid, like rearrange Corey's face.

"What the hell is going on here?" Alex's voice barely cuts through the haze of red. "Bishop, stop fucking around. King, why the hell aren't you suited up? You need to be on the ice in two minutes."

"Just messing around. He's on it, Coach." Bishop releases me and claps me on the shoulder. "Channel the anger on the ice. Every puck coming at you is that fucker's balls."

I run my hands down my face, trying to find some calm. I don't like the way Corey is suddenly trying to get under my skin. It's obviously intentional, and I'm not sure what the purpose of it is.

I finish dressing and try to clear my head and get in the zone. Once I hit the ice, I search for Queenie in the arena. I spot her up in the box with the rest of the girls. Which is good: she'll be too close to Corey if she sits behind the bench.

I take my place in net and focus on the game, not the one player who gets under my skin. I guess now I know how Bishop felt when he and Rook weren't seeing eye to eye. It's hard not to be preoccupied.

I take a few deep breaths and remind myself that later tonight I'll have Queenie in my bed, under me—or on top, or both—and that she's finally admitted how she feels about me. She's my raging rapids, and I'm her calm lake at dawn. We're good. Perfect. She's going to meet my family, and they'll love her. Corey can't touch what we have.

I do what Bishop suggested and channel all the negative energy into protecting the net. It's incredibly effective, especially the part where I envision Corey's flattened face on the puck every time it gets close to the net. We end up with a shutout, which means I feel fantastic about the game, and most of the negative energy seems to fade away with the back pats and my teammates complimenting me on a job well done.

I'm in a great mood as I shower and get ready to meet up with the girls, who are likely already at the bar. Corey's too busy with whatever's happening on his phone to pay attention to me, which is probably good for both of us. I'm riding a high, and I would gladly knock him out if he decides we need to have a go at each other.

"You're going to stay for a couple of beers tonight, right?" I ask Bishop as I shrug into my dress shirt.

"That's a rhetorical question, right?" Bishop makes an adjustment in his underwear. They always have a ridiculous pattern on them. Tonight it's a pineapple and olive dancing together. It's hard not to look at them.

"Uh, just making sure. I think I might have a drink." I fasten the top button on my shirt and make sure the collar is smooth.

Bishop's brow quirks. "You all right?"

"Yeah. I'm great, actually. My family's coming to visit, so Queenie'll get to meet them, and I told her how I feel about her, and she feels the same, so we're solid. It's good. Everything is perfect. I think I might ask her to move in with me. For real this time. Maybe after the holidays. That's not too soon, is it?"

Bishop holds up a finger, taps his lips a couple of times, and then looks at me like I'm the stupidest person on the face of the earth. "You realize I'm the last person you should ever ask for relationship advice, right? I told the woman I'm married to that her face was a boner killer."

I cringe, because that's a horrible thing to say, let alone to the woman who willingly sleeps beside him every night. "That was before you realized who she was, though."

"Yeah, but the point is, I'm not the person you want to ask for advice. I mean, I'd tell you to pin her the fuck down before she realizes she's made a mistake, if you were me, but you're not me. You're likable and friendly and shit. I'm lucky I'm nice to look at and that I can give my wife multiple orgasms; otherwise I'd be fucked, man."

"Is that a common thing?"

"Is what a common thing?" Bishop works on tying his tie.

"Multiple orgasms."

He looks away from his reflection for a moment. "You asking me for pointers in the bedroom?"

"No. Of course not. I know what's effective with Queenie. I just didn't realize multiples were that common." I'm actually a little disappointed. Although I won't admit that to Bishop, or anyone else. Jessica was always very . . . proper. And basically silent. It didn't matter how many questions I asked, how much direction I sought, everything was always "fine" or "nice."

Queenie is the opposite. Which I love. She'll tell me exactly what she needs and how she needs it. And she seems to really like that I seek direction from her. I can only learn her body if she shares with me what makes her feel the best.

"Can I ask you something without offending you?"

"As long as you're not disrespecting Queenie, sure." I tie a windsor knot without looking in a mirror.

"Are you, like, missionary only?"

"Pardon?"

"Positions. Do you have more than one you like?"

I meet my best friend's questioning gaze and consider how much information I want to give him about my private, personal life. "I can appreciate all views."

His eyebrows climb into his hairline. "I thought I knew you."

"You do know me." I shrug into my suit jacket and check for any lint I missed.

"Queenie's good for you, though, because this isn't a conversation we would've had a year ago."

"I'm not being disrespectful."

He puts his hand on my shoulder. "No, man, but with Jessica there wasn't ever a conversation, about anything. She was an accessory. Queenie is a partner. She's the olive to your pineapple."

"That sounds awful."

"It's actually not that bad on pizza, but you need hot peppers, bacon, ham, and pepperoni to balance it all out. The pizza isn't the point. It's that you found someone who lights a fire under your ass. It's a good thing. That's all I'm saying. And multiples are the fucking bomb." Bishop makes a fist and approximates a jerking-off motion before he realizes Rook is watching him. "It's good for everyone."

"Especially my ego," I agree.

"Fucking shit!" Corey barks from across the room. He punches at his phone and brings it to his ear. "What in the actual fuck, Sissy? I told you I'd take care of it. What the hell were you thinking?" He screws his eyes shut and exhales heavily through his nose. "This is going to be a nightmare to manage. What? No. Don't do that!" he snaps, then changes his tone. "Come on, baby, that's a bad idea. Where are you now? I'll come get you. We'll figure out how to fix this." He pushes up off the bench and stalks out of the locker room.

"I wonder what that was about," Bishop mutters.

"Sounds like there's trouble in paradise." We gather up our things, and Rook falls into step with us.

"If there were two people who deserved each other, it's Slater and Sissy," Bishop says. "She's the perfect nightmare for Corey to end up with."

"The douche factor and the crazy pair nicely, that's for sure," Rook says. "At least she's not trying to siphon jizz out of used condoms anymore."

"I'm sorry, what?"

"I made the mistake of hooking up with her once back in my rookie days, obviously long before I met Lainey," Rook replies, his expression a mix of embarrassment and regret.

"Oh, man, I remember that! Didn't she fake a pregnancy? Took pictures on social media and tried to blackmail you or whatever?" Bishop asks.

"That she did. Used the plaster casts from her sister's baby belly to stage photos."

"That's just . . ."

"Certifiable?" Rook supplies.

"Yeah." I can't imagine getting involved with someone that unbalanced. It's why I'd never had a one-night stand until Queenie. It obviously turned out a lot different than either of us expected, but it could've gone very badly had she been a Sissy.

We leave the arena and head across the street to the bar we usually meet up at after home games. I decide tonight I'm going to indulge in one of those fun drinks Queenie and I had that first night we met, between the shots. The white russians. Those were tasty.

My phone buzzes in my pocket repeatedly as we enter the loud, hectic bar. I slip it out of my pocket, wanting to send Queenie a message and find out where they're sitting so we're not searching the whole place for them.

"What the heck?" Message after message comes in from my family chat. I open the feed and try to make sense of what's going on, but they're coming in too fast.

"Oh shit, I think we've got some trouble." Bishop elbows me in the side.

I look up from my phone and follow his gaze across the crowded pub to the bar. Where my girlfriend is being yelled at by Slater's pregnant fiancée.

# CHAPTER 22

## BROKEN VOWS

*Queenie*

I cannot believe this is happening.

Actually, I can. Because my life is one big shitstorm after another, so why wouldn't I get called out in a bar, in front of my friends, and a bunch of strangers, by a pregnant woman?

"You had your chance, and he doesn't want you. He wants me." Sissy, Corey's lunatic fiancée, points to her chest and then waves her hand around in the air. "You see this diamond? He spent over fifty thousand on this! He told me he didn't even get you a ring at all, so that shows you exactly how important you were to him. I'm the one who's having his baby, not you!" she screams.

"I think you're confused. Queenie's dating Ryan Kingston, the goalie." Stevie holds her hands up like she's trying to ward off a wild animal. Or perform an exorcism.

Speaking of King, I spot him pushing his way through the crowd, trying to get to me. Which is not what I want at all. In fact, it's the very last thing I want to happen. I was supposed to have had time to tell him tonight. When we were back at his place and all our friends and a whole bunch of strangers weren't around to witness it.

"Does he know you're *married* to my fiancé?" Sissy continues to scream at ungodly volume.

Kingston is right behind her now, and, based on his confused expression, he definitely heard her, as did everyone else within a fifty-foot radius.

"I hope he dumps your stupid ass! You better give Corey that divorce or I will kick your skinny ass right after I've had this baby! He's spent more than a hundred thousand dollars on our wedding already, and we have all sorts of famous people coming, so you better not fuck this up for me. And you can't have any of his money either. That's for our baby!"

There are too many people looking at us. My face feels like it's on fire, and I'm sweating. I raise my hands in submission. "Look, I understand that you're upset, but there's been a misunderstanding. Can we go somewhere else to talk about this? In private?"

"Absolutely not! Everyone should know you're a lying, cheating slut! He told me you're the one who took off on him. You've been cheating on him for *years!*" she sneers. "And I exposed you for the money-grubbing fraud you are." She holds her phone up in front of my face.

I can't hear what's playing on the screen, but the caption "Wedding Dreams Crushed by Vengeful Estranged Soon-to-Be Ex-Wife" says it all. It's one of those horrible tabloid-style media sites, but it's still out there, for everyone to watch. And Sissy is an overdramatic nightmare, so it will definitely garner attention.

"Sissy, baby, what're you doing?" Corey comes barreling through the crowd, pushing people out of the way.

She whirls around. "Fixing the problem, since you won't! I told her she needs to give you the divorce so she doesn't ruin my wedding."

Corey looks like his head is going to explode. I sincerely hope he falls into the dump truck of bullshit he's thrown at me with this freak show.

Kingston reaches around Sissy for me and brushes her shoulder in the process.

Sissy smacks his arm and whirls around, shoving her finger in his face. "Do not manhandle me! I'm pregnant!" As if we couldn't tell with the disco ball–style sequined dress she's wearing. Which is totally not reasonable for a hockey game, or even a New Year's party in Vegas.

She looks over her shoulder at Corey, who seems like he'd rather be anywhere but here. "Are you going to let him put his hands on me like that?"

All hell breaks loose—not that it wasn't loose already, but it's suddenly that much worse when Corey tries to come at Kingston. Bishop gets in the way, and Sissy starts slapping him. It gives Kingston the opening he needs to pull me out of there.

"Just go." Bishop tips his chin up. He's holding Corey at arm's length while Sissy continues to swat at him.

She suddenly stops and grabs her belly. "Oh! Something's happening in there! If I go into labor early I'm suing you!" she screams at me.

Kingston wraps his arm around my waist and lifts me up so my feet aren't touching the ground anymore and carries me out of the bar.

"You can put me down now," I say when we're halfway down the street, heading in the direction of the arena.

He doesn't respond, just continues to carry me like a child, across the street and to the private lot where the players park. Even when we reach his car, he doesn't put me down. Or speak. Which is starting to worry me. As is the way his jaw keeps ticcing. He unlocks the car, opens the door, and deposits me in the passenger seat. I jump when he closes it rather firmly. He stalks around the front of the car and gets in the driver's side.

But once he's in the car, he doesn't make a move to buckle up, or check all the mirrors, or turn the engine over. He's breathing heavily, and he grips the steering wheel, knuckles almost white.

"Kingston?"

"Is it true?" His voice is thick.

"Yes. But it's not what you think."

He closes his eyes, and his hands flex on the wheel. Prying one free, he rubs his chin, and when he turns his gaze on me, I feel like I'm looking at a stranger. "You're *married*. I've committed adultery with you. Repeatedly." It makes sense that this is where his mind has gone. Kingston is unfailingly loyal. He's also very much about following rules, doing the right thing, and being a good person.

"I shouldn't be. I'm not supposed to be. Married to Corey. I'm not supposed to be married to him." I take a deep breath, trying to manage my anxiety and my mortification over the fact that I've been painted as a home-wrecker on some horrible third-rate tabloid show. "It'll make more sense when you hear the whole story."

"Can you explain then, please?" he says, his voice shaking.

"We met in my first semester of college. He pursued me, invited me out with him and his friends all the time. He played hockey, and I knew a lot about it. I was eighteen. I had decided I wanted to wait to have sex. I mean, I don't think I necessarily planned to wait until I was married; I just . . . my dad and I talked about the importance of making sure I was ready for the consequences and the responsibility, and for him, that had been *me*." There's more to it than that, obviously. So much more, but I figure I'll give King the abridged version before he cracks all his teeth from grinding them together.

"Anyway. I'm impulsive and Corey isn't super smart. I was even more impulsive then than I am now, which I know might be hard to believe." I laugh nervously, but when Kingston doesn't join in, I clear my throat and barrel on. "We'd only been dating for a month when he proposed." With a twist tie.

"And I stupidly said yes. We went to a justice of the peace, got married in secret, and figured we'd wait until the holidays before we told anyone." That was Corey's idea. "I moved in with him, except he lived in one of the off-campus frat houses. It was a constant, unending party.

And disgusting, because college boys don't clean anything, especially not bathrooms."

I wring my hands, remembering how awful it had been. "I'd realized pretty much right away that it was a mistake. He'd proposed on a Friday night, and he'd been doing keg stands." I'm pretty sure we were both either still half-drunk or at least very hungover the next morning when we took the trip to the justice of the peace. "None of my friends were there. He asked two guys on the street to be our witnesses for fifty bucks."

"Jesus, Queenie. What were you thinking?"

That if I was married, then my dad would stop worrying about me. That he'd start living his own life. That I would have my own person. And I was hungover, so that didn't help. "I don't think I was" is my stellar reply.

He scoffs and shakes his head.

I don't tell him the worst part. That we stopped at a drive-through burger joint on the way back to the frat house after it was done. And then he took me up to his room and "made love to me." His breath tasted like onions and beef, which he panted all over me between sloppy kisses. It lasted three minutes. At least it wasn't painful, because of his pencil penis.

"Two weeks after we tied the knot, I came home from the library, because studying in a frat house is impossible, and found him screwing one of the bunnies who was always hanging around." She was pretty much their communal fuck toy. Which was horrible, but then, they were not a nice group of guys.

"He cheated on you?" I love that he sounds appalled, likely because it's something he would never even consider.

"I don't know why I was surprised at the time. I should've expected it, but I made a reckless, impulsive decision, and those have consequences."

"Was he even sorry?"

"No. He wasn't." He'd told me I should've knocked first, and then he told me to get out. *Get the fuck out.* Like I was nothing. Because to him I was.

"So I consulted a lawyer about getting a divorce—we didn't qualify for an annulment—and got all the paperwork together, which is a huge pain in the ass, by the way. All you have to do is sign a few papers to get married but to undo it is a giant headache." I rub my temple, feeling one coming on. "Everything was signed. All he had to do was pay his half of the filing fee and it would've been done. I thought it was taken care of. But he told me today that we were still married, and he doesn't remember if he paid the fee. So here I am, six years later, still married to the biggest asshole I've ever had the misfortune of dating. All this for the hundred and fifty dollars he didn't pay. I don't know why I didn't just pay the whole thing." Tears leak out of the corners of my eyes, and I wipe them away with the back of my hand. "I was going to tell you tonight, when we got home after the game, but his stupid fiancée had to go and broadcast it to the damn media."

My phone buzzes from inside my purse. The ringtone tells me exactly who it is. "Oh my God, my dad is going to lose his mind."

"You never told him." It's not a question. The anger is gone from Kingston's voice. Now he just sounds flat.

I shake my head and press the heels of my hands against my eyes, as if that's going to keep the tears at bay. "I didn't think I'd ever have to. I thought it was done and over with and I wouldn't have to deal with it or Corey again. As soon as I signed the papers and gave him my share of the money, I went home. I quit right in the middle of the semester."

And I moved right back in with my dad. He'd started dating someone while I was away, but as soon as I came home, he ended it. I enrolled in courses in the winter semester at a local college, and he never once gave me a hard time about the money he'd spent and lost on that semester. Or the other programs I later didn't finish either.

"Do you want to answer your phone?" King asks.

"No."

"Let me rephrase that—*should* you answer your phone?"

"Yes, but I can't have this conversation over the phone." I tip my head back. All I want to do is run away from this problem. Like I did when it happened in the first place. Back home. I've been doing that for the past six years. "He's going to be so disappointed."

"Why do you think that?"

"Because I made a stupid mistake, and now I'm all over social media. It's a PR nightmare for him."

"He'll know how to deal with it."

"But he shouldn't have to deal with it. He shouldn't *have* to deal with me. I should have my own place and a regular job. He bought that house specifically because it had a place for me if I needed it. And the pool isn't for him; it's for me. It's like he knows I'm going to keep fucking my life up. Why can't I get my shit together and keep it together for once?" I bang my head on the back of the seat. "I should've known something like this would happen. Everything was too good to last."

My phone rings again.

"I'll take you to your dad's." Kingston starts his car and pulls out of the parking lot.

The rest of the trip is silent apart from my occasional sniffles.

He pulls into the driveway and shifts into park.

"Thank you for bringing me home. I'm sorry about . . . this whole thing. You really don't need my stupid drama."

"I can handle drama, Queenie. My sister is my mom, remember?"

"It wasn't your choice to have that secret kept from you, though. And it wasn't a mistake you made. It was someone else's. This one is on me." I sigh, my stomach flipping as the front door opens and my dad's silhouette fills it.

"Do you want me to come in with you?"

"That's kind of you, but I need to talk to my dad on my own. He's probably going to be angry that I kept this from him, and I don't think you'll be an impartial mediator."

"Okay." He nods once.

I unbuckle my seat belt and reach for the door handle.

"Hey." Kingston's warm, rough fingers wrap around mine, and he squeezes. "We'll figure this out, okay?"

"Okay. I should go." He doesn't make a move to kiss me, and neither do I. I'm not sure how much he's placating me because he feels sorry for me and how much he really means it. I can't say that I would blame him if he decided I'm too much for him.

It's usually why my relationships end.

# CHAPTER 23
## DAD DISAPPOINTMENT

*Queenie*

My dad steps aside to let me into the house. I feel like a teenager who's been caught drinking. Except I got married instead. Which is infinitely worse. It would probably be better if I got caught robbing a bank than the situation I currently find myself in.

"I think you have some explaining to do." He closes the door, cutting off the view of Kingston's car, which is still idling outside the house. I watch through the window as he pulls away from the curb, and I feel like my heart's been run over.

And it's all my fault.

If I'd stayed and made sure Corey paid the fees, I wouldn't be here now, in this horrible situation. But I didn't make sure everything was taken care of, because I wanted to run away from my problem and never think about it again. And now I have to face the consequences, which are a hell of a lot steeper than $150.

"I'm sorry." It's the only thing I can think of to say. And I mean it. Wholly. Truly.

I'm sorry for so many things.

I'm sorry that my biological mother tricked him by lying and telling him she was on the pill when she wasn't. I'm sorry that my dad was too hormonal to make a better, more informed decision and didn't rubber up anyway. I'm sorry my mom bailed when I was a few months old. I'm sorry that my dad is such a good guy and decided he was going to raise me on his own.

He stands in the middle of the living room, looking like he's been to hell and back. "I don't want an apology. I want you to tell me what happened. Did you really marry him?"

I can handle so many things—his anger, his frustration, his irritation—but the look on his face right now is more than I can take. It's not disappointment.

It's failure.

I tell him everything I told Kingston, even the part when I walked in on Corey with someone else.

"Why didn't you tell me? Why would you keep this from me?"

*Because then I would've had to explain why I did it in the first place.* I was wrong to be worried about his disappointment or anger. His hurt is far worse. I take a seat next to him. "I was embarrassed, and I didn't want you to be disappointed in me."

"I'm not disappointed, Queenie; I'm confused. I don't understand why you made such a huge life decision on a whim and then kept it a secret for six years."

"We're not supposed to still be married." I explain what happened with the divorce paperwork and why it never went through.

My dad rubs his temples. "It's not the paperwork that's a problem, Queenie. We can work on getting that taken care of starting tomorrow. It's the fact that you were in that situation in the first place, and I had no idea. That's my issue."

I twist my hands in my lap, feeling very much like the eighteen-year-old girl I was when all this happened in the first place. "I thought if I had someone, you might try to find someone too."

"Why would you think you needed to get married, though?"

"Because I was eighteen and an idiot." And hungover at the time. "And I thought marriage and stability were synonymous with each other. It was an impulsive, bad decision, one I can't ever undo, no matter how badly I wish I could, but at the time it seemed like a good solution. All you did was work and take care of me. I got caught up in the idea of having my own person, thinking it might help you move on too." And he had started to, until I came back home.

My dad's smile is sad. "Oh, honey, I chose to focus on you and work because those were the two things I cared the most about. I wasn't ready to bring someone else into the mix. I wanted you to always be my top priority, especially since your mother wasn't really in the picture, and when she was, all she did was cause you heartache."

I can only imagine what she's thinking now if she's seen the media coverage of this train wreck. I'm sure she'd be gleeful over the fact that I married a hockey star and then botched up the divorce. "I didn't want you to put your life on hold for me anymore."

"I wasn't putting it on hold for you, Queenie." He takes my hand. "I didn't trust myself to find someone who would be good for us. The last thing I wanted to do was bring a woman into our lives who was going to wreak more havoc on it. I tried dating on and off over the years, but I didn't like the way it upset the balance."

"I feel like that's my fault. I sure didn't make it easy for you."

"You were a teenager; you weren't supposed to make it easy. And maybe I should've tried harder to make one of those relationships work, but I wasn't willing to risk making you feel as if you weren't impor-tant. It was always us against the world, and I refused to let anyone who wasn't worthy compromise our relationship." He gives my hand a squeeze. "I was a kid raising a baby, and then I was a thirty-three-year old with a teenager. I made mistakes with you: ones I might not have made if I'd had maturity and life experience on my side. So I'm sorry that I failed you along the way."

"You didn't fail me, Dad."

"But I did. Somewhere along the way I failed to communicate that my lack of relationships wasn't because of you; it was because I wasn't ready to settle down."

"I guess in my eighteen-year-old brain I thought me being married would give you the push you needed."

My dad laughs. "Sending me links to dating apps would have given me a similar push."

Both of our phones buzz—his from the table beside his recliner and mine from my purse. He nabs his, expression sobering as he scans the screen. "I've arranged a meeting with Corey and his agent so we can figure out the best way to deal with this. He'll be issuing a public statement to help smooth things over; I can tell you that much. And we'll get the divorce papers filed correctly, so that's dealt with too."

"This is going to be such a PR headache."

"Slater is always a PR headache. If I'd known he was going to be such a constant problem for the team, I never would have agreed to the trade."

"I should've told you as soon as you signed him. Well, I should've told you as soon as I dropped out and came back home six years ago, but I was pretty embarrassed by the whole thing."

"We'll get it dealt with so you can move on from it." He taps the arm of the couch. "How's Kingston handling it?"

"He's . . . handling it like he handles everything, I guess." But that's not necessarily true. I've never seen him as upset and angry as he was tonight, before I explained what happened.

"Does that mean the two of you are okay?"

"For now, I guess."

"For now?"

"It's a lot to deal with." *I'm a lot to deal with.*

"He cares a lot about you, though, Queenie. I can see that. He'll weather this storm with you."

I want to believe my dad is right, but the problem is, *I am* the storm. And I worry that after a while, Kingston will want to trade the cyclone that is me for someone whose calm matches his.

# CHAPTER 24

## BUSY BODIES

*Kingston*

"What kind of girl gets married at eighteen in secret?"

"This is soap opera level off the hook!"

"She's way more exciting than Jessica, that's for sure."

"Do not encourage this, Gerald! Ryan does not need this kind of drama in his life."

I scrub my hand over my face. This call has been going for a good ten minutes. My whole family is on the call, so it's a lot of loud voices and opinions being shouted at me. It's giving me a headache. "Can you all stop talking over each other, please? And I think I get to decide how much drama I need in my life, Mom." Despite her being my grandmother biologically, she's still Mom to me. I can't unlearn that. And unless it's a private conversation, I still refer to my momster as Hanna.

"How well do you really know this girl? She's still legally married to another man. You can't continue to date her," Mom replies.

That gets a few coughs and some muttered agreement.

"I respect your opinion, and your concerns, but that's not a choice you can dictate for me." Although I will admit it's a bit of a mind-bender to find out that I've been sleeping with a married woman, regardless of whether or not that marriage should have been dissolved more than half a decade ago. It's bringing up a lot of conflicting emotions, like guilt and anger, and in some ways it feels like another betrayal.

"Where is your head, Ryan?" Mom snaps. I can envision her, sitting at the kitchen island with the glass bowl full of fake fruit in front of her.

"She must be a wild one in the bedroom if you're willing to take on this kind of press." I bet a million dollars my brother is smirking. He's also not wrong, but it's about a lot more than how compatible we are between the sheets.

"Gerald Joseph Kingston, that is not appropriate," Mom chastises.

"But it's probably true," says Gerald. He's ten years my senior and acts like he's still seventeen.

Mom decides to ignore that comment. "I understand that maybe you needed to sow your oats, Ryan, and now that you've done that, I think you should consider getting back together with Jessica. I know you went through a rough patch, but it's clear she still cares about you."

"We're not having a discussion about my relationship with Jessica right now, Mom."

"But you have years together. She's already like a daughter to me. Have you spoken to her?"

"Not recently." And I don't plan to, either, but telling my mother that is like telling a religious fanatic that their belief system is flawed: pointless and asking for trouble.

"Well, I saw her last week, and she asked how you were doing. I told her you would come to your senses soon enough. You don't want to wait too long, or she'll move on and find someone else. I would hate for her to settle, or for you to do the same."

"This isn't about settling." I pinch the bridge of my nose, frustrated and trying not to go off on her. My head is a mess over this, and I can see the damage Queenie's mother did to her self-esteem and self-perception by constantly telling her she wasn't ever going to amount to anything. I'm beginning to understand Queenie better, and this situation gives me a much clearer picture of why she's so damn hard on herself. It also makes me wonder what it's going to take for her to get past that, and if she even can, considering she's spent the past six years hiding this mistake from the people who are most important to her.

"I think we should come up to visit earlier than planned. We need to deal with this as a family," she declares.

That statement is followed by Gerald saying he might have trouble getting the time off work.

"Maybe it would be better if we put a hold on the family visit," I counter. While this conversation is taking place, I have private messages coming in from Hanna, who is also on the call but has remained silent for the most part, other than occasionally telling Gerald to can it.

"I don't think that's a good plan at all. If anything, we need to come out there now more than ever. You need the emotional support."

"That's not a good idea. I'm not in the headspace for a family intervention." I just found out my girlfriend is married to a complete jerk. Yes, it's a technicality, and in some ways I can understand why she didn't say anything about it, but this isn't something I'm going to get over in five minutes like everyone probably expects me to. The last thing I need is my family thrown into the mix, giving their opinions while I'm still trying to form mine.

"Which is precisely why you probably need one," Mom says.

"Look, I appreciate that you're concerned, and likely shocked, but dropping everything to come out here is not reasonable. I need time to deal with this. Besides, I'm leaving for away games, so you coming out here is pointless."

"Okay. Fine. But we're still coming at the end of next week," Mom concedes.

"Okay. It's been a long day; I need some sleep. I'll talk to you all tomorrow."

It's a chorus of good nights and I love yous before I end the call. Three seconds later my screen lights up again. This time it's just Hanna. I accept the video-chat request, and her face pops up on the screen.

"You handled that well," she says.

"Thanks."

"How are you really doing?"

"Honestly? I have no idea."

"Do you want to go through what exactly happened without all the color commentary? That way I can get a better picture of what you're facing."

"Yeah. Okay." I give her the full rundown of the day—well, mostly the full rundown, minus any private moments. "You know, I can appreciate why she didn't want to say anything to me before I got on the ice tonight. I can even understand why she lied and said Corey didn't corner her when obviously he did, but she could've told me the actual truth about their relationship when he first joined the team. It was an intentional omission, and technically that's not a lie, but it's certainly a choice, and it feels a lot like the same thing."

"Okay, I can see your point, but I want you to put yourself in her shoes."

"I would never do something like that."

"Lie by omission? I'm pretty sure you just did that when you told our family you're okay, since you're clearly not."

"This isn't the same thing at all, and I mean I wouldn't have gotten married at eighteen and then hid it from everyone."

"Well, of course not, King. Look at how you were raised. There was a lot of negative role modeling going on. I love Mom and Dad, but you were an easy kid, and you toed the line because you didn't like getting in trouble and you didn't want to end up in the same situations as your brother. Uncle. Whatever. They used fear to keep you in line, and it worked. Guess who it didn't work for?"

"You and Gerald." I push up off the couch and take my phone with me to the kitchen. I could use a drink.

"Exactly. I mean, Gerald got caught growing pot plants in Mom's garden, and how many times did he and our cousin Billy get caught drinking underage?"

"I can't remember. I was pretty young."

"The point is, you have always been a rule follower, and that's worked well for you, except now it's not because you're sitting in a very gray area. It's easy to say she lied by omission, but would you really want to tell her that you'd been married at eighteen, for what was supposed to be all of a handful of weeks, filing fee notwithstanding?"

"Well, no, but—"

"But what, then?" She doesn't let me finish, though. "You've had a rough year, between ending things with Jessica and finding out that I'm your mother, Ry. It makes sense that you're hypersensitive to omissions, because we all lied to you for three decades. I'm partly responsible for that. But then so is everyone else, our parents included."

"Yeah, that might be part of why I'm struggling," I admit as I pour myself a glass of milk, then pause when I see the bottles of vodka and coffee liqueur in the door of the fridge. Queenie brought them over the second time she slept here, and sometimes she'll make me a white russian to help me "loosen my reins." I don't know what the milk-to-alcohol ratio is, but I'm sure it's not that hard.

"What in the world are you doing?"

"Making myself a white russian."

"Wow, you must be stressed if you're drinking."

"Queenie was supposed to stay over tonight. Neither of us have to be up early, and she usually makes me one of these on occasions like this, except now she's dealing with her dad and I'm—"

"Talking to your momster on video chat, trying to make yourself an alcoholic beverage."

"Yeah." There's a shaker thing in my cupboards somewhere, but I don't feel like looking for it. I pour some vodka and some coffee liqueur into my pint glass and stir it up with a spoon. It looks like chocolate milk, but it's not frothy, and there's no ice. I take a sip. It's not half as good as the ones Queenie makes for me, but I can suffer through it. "You know, I think with a little time I can get over this whole thing, but I'm not sure about Queenie."

"How do you mean?"

"I can handle the media going squirrelly and all the ridiculous crap that Corey's fiancée said on that crack-pipe show, but I think Queenie is going to have a hard time with it, and from what I've seen, her response to problems is to run away from them."

"So be someone safe for her that she can run to."

"I want to be able to be that for her."

"But?"

"But I'm angry."

"Okay, and that anger is understandable. But what exactly are you angry about? The situation? The omission?"

"All of it, I guess? I don't know. She says she loves me, but she doesn't trust me enough to tell me she was married to that jackass." And that truly is the crux of it, I suppose. I feel . . . let down. Again. Something important was withheld from me by someone I love, and it's compounded and magnified by the family secret that was dropped on me like a bomb this summer.

"Oh honey, I love you with all my heart, and I couldn't tell you I was your mother for three decades. The only reason it came out was because my asshole ex wanted to go out in a blaze of glory. I'd like to think I would've eventually had the gumption to go against what Mom wanted and tell you, but there were too many layers of complication. I wanted to tell you a million times, but I didn't want to upset the balance, or run the risk of losing the special bond I already had with you. Can you see, at all, how it might be the same for Queenie?"

I squeeze the bridge of my nose. "I guess, when you put it that way . . ."

"I'm not telling you not to be angry. You have a right to be upset with a lot of people right now, but you're an incredibly empathetic soul, and that's as wonderful as it is difficult, because it means you put other people's feelings ahead of your own. So be angry if you need to, but also be compassionate and gentle."

"I'm going to try my best." I drain half my drink in two gulps. It's definitely not as good as the ones Queenie makes for me.

"Do you need me to come visit this weekend?"

"I'll be all right until you come out with the family."

"Okay. I always have your back, Ryan, no matter what."

"I know. You always have."

Sleeping on it gives me the perspective I need. Or restlessly rolling around in my empty bed, wishing Queenie were next to me, married to a jerk or not, is enough for me to conclude that I can get over this, because I don't like the alternative. The next morning I pop into Queenie's office before I head to the gym, but she's not there. Jake's door is open, though, so I knock.

He gives me a strained, tired smile. "I assume you're looking for Queenie."

"I am, sir."

"She's not here."

"Is she okay?"

He sets his pen down on his desk and runs a hand through his hair—based on the state of it, he's been doing this a lot today. "That's a loaded question."

"I'm sure it is. She's had a difficult twenty-four hours. Does that mean she's at home?"

"She is. She's going to take some time off." I can see where she gets her reticence from, seeing as Jake likes to provide limited answers much like his daughter does. Although it's very possible he doesn't have an actual answer.

"More than a few days?"

"I'm not sure. She's pretty upset right now, and facing the team after what happened last night won't be easy for her if she decides coming back is what she wants to do." He sighs and leans back in his chair, lacing his hands behind his neck. "And I honestly don't know if having her come back *is* the right thing to do."

"What happened wasn't her fault!" I snap. "None of this is."

His left brow rises. I should probably apologize for my tone, but someone has to defend Queenie, and if her own father won't, I sure as hell will. "I know Queenie can be impulsive, but she was eighteen, and from the little she's confided, she didn't have a reliable mother figure to help her navigate relationships. And that's not to say you didn't do your best, but it's not the same."

I should definitely stop talking, but now that I'm on a roll, I can't stop. And it feels really good to say exactly what's on my mind, even if it's going to cause problems for me later. "She feels an extraordinary amount of guilt for the mistake she made, and I believe she also feels like she's been an anchor in your life, rather than a buoy. She has so much potential and incredible talent, but she doesn't believe in herself, which is a travesty. And so is telling her she can't come back here. Especially because of a mistake she made six years ago that someone decided to twist around and throw back in her face in a horribly public way. That's not going to help her at all."

He holds up his hand. "I'm aware she's not at fault. And I would never tell her she couldn't come back to work here, but I have a feeling she's not going to want to, and I can't say that I'd blame her at all."

"Oh." I pause, realizing my error. "I'm sorry, I must have misunderstood."

"Don't apologize for standing up for my daughter. I don't think she's had enough people in her life willing to do that for her. And one of the people who was supposed to be the most supportive took every opportunity she could to cut her down."

"Her mother."

He nods. "She's done nothing to earn that title." He's silent for a moment before he continues. "She was, and still is, a very selfish, self-absorbed person. Her concerns revolved around herself and what she wanted, not what Queenie needed."

"I've gathered that from what Queenie's said about her." And how she reacted to the phone call from her when exhibition games first started.

"The only thing she's ever done for Queenie is cause upheaval in her life." He tosses his pen on the desk and scrubs a palm over his face. "Look, King, I'm probably overstepping every single boundary there is right now, but I know my daughter. She's used to people leaving and letting her down. And while I've done everything in my power to make sure she's taken care of, clearly I can't always protect her. And I feel like I'm a big part of the reason she's in her current predicament. So if you're really in this like you seem to be, don't let her push you away. And trust me: she'll try."

"I'm prepared for that, sir."

He smiles, but his sadness weighs it down. "I figured you would be."

◆  ◆  ◆

I take my chances that Queenie is going to be at home and head to her place without texting first. It's purposeful, since I fully expect her to avoid me or do what Jake said and try to push me away. We have a series of away games coming up, and there's no way I'm leaving things the way they are when I'll be gone for several days.

Loud, melancholic music makes the windows rattle as I approach her front door. I knock and peek through the curtains. I can see her in the kitchen, standing in front of her easel, paintbrush in one hand, palette in the other. I'm almost relieved to see her doing something constructive, after yesterday. But another part of me feels . . . sad that this part of her is something she hasn't been comfortable enough to share with me, and I believe that these two facets of who she is are somehow intertwined.

I want all of her, and she keeps tucking little pieces away, hiding the things she's afraid to let me see.

I knock again, harder this time. She startles and curses, dropping her brush on the floor. She bends to pick it up, giving me a quick glimpse of the piece she's working on before she eclipses it with her frame again. It's not enough time for me to decipher the content, only enough to get a blur of green and black. She drapes a sheet over it and drops the palette on the table and the brush in a murky glass of water.

"Coming! Hold on!" she calls out as she surveys the mayhem. I see the moment she decides there's nothing she can do about it and rushes to answer the door, tucking a bra under a couch cushion on the way.

The door flies open, and her eyes flare with surprise. "King, hi, I didn't . . . hi."

I take her in, messy bun knotted on top of her head, black and green paint streaked across her cheek and the oversize white buttondown shirt she's wearing. I don't detect shorts or any other bottoms, although the shirt does hit her midthigh. "Hi."

"I wasn't expecting company." It sounds like an apology. She glances over her shoulder at the disarray inside her house.

"Do you mind if I come in? So we can talk." I hook my thumbs in my pockets so I'm not tempted to tuck her hair behind her ear, or make unwelcome physical contact. What I want is to wrap her up and protect her from Corey and the hell this is probably wreaking on her.

Her shoulders curl in and her head drops, eyes on the floor. "Sure. Of course." She steps aside and lets me in. Then rushes to make room for us on the couch, which is littered with blankets, a few sweatshirts, and a couple of pairs of socks. The state of her place is significantly more chaotic than it was the last time I was here.

"Have a seat." She motions to the now mostly clothing-free couch and wrings her hands nervously. "Can I get you something to drink?"

"I'm okay, thank you. Come sit with me." I pat the cushion beside me.

Queenie chews her bottom lip for a few long seconds and finally drops down, but she leaves a cushion of space between us.

"How are things with Jake?" I felt awful leaving her last night, but I also knew she was right and that I wouldn't have been an impartial mediator at all.

She plays with a loose string on her shirttail. "They're . . . okay. He was hurt more than anything."

"Because you kept a secret from him?"

She nods. "He's angry at the situation, though, not me."

"I'm not angry with you, either, Queenie."

She exhales a shaky breath and lifts her eyes to meet mine briefly. "But I understand that this is all too much for you. You don't need my drama."

"Queenie—"

"It's okay." She reaches out and squeezes my hand before withdrawing hers quickly. "You don't need to explain. I completely understand. My life is a mess and yours isn't. It's probably better if we end things now so you don't get dragged into more of my bullshit."

A hot spike of panic slides down my spine. "Is that what you want? To end things?"

Her gaze lifts again, eyes red rimmed. She looks exhausted and so, so sad. "Isn't that why you're here?"

I realize I need to tread very carefully here, that I can't direct my anger and frustration over this situation she's found herself in at her, since the fault doesn't lie with her. "No."

"But I thought . . ." She trails off and brings her fingers to her mouth, nibbling on a ragged nail.

"That I came here to break up with you?" I finish for her.

She lifts a shoulder in a half shrug. "I wouldn't blame you if you did. I'm a lot to deal with on a good day, and this is even more than I know what to do with."

I pinch the bridge of my nose, uncertain as to whether I'm more sad, angry, or frustrated at the moment. Because one of the people who was supposed to love her and embrace her wild, passionate soul made her feel like those were flaws she needed to apologize for.

"Come here: you're too far away." I don't wait for her to move closer. I simply grab her by the waist and settle her in my lap.

Silent tears glide down her cheeks, and her chin trembles. She smells like paint and laundry soap and fresh rain. I wipe away the tears as they fall, but there's more behind them. "Baby, I want you to listen to me and really hear me, okay?"

"Okay. I'll try," she whispers brokenly.

"I love you."

"That doesn't change all the crap I'm bringing into your life."

"You're not hearing me." I cup her face in my hands and press my lips to her forehead, her cheek, the tip of her nose, and finally her lips. "You can push me away as much as you want, but it's not going to stop me from wanting you. I love you because of all these perceived flaws you have, not in spite of them. I know you've been let down a lot, and I don't plan to be one of those people in your life. Give us a chance to get through this together, Queenie. Let me catch you when you fall. Let me be your safe place to land."

She covers my hand with hers and nuzzles her cheek into my palm. "I'm a mess right now. My life is a mess."

"You made a mistake, Queenie; it doesn't make your entire life a mess. Is the situation messy? Most definitely, but you're not at fault for that." I brush away more of her tears.

"I'm sorry I didn't tell you, but I didn't think I'd ever have to tell anyone. It's embarrassing."

"I understand why you didn't. At first I was hurt—"

"Because I kept it from you."

"Because I thought you didn't trust me enough to tell me. Everyone has secrets they keep from others, even from themselves. I know this is hard for you and that you're very used to being let down by the people who are supposed to lift you up, but I want you to know that I'm not going anywhere, Queenie. I want all your dark secrets to be mine to keep. I want all your pieces, all the things that make you who you are. I don't care if you think you're bent or broken; let me love all of you."

She gives me a soft smile, and her warm palm settles on my cheek. "I'll try my very best."

# CHAPTER 25

## THE POWER OF ESTROGEN

*Queenie*

I think I've eaten twenty bags of sour cream and onion chips over the last three days. My skin feels tight from the salt. I almost wish I craved sweets, because I think it would be a lot better than the salt swelling that's currently going on.

It's good that King is on an away series, since my breath smells like a field of chewed-up green onions. And that's about the only reason his being away is good. After our talk I felt better. Like things are going to be okay.

And then he got on the plane, and I stayed behind so I could clean up the mess that is my life and make some much-needed changes. I've started doing both of those things, beginning with finding my dad a replacement assistant who is technologically savvy. So far I've found six promising prospects, whose references I plan to check thoroughly.

The downside of the guys being away is that aside from some light paperwork, I don't have a lot to occupy my time or my mind. So I went online. And fell down the horrible, disturbing rabbit hole that has become the biggest embarrassment of my life.

Also, Sissy is an absolute loon. But the way I've been smeared all over the worst of the worst tabloids and the horrible rumors all over the hockey sites and bunny forums are . . . mortifying.

And I'm supposed to meet King's family next week. I'm not sure it's a good idea anymore. I'm convinced they're going to decide I'm not good enough for him.

And I sort of believe I'm not, which isn't helpful.

Maybe Corey is right. Maybe I am a nightmare of a girlfriend. Maybe Kingston is only staying with me because he feels sorry for me and he doesn't want to hurt my feelings. Half of me can't wait for him to be home so I can shake the uneasy feeling that being away from him incites. The other half doesn't want him to come home, because that will mean his parents and momster and brother are coming to visit, and I will have to meet them and impress them. After I've been painted as a home-wrecking, money-hungry puck bunny.

I feel like my current insecurities are fairly warranted.

The game doesn't start for several hours. I should tackle some of the laundry that's piled up over the past few weeks. But I don't feel like it. I honestly don't feel like doing much, other than eating chips and surfing the net, looking for the newest horrifying article about me.

I prop my feet up on the coffee table, and empty chip bags crunch under my heels and a couple fall to the floor, crumbs scattering on the carpet. I survey my bungalow and consider how the disarray very much matches me on the inside. I make sure I have my box of tissues before I flip open my laptop.

I'm about to start searching hashtags when there's a knock at my door. I'm not expecting company, so my first thought is to ignore it. But whoever it is knocks again.

"I can see you sitting on the couch! Open the door, Queenie!" Stevie yells, and she knocks on the window behind my head. "Ow, shit!" She must have bumped into the rosebush, since she's standing in a flower bed. The roses are long dead, but the thorns are still there because the bush hasn't been pruned.

I open the sheer curtains and crack a window. "What're you doing?"

"Staging an intervention," Violet says from behind her. "Now open the door and let us in. It's raining."

"This is Seattle; it's always raining," I mutter, but I get my ass up off the couch and weave my way through the crap strewn all over the floor so I can get to the door.

I throw it open to find Stevie and Violet standing on my front porch with a grocery bin full of stuff.

Violet steps in front of Stevie. "Kingston was right to call us. Enough of this self-imposed exile bullshit. You've fulfilled your moping quota for the rest of the year." She steps over the threshold and into my bungalow, gags, drops the bin on the floor, slaps her palm over her mouth, and retreats back outside. "What the hell is that smell?"

"Sour cream and onion chips, dirty laundry, body odor, and there might be something rotting in the garbage."

"Right. Okay. New plan." Violet addresses Stevie. "We get this one in the shower so she doesn't smell like the inside of a jockstrap and take this party back to my place." She pulls a spray bottle out of her bag and starts spritzing around me.

I cough and wave my hand in front of my face so I don't inhale it. "What is that?"

"Menthol spray." She nudges past me. "Get in the shower, unless you want me to drag you outside and hose you down. We have a schedule to keep, and I've timed everything so that we'll be home right before the game starts."

I want to argue, since the game doesn't start for another three hours, but instead I do what I'm told. Also, it's not that warm out, and being sprayed down with a hose seems a lot like something that would happen in prison.

The hot water feels heavenly, so I stand under the spray for a long time. When I'm done washing off the past few days of melancholy and sour cream and onion chips, I turn off the shower, wrap myself in a towel, and open the door. Stevie nudges Violet out of the way and thrusts a pile of clothes at me.

"Where did those come from?"

"Your closet. We weren't sure if the hills of clothes lying all over the place were clean or dirty, so I felt like if it was hanging up, it might be safe."

"Okay." There's a very solid chance something on a hanger would be clean. Or cleaner than anything lying on the floor or draped over the back of a chair. I dress quickly in a shirt I haven't worn in three years and a pair of equally old jeans. But they don't smell like onions, and I don't either anymore. I brush my teeth and rinse with mouthwash to help with the bad breath, but my mouth still tastes like onions. Minty ones, though.

When I'm done putting myself together—I definitely look better, and I feel better too—I step out into my living room and freeze. "What's happening here?"

There's a woman I don't recognize in my kitchen, cleaning it.

"Queenie, this is Aurora. Aurora, this is Queenie."

She flashes me a bright smile and extends her hand. "Mr. Kingston requested I come by to help clean up."

"King sent someone over to clean my house?" I ask no one in particular.

Aurora scans the absolute mayhem. "He intimated that you've been busy as of late and the assistance would be helpful."

"Right. Yeah. Okay." I motion to the corner of the room, where my easel and canvases are stacked. "Just don't touch those, please."

"Of course not. Mr. Kingston already informed me as such."

She sounds like Mary Poppins; thankfully, she looks like a slightly younger version of my grandmother. I hope she hasn't had to deal with our pile of sex sheets. I wonder if King does those himself. It seems like something he might take care of so someone else wouldn't have to.

"Okay, well, thanks so much, Aurora, for tackling this. We need to get a move on if we're going to make it to the spa on time for our mani-pedis." Violet consults her phone.

"Mani-pedis?" I parrot.

"Kingston set up appointments so we could all go together. He thought you might need a little pampering, and we were inclined to agree." Stevie motions between herself and Violet.

"Kingston set this up?" I don't know why I'm even surprised by this. It's 100 percent something he would do.

"Yup, pretty sweet, huh?" Violet grins.

And because I'm an emotional mess, I burst into tears.

"We got you, girl." Stevie gives my shoulder a squeeze, grabs a few tissues and my purse, and steers me out the door so I can have my breakdown without Aurora witnessing it.

We pile into Stevie's SUV; I'm in the passenger seat, and Violet sits in the middle seat in the back so she can stick her head between the seats. "You're staying off social media, right?" Stevie asks as she pulls out of the driveway.

"Uh, well . . ." I chew on the inside of my lip when they both give me a *What the hell?* look.

"Oh God." Stevie and Violet share a glance in the rearview mirror. "Queenie, rule number one is to never, ever look at social media."

"I wanted to see how bad it was," I mutter.

"Social media is a cesspool of angry bunnies and jealous bitches. We've all been raked over the coals at some point, right, Stevie?" Violet says from the back seat.

Stevie glances in the rearview mirror. "Yuppers. My ex took a video of me and Bishop kissing—"

"Mouth fucking. *Kissing* sounds sweet, and you two were fucking each other's mouths with your tongues and pretty much dry humping each other. In public."

"Would you like to tell the story?"

"Sure. My version is always more exciting anyway." Violet props her fist on her chin and launches into the story of how Stevie and Bishop met and ended up together. Including how the mouth-fucking video came to be.

"The point is, all of us have had to deal with at least one social media shitstorm. I mean, Alex told the entire hockey-watching nation that we were just friends, when that clearly wasn't the case. We mouth fucked all over the damn place. And we were dating. And he'd asked me to move in with him—while playing naked Scrabble, but that's another story. What I'm saying is that we get that it sucks, but you're not alone, and you don't have to hide from the world and wait for the dust to settle."

"It's embarrassing."

"Have you met me?" Violet points to herself. "I'm a walking embarrassment. I can't go anywhere without saying something regrettable. Alex has to script everything I say when we do interviews—which I hate, by the way—and I sound like a robot. And even then there's a good chance I'll accidentally say something I shouldn't. You got married when you were eighteen, and that douche nozzle screwed up the divorce papers. Everyone in the hockey-watching nation knows that Corey is an asshole and that his fiancée is a loon. Unfortunately, that combination makes for great headlines."

What Violet is saying makes sense, and I know all of this will eventually blow over, but it's more than that. It's all the other pieces that are the problem. It's the fact that I got married on a whim in the first place, that I've been relying on my dad for a job, that I'm still living in his house, that I'm too afraid of failing to even bother trying to do what I really want. Because one of the people who was supposed to encourage me liked to tear me down instead. And now Kingston's family has a horrible impression of me.

The mani-pedis are a nice distraction from the shitshow that is my life. Stevie and Violet tell me all kinds of embarrassing stories, which definitely makes me feel better about everything. I'm still stressed about the meet-the-parents situation, but at least I have a sounding board that isn't my dad and my boyfriend.

When we get to Violet's, plans change a little. Her brood and Lainey's son, Kody, are in the theater room, already watching the game with Lainey, who couldn't make the mani-pedi session.

Violet's oldest, Robbie, is reading a book in the back row with his feet propped up on the back of the seat in front of him. Maverick is watching the game at the front of the theater, and so is Kody. Well, Kody is sort of watching, but he keeps looking over his shoulder at River and Lavender, who are sitting at a round table covered in art supplies. River hands Lavender crayons, his attention half on her, half on the game.

When Lavender realizes her mom is home, she pushes back her chair and rushes over, wrapping herself around Violet's leg.

"I hope you still love me this much when you're a teenager." She tugs on her ponytail.

When Lavender spots me, she abandons her leg and rushes over to me, giving me the same hug treatment. Then she takes me by the hand and tugs me toward the door.

"Where are we going?"

"My room! I show you my wall!"

"Do you have new art?"

She nods and pulls me along, practically skipping. When we get there, I can see she's been busy with paints, and of course she insists that we make something together. Violet comes up and tries to persuade her that I'll come back another time, but Lavender won't hear it, and I'm more than happy to lose myself in finger painting for a while. I miss all of the first period of the game, but it's 100 percent worth it. Lavender is extremely chatty when she feels safe in her element, and her art room definitely provides that.

She tells me all about the things she loves: that she wants a pet cat but her dad is allergic and that she likes dogs but they lick their bums and then your face, and that's gross. She also tells me that her friend in her art class has a dog, and it ate his favorite stuffie, and he cried.

When we've finished our masterpiece, it's already eight o'clock, and I have to remind her not to rub her tired eyes with her paint-covered hands.

We wash up, and she gets ready for bed on her own, although it looks like her pajamas might be on backward. Violet puts her and River to bed. Kody's already passed out on one of the mats on the floor, and Maverick is sprawled across the front seats, eyes popping open every once in a while, but it's clear he's ready for bed. Robbie seems to have disappeared, likely to his room.

We set ourselves up in the back row with drinks, and the girls fill me in on what I missed while Lavender and I were finger painting.

Violet drops down into the seat beside mine a few minutes into second period. "Thank you so much for indulging Lavender: she would spend all day in that room if she could, and she adores you."

"It was really my pleasure. And I adore her too," I tell her. "How long have you had the art room?"

"Alex had one of the spare rooms converted about six months ago, when we started taking Lavender to art therapy classes with Kody."

"They go together? That's so cute."

Lainey nods. "We thought we'd give it a try. Kody likes working with clay the most because he's more kinesthetic, and he only makes hockey pucks, but it's been so good for his anxiety, and mine to be honest," Lainey says.

I know this about Lainey, that she worries a lot. She's brilliant, has three master's degrees, and has already completed a PhD, but she wants to start a second one. She's kind and sweet and lovely, but crowds are not her thing.

"Lavender loves it, and it's definitely helping bring her out of her shell." Violet then addresses me. "She's constantly asking about you, so feel free to drop by and get your finger paint on anytime."

"I'd love to, if you're serious."

"I'm totally serious. She likes the instructors at the therapy center, and she's making such great gains with the other kids, but for one on one, we still can't find someone she's willing to open up to."

"I'd be happy to come over anytime." I drum on the arm of the chair for a few seconds before I confide, "I actually went to college to become an art therapist."

"Why aren't you doing that now, then? You're amazingly talented, and you're like a kid whisperer. They love you," Violet says. "I poked my head in while you two were doing your thing, and Lavender was talking up a storm. She only ever does that with us. We've tried three different therapists, and no one has gotten her to open up like *that*."

"I didn't finish the degree, but I made an appointment with one of the course counselors at the college to see what classes I still need and if they have any openings in their program."

"How long do you think it will take to complete it?"

"Not long: a semester, plus an internship."

"We're taking Lavender and Kody to the art center tomorrow if you want to check it out with us. She'd be over the moon if you came along."

"Yeah. Okay. That would be great."

I can't fail if I don't try, but I can't succeed, either, and this seems like a baby step in the right direction.

# CHAPTER 26
## DONE DEAL

*Queenie*

The next morning Violet gets the two older boys off to their respective activities. Robbie requires zero prodding. He wanders around the kitchen with a book in front of his face, barely sparing a glance at the bowl as he fills it with some kind of homemade granola, covers it in almond milk, and slowly shovels it into his mouth while still reading.

Maverick isn't so easy. He complains about not being able to eat Froot Loops for breakfast and then points to the Pop-Tarts sticking out of her purse, saying he knows those ones aren't for Lavender and River, because they only like the strawberry ones. Eventually Violet gets them ready and sends them on their way with their nanny.

Lainey shows up five minutes later in her giant seven-seater SUV. Kody's sitting in the middle seat—he only has a booster now because he's freaking huge for his age. I help get Lavender's seat secured and get her buckled in while Violet argues with River about where he's sitting.

She finally says something to him that seems to placate him, and he gets in the car, albeit grudgingly.

When we get to the art center, Lavender wants to show me around. When she reaches for River's hand to drag him along, he crosses his arms and plops into a chair, sulking.

Lavender shrugs and leaves him there, too excited to be bothered, I suppose. She shows me all the pieces she's done since she started coming here. Once I've had the full tour—it's an amazing space—Lavender grabs a smock and takes a seat at one of the painting tables, and a still-grumpy River does the same, settling in the chair beside his sister.

Kody heads for the clay tables. Once they're settled at their stations, we hang back and watch them for a few minutes.

"Do they always come together? The three of them?" I ask.

Violet shakes her head. "I only bring River about fifty percent of the time, because I think it's important for Lavender to do things on her own, without him. It forces her to have her own voice and not rely on him so much."

One of the staff comes over to say hello, and Violet and Lainey issue an introduction. We start talking about their programs, how they have informal drop-ins, classes, and a special art therapy program with both group and private sessions.

By the end of the half-hour session, I've already filled out their volunteer forms and assured them I can make the three-month minimum commitment. I'm excited by the prospect of volunteering in a place that's in line with what I've always been passionate about.

After I'm dropped off at home—we go for lunch first—I call back the top potential candidates to replace me as my dad's assistant, narrow it down to three, and schedule in-person interviews for when my dad gets back from the away series.

I'd do all the interviewing myself, but I know my dad, and he'll want to be part of the process, especially since it will be him working with whoever gets hired.

The team is scheduled to return this evening, and as much as I'd like to spend the night with Kingston, I have to be at my lawyer's office early tomorrow morning so we can sign the paperwork and make the divorce final.

Kingston calls as I'm getting ready for bed, on a video chat. Based on his current state of dress and the fact that I'm propped up on his folding table and he's unloading his duffle directly into the washing machine, he just got home. It means my dad will also be home soon.

"How's my queen?" His gaze moves over me, a slow sweep that heats as he takes in my bedtime attire.

"Good, tired, missing my king." We are so cheesy, and I am totally okay with that.

"I miss your lips."

"Which set?" I am totally using sex to deflect all the other anxieties that are currently eating at me.

A half smirk curves the corner of his mouth, and his tongue peeks out to touch the chip in his front tooth. It's a completely subconscious action that I find incredibly sexy for whatever reason. "Both, actually. I could come to you. I don't have to stay the night. I can drop by for an hour, kiss those pretty lips of yours."

"Both sets, obviously."

"Mmm. I'd divide my time equally, so neither feels underappreciated."

I laugh breathily. "I would honestly love that, but if you're home, that means my dad will be home soon, and we have to go to the lawyer's tomorrow morning. And let's be real: nothing ever lasts just an hour with you, especially when you've been away for four days."

He frowns and taps his lips, the lust in his eyes fading quickly. "I could come with you to the lawyer's in the morning. I should be there."

I make a face. "I'm not sure I'd agree with that. As much as I appreciate your support, I need to do it on my own. My dad is driving me there, but he's not coming in when I sign the papers. I need to see this through, and I can't imagine Corey being anything but an antagonistic ass no matter what, but he'll be a million times worse if you're there with me."

He seems to want to fight me on it for a few seconds, but eventually he says, "I guess I can see your point. And if he's a jerk, I'll want to punch him, and that will make things even worse."

"Punching him would feel good, but yeah, it definitely wouldn't help the situation."

"Will you call as soon as you're done and tell me how it went?"

"Of course."

He nods, resolute. "Okay. I miss you. I need to find a way to get some alone time in with you, regardless of whether my family is in town or not. How are you feeling about meeting them tomorrow?"

"Honestly? Nervous." I'd like to say I'll feel better when the divorce is final and King's no longer dating a married woman, but I'm not sure even that is going to settle my mind or my nerves.

"It's going to be great, Queenie. Momster is so excited to meet you in person."

"I'm excited to meet her too." And I am.

The flash of headlights in the driveway draws my attention. "My dad just got home. I should probably let you go."

"Okay." He exhales a long breath. "I love you."

"I love you too."

He smiles. "My favorite words from your lips. Sleep well. I can't wait to see you tomorrow."

"Me too." It's the rest of his family I'm not excited about.

"You're sure you don't want me to come in with you?" My dad taps restlessly on the steering wheel, gaze shifting between the lawyer's office and me.

"I'm sure. I need to do this on my own, and it's awkward enough for you having to deal with Corey on a business level; I'd prefer if my personal stuff doesn't interfere more than it already has."

"Yeah, well, if his train wreck of a fiancée could learn when to keep her damn mouth shut, we could've avoided a whole hell of a lot of unnecessary bullshit."

He's definitely not wrong about that. "He certainly knows how to pick 'em, doesn't he?"

"Don't do that, Queenie. You were eighteen years old, and you made a mistake that you tried to rectify, on your own, without support. It was one bad decision, and it doesn't define who you are as a person."

It's not the one bad decision I made six years ago that's the issue now; it's that I've kept making decisions that haven't gotten me any further away from the dependent part of my personality that I can't seem to shake. But I'm trying to change that. Baby steps.

And doing this on my own is one more step in the right direction. I lean over and kiss him on the cheek. "I know. I appreciate you driving me here and being so supportive."

I can tell he wants to say more, but I also know he wants to give me the chance to deal with this in my own way. "I'll be here when you're done."

"You honestly don't have to wait. I can Uber home."

"Not a fucking chance, Queenie. If Corey pulls any bullshit, I'll be right here."

"I'll be fine." I shoulder my purse, checking again for the file folder. I've been doing that compulsively since I got in the car, as if it's going to magically disappear and I'll be married to Corey for the rest of my life.

Last night I had a dream that we were chained together and that our skin had started to fuse and I could never separate myself from him. I woke up screaming at four a.m. and did not go back to sleep. Hence I'm jittery, since I've had about seven cups of coffee.

Corey ends up being twenty minutes late, which is not a surprise. He also brings his fiancée along.

"Is the entourage necessary?" I ask as he drops down into one of the chairs at the table, not bothering to pull out a chair for Sissy.

"I want to read everything over to make sure you're not trying to take my baby's money," she snaps.

I roll my eyes. "All I wanted six years ago was to separate myself from him completely, and if Corey hadn't messed it up by not paying the damn filing fee, we wouldn't be sitting here at all—"

"Ha!" Sissy barks out a fake laugh. "Of course you're trying to make it Corey's fault! We all know that it was you who took off without making sure the papers were properly filed. And he told me it was you who didn't pay the fee, not him!"

Of course he's spun it so it's on me and not him.

"Is that what he told you?" I wave my own question away. "You know what? It doesn't matter. You'll find out soon enough what you're getting yourself into."

"What's that supposed to mean?"

Corey clears his throat, looking somewhere between annoyed and uneasy. "She's trying to get under your skin, Sissy. Maybe you wanna go get yourself a coffee or something?" He pulls his wallet out of his back pocket and peels off a hundred-dollar bill.

Sissy snatches his entire wallet and pulls out a handful of bills, then tosses it on the table. "Coffee makes me have to pee. I'm going to Saks. Pick me up when you're done." She waddle-flounces out of the room.

"Hope you got a prenup." I turn back to the lawyer, whose time we're wasting. "Okay, let's make sure this is done correctly this time so I don't end up smeared all over the news for keeping you 'tied down' for another six years." I make air quotes at Corey.

"You're the one who ran away." He takes the papers his attorney's given him and flips through. "Whoa, hold on a second here. What's this about a hundred K? I'm not giving you shit."

"You might want to reconsider that, Corey, since you're the reason we're still married, and your fiancée launched an unfounded public smear campaign, which means I can no longer work for the team."

"That doesn't mean you deserve money!"

I snort, because that's an epic joke. "The crap I'm dealing with as a result is the opposite of wonderful. The ironic thing is, if your fiancée didn't air our dirty laundry to anyone who would listen, I would've signed these papers and asked for nothing. But now, after all this, asking for a hundred thousand dollars is small in comparison. I'm sure you can spare it from your endless bank account to help right your wrongs." He opens his mouth to speak, and I hold up a finger. "Choose your words carefully, Corey, particularly in front of our lawyers. Do not think for a second that you can push me around or belittle me. I am not an eighteen-year-old girl anymore, and your BS isn't something I intend to deal with ever again, after today. Remember, we've been 'married'"—I use air quotes again for emphasis—"for six years, and we did not have a prenup. My lawyer told me I could technically go after half of your income from all those years if I wanted to. So do not push me."

He has a whispered conversation with his lawyer, frowning the entire time. Eventually he huffs a breath. "Fine. You can have a hundred K: that's chump change for me. Don't spend it all on new tits."

"Wow. You are absolutely disgusting. Good to see some things don't change." I scribble my signature on every page, slide them aggressively toward Corey, and slam the pen down in front of him, wishing I could stab him in the hand.

I wait until Corey signs each page, which takes forever since he writes like a six-year-old who's half-asleep. Then he wire transfers the money directly to my account while my lawyer's paralegal makes a copy of the papers for me. I gather my things and push away from the table, shaking the lawyer's hand. "Thank you for freeing me from the shackles of misery."

"You're welcome." He fights to hide a smile.

I hightail it out of the office and speed walk as calmly as I can down the hall. I just want to get as far away from Corey as possible.

"You still think your Boy Scout is gonna want my used goods?" he calls out after me.

I want to turn around and kick him in the balls, but we're in a law office, and that would be grounds for some kind of charges, so instead I ignore him and keep walking.

I know I've made the right decision. While some may think I'm being opportunistic in asking him for that money, he cost me my job and a whole lot of dignity with the horrible things Sissy said about me. I have a right, after the public humiliation that follows me online and will probably follow me forever now. If anyone were to do a search of my name, they'd find this, and who knows what future damage that could cause.

I push through the door and step out into the cold, rainy day. I don't run across the lot in a bid to outrun Corey, because he's definitely faster than me, and also, running is exactly what he wants me to do. So I pop my umbrella, almost hitting Corey in the face with one of the sharp ends, and begin a leisurely saunter across the lot.

"Your Boy Scout coming to pick you up?" he mutters, then spots my dad's car. "Or has he already dumped your crazy ass, and now you're gonna live in your daddy's pool house forever?"

I spin on my heel and tip my chin up so I can look him in the eye. "I wonder how you'd feel if you had a daughter and you heard someone speaking to her the way you are to me, right now. I hope Sissy has a girl, and I hope you actually give a shit about her so you'll understand what it's like to legitimately want to protect someone from others' harm. I will never understand why you need to constantly tear people down to make yourself feel better about who you are."

I don't wait for him to process that comment, because I'm not sure he actually can. The driver's side door of my dad's car opens, and

I physically feel Corey back off. The air is suddenly lighter, and it's not such a struggle to move.

My dad rounds the hood, glancing in Corey's direction. "You okay?"

"Fine. Good. Let's just go."

He opens the passenger-side door for me, and I slide into the seat.

"Queenie." He's gripping the frame of the car like he wants to tear something apart. Namely Corey.

I meet his gaze. "It's done. I can't move on if you can't, so please, let it go."

He exhales a breath through his nose but does what I ask. It isn't until we leave the parking lot and are headed back toward my dad's place that I allow all the emotions I've been holding on to out.

"Hey, hey, what's wrong? What happened?" My dad glances at me and back at the road as he reaches across the center console to squeeze my hand.

"I'm just relieved it's over. That's all. I want to be able to move forward, and having this whole thing hanging over my head this past week has made that impossible. Like there's been a weight on my chest, and I can't breathe."

"I think it might be similar to how I felt when your mother finally signed over full custody. My whole life felt like it was suspended until that moment, so I get it, Queenie. I'm so sorry that you had to go through this at all."

"Well, it's done now, so we can leave it in the past, where it belongs." I tap on the armrest, gathering my courage. "I asked for money and I got it. Not a lot. I mean, it's a lot for me but not for him. I can pay for college now. I can finish my degree, and you won't have to worry about helping me financially."

"You didn't have to do that. I will always be here to support you."

"I know. But he owed me after everything that happened, and I know that you'll never tell me I can't come back and work for you, but

I don't think I should. I love you for helping pick me up every time I fall, Dad, but this was always supposed to be temporary. It's too many layers of complication: for you, for me, for Kingston."

"I understand, and I think it's brave and ballsy of you to go in there on your own and face that douchebag. If I could take back bringing him on the team, I would."

My dad drops me off at home, and I message Kingston to let him know everything went okay this morning before I tackle the slew of messages in my group chat with Stevie, Lainey, and Violet. Never in my life did I think that sending a message announcing my official divorcée status would garner so much excitement.

Things are finally looking up.

# CHAPTER 27
## UNPLEASANT SURPRISES

*Kingston*

Queenie messaged to say she was home from the lawyer's and that she is no longer married. So I'm standing outside her door with a bouquet of flowers, a box of chocolates, and a helium-filled unicorn balloon that reads **CONGRATULATIONS**. Seems appropriate, all things considered. Besides, she and I both need a little levity after this crap situation.

She throws open the door. "Hey, hi." Queenie looks beautiful, exhausted, and nervous.

"How's my queen?"

All the relief that comes with seeing her disappears when her chin quivers and her eyes pool with tears. She lifts her shoulder in a wordless shrug. I drop the flowers and chocolate on the closest available surface, which happens to be her clean counter.

I open my arms and Queenie steps into me, her low, soft sob getting muffled by my shirt. I hold her against me, cupping the back of her head, and drop my mouth so it's at her ear. "What's wrong; what happened? How can I fix it?"

"You've already fixed it: you're here."

After a few minutes of just holding her, I cup her face in my palms and tip her chin up, brushing away the tears. "Why so sad?"

"Not sad." She shakes her head. "Just emotional. I'm glad it's over and happy you're here."

I brush my lips over hers. "That makes sense. So it's official? The papers are all signed?"

"They are."

"And Corey didn't give you a hard time?"

"I held my own." She smooths her hands over my chest. "I left tearstains and snot trails all over your polo."

That's not the answer I'm looking for, and it's clear she's trying to distract me, but I don't push because I know it's been difficult for her.

"I always have an extra one in my car, so nothing to worry about."

"Of course you do." She laughs and then gives me a small, slightly sad and rueful smile. "You're officially dating a divorcée."

I tip her chin up. "I like it. Makes me feel like a rebel."

This time her smile is genuine. She chuckles and shakes her head. "Only you, King."

"I missed you." I skim her throat, and her pulse hammers under my fingertips.

"Me too. I mean, I missed you, not myself." She links her hands behind my neck, bringing her body flush with mine again. "I was worried this week."

"About?"

"All the time you had to think while we were apart. I wasn't sure if you'd come to your senses or not." She huffs a laugh and looks away, so I can't see her vulnerability. She doesn't give me a chance to ask what she means. Instead she tugs on the back of my neck and brings my mouth to hers.

The kiss is soft for a few strokes of tongue before need takes hold. Her nails dig into my nape, and she moans into my mouth. I pick her up and deposit her on the counter. She lands on the box of chocolates, crushing the corner. I shove them out of the way and step between her legs.

"Thank you for the flowers and the chocolate."

"You're welcome," I groan when she bites the edge of my jaw.

"And the . . . unicorn balloon? Does that say 'Congratulations'?"

"They don't have 'Happy Divorce' ones, interestingly enough." I tug her blouse over her head. It's pale green and pretty, as is the green lace bra underneath. I cup her breasts in my palms, then glance around the bungalow. The curtains are gauzy and not the best at keeping prying eyes from seeing things they shouldn't. "Is Jake at the arena?"

"Yeah, he dropped me off and headed there right away. How long do you have before you have pregame skate?" She tugs my polo free of my khakis and goes to work on my belt.

I check the clock on the stove. "About an hour and a half, but you have an appointment in an hour, so this'll have to be a quickie." I find the zipper on her skirt and pause. "Is that okay? I promise I'll take better care of you later."

"Your version of a quickie is not the same as everyone else's, King. And yes, it's okay. And you take amazing care of me, always." She flicks the button open on my pants. "Wait, I don't have an appointment."

"I set up a pampering session for you and Stevie before the game tonight. I thought you might need some extra TLC, and since I can't provide it in the form of excessive orgasms, this was the next best thing."

"You are the most amazing boyfriend." She slips her hand in my pants. "Now please get inside me so I can have at least one of those orgasms you keep taunting me with."

Thirty-seven minutes and two orgasms for Queenie later, we're dressed again and in my SUV, on the way to the spa.

Except when we arrive, there are all sorts of media vans parked in front of it. "What the heck is going on?"

"I don't know. Maybe they got wind that there's a celebrity around or something?" I say as we pass the spa. It's an exclusive one, and very expensive.

The last time I sent Queenie there, she told me the lead singer of a local band was getting a facial. They're usually really good about keeping celebrity clients under the radar, but occasionally someone posts something and forgets to shut off their locator, and the media jumps all over it.

"Maybe." I park around the corner. "I'll walk you in to make sure it's nothing we need to worry about."

"Okay. Sure. That would be good." Queenie nibbles on the end of her fingernail.

I hop out of the SUV and meet Queenie on the sidewalk. I thread our fingers together and give her hand a squeeze. "I'm sure everything is fine."

Except as we round the corner, the throng of media vipers suddenly turns and moves toward us in a wave. I look over my shoulder, expecting to see someone notable, but then famous people often wear hats and big shades to hide who they are. And then I realize what's happening, because the reporters start yelling. At us.

"Ryan Kingston! Are the rumors true? Did you get the general manager's daughter pregnant?"

"Are you being blackmailed?"

"Did you really take all of Corey Slater's money in the divorce?"

"Are you dating the GM's daughter as a PR stunt?"

"Did you know that Queenie Masterson was married when you two started dating?"

"Is she going after all your money too?"

"Oh my God." Queenie tucks herself into my side, trying to hide from the flashes and the microphones suddenly pointed in our direction. Stevie's aqua hair appears as she shoves her way through the crowd, Bishop's mammoth frame hulking behind her.

He spins around and holds out his arms. "What? No questions for me? Me and my wife aren't exciting enough for you?"

"We gotta get Queenie out of here. They're sending one of the stylists to our house. We showed up early, and Bishop thought he was being funny posting about ball waxing. The media showed up because you two have your bromance going on."

One of the reporters asks him if Stevie's pregnant.

Bishop jabs a finger in the reporter's direction. "Yes. With sextuplets, because my army of sperm is the motherfucking bomb. We're gonna start our own damn hockey team in one fell swoop." He raises his arms in the air like he's preaching a sermon.

"Oh, for fuck's sake. My brother is going to shit a brick when this goes viral." Stevie spins us around and flanks me as we head back to my SUV. She and Queenie duck into the back seat and I get behind the wheel, soon pulling out into traffic before the reporters can surround us. Bishop does a good job of distracting everyone, letting us make a quick getaway.

"Oh my God, oh my God, oh my God." Queenie's eyes are wide, her fingers at her lips, and she looks like she's about to cry. Again.

Stevie meets my concerned gaze in the rearview mirror and throws her arm around Queenie's shoulder. "It's gonna be okay. It's just fresh gossip."

"I can't go to the game tonight. I can't face that kind of mob."

"It'll be fine. We already have a plan to get into the arena tonight. And you don't have to worry because we'll be in a box and reporters can't get to us; plus, now that I'm pregnant with sextuplets, no one is going to care about your divorce from Douchey McDickface."

"I can't believe Bishop did that. You hate media drama."

"I hate it when they use baseless facts to railroad people more. Let them have a heyday with that. I'm sure I'll get knocked up sooner than later, and someone will say it's someone else's baby."

I want to stick around and make sure Queenie is actually okay, but I'm out of time and I need to head to the arena, so I'm forced to leave her in Stevie's capable hands. So much for a relaxing afternoon for her.

Obviously I'm worried about Queenie, and distracted. I check in with Queenie after I get to the arena, and she assures me she's okay, sends me a shot of her team-color-themed manicure, and tells me that she's still coming to the game, which is a relief. I'm grateful for Stevie and the other wives, because today has been tough enough for her as it is. I just want things to go smoothly tonight.

Most of my family has already arrived in Seattle, apart from Hanna, who's coming in through LA because of a conference she was attending, and her flight was delayed by a couple of hours, so she'll miss the first half of the game.

I check my messages on the way from the parking lot into the arena. Based on the family chat, they've already dropped their stuff off at the house, fought over rooms, raided my fridge, and made fun of my lack of exciting beverage options for anyone but toddlers. They obviously haven't found the liquor that Queenie brought over. Or the stocked beer fridge in the garage.

I have a new message from Hanna letting me know she's finally on her way to Seattle and that she'll see me after the game—that one was sent about ten minutes ago.

There are private messages from my mom telling me she has a very special surprise and that everyone is very excited to see me. "Special surprises" are not a rarity and often take the form of a hand-knit sweater, or a beanie, or a scarf. I have a closet full. I message back to let her know I'm excited to see everyone and that I look forward to the surprise before I pocket my phone and push through the doors to the arena.

I pass the hall leading to the offices and use the back entrance to access the locker room. Normally Bishop and I would have ridden in together, but with my family coming it made more sense for us to come separately.

Bishop is already there, in his underwear. They have a strange print on them that I don't want to inspect too closely, because it looks like there's a woman hugging his junk, and it's magnified thanks to the cup he's wearing under them. The woman actually looks like Stevie when her hair is pastel purple.

I drop down on the bench in front of my locker. "Thanks for helping us out earlier."

"Least I could do. It was my fault the media showed up in the first place. Ten fucking minutes after I posted about getting my junk waxed, a million freaking reporters showed up, being assholes, asking stupid questions. I shoulda known better, considering what's been going on today." He nods in Corey's direction.

He's sitting on the bench on the other side of the room, looking rough. He was quiet during pregame skate, which was highly unusual.

"I saw him in his car earlier; looked like he was getting chewed out by the fiancée about something. You'd think she'd be happy now that there's nothing standing between her and his bank account anymore." Bishop slides his feet into his skates and starts lacing them up.

"You don't think it has anything to do with the actual divorce?"

"Based on how she tried to blackmail Rook back when he started out, and the number of players she's been on the arm of over the years, there's a good chance she's looking for an easy meal ticket. Besides, you've been in the shower with him: there sure isn't anything to get excited about." He motions to his crotch.

He has a point. Corey is about as well endowed as a Chihuahua.

"What the hell are you two talking about?" Rook reaches around Bishop and steals his deodorant out of his locker.

"Hey! What the hell, man?"

"I ran out. I'm borrowing. You're family."

"Uh, no, in-law is not the same as a blood relative. And even if you were my blood, I would not lend you my fucking deodorant." Bishop tries to snatch it back, but Rook's on his feet and Bishop's skates are only half-laced.

He pops the cap off, and it hits Bishop in the chest. He grins as he lifts one arm high in the air and rubs the stick all over his armpit.

Bishop makes a gagging sound, then smiles right back. "Reverse cowgirl."

"What?" Rook frowns.

I elbow Bishop in the side before he can repeat himself, aware that this conversation isn't going anywhere good. "I have a brand-new one in my bag. Rook, you can keep that one."

Rook's eyebrows pop as he finally digests what Bishop's said. "You son of a bitch!" He hurls the deodorant at Bishop, who ducks out of the way. It ricochets off the wall behind him and lands on the floor.

"I'm fucking kidding, man, but you asked for it. Borrowing deodorant is like borrowing underwear or a toothbrush. The only person who gets to do that is the one whose tongue is routinely in my mouth, and that person happens to be your sister." Bishop is still grinning, aware he's skating near the edge.

"Even that was more information than I needed."

"Well, maybe you'll think twice before you go around borrowing deodorant."

"Winslow, Bowman, you're worse than a couple of toddlers fighting over the last cookie. Give it a goddamn rest or I'll change the starting lineup, and one of you isn't going to be happy about it." Jake has the uncanny ability to appear out of nowhere, generally when those two are in the middle of one of their bitchfests. Since Queenie made the suggestion, they've been putting them on the same line for home games to change things up, and so far the results have been highly favorable. While Queenie might not always believe it, it's clear that she has good instincts and she sees solutions or possibilities that others might miss.

"Rook used my deodorant."

Jake grimaces. "That's just wrong."

"He divulged personal information about my sister's sexual-position preferences." Rook thumbs over his shoulder at Bishop.

"I was joking, and I only said it *after* you used my deodorant."

"Just get your asses dressed and game ready." Jake turns to me. "King, you good?"

"Yes, sir."

He gives my shoulder a squeeze. "It's been a rough week; thanks for sticking by her," he says quietly.

"I wouldn't have it any other way, sir."

He nods, then continues on over to Corey, expression stoic. I can't even begin to imagine how difficult it's been for Jake to deal with him through all this.

Bishop and I finish getting game ready. "Hey, check this out."

He shows me his phone. There's a picture of Queenie with Lainey and Stevie, hair done and dressed in my jersey and a pair of jeans, and she's smiling. It looks genuine.

Once we're on the ice, I scan the arena, look for the girls, and find them up in a box. At least Queenie is here, even if she's not close enough to steal a kiss from. I find my family in another box on the other side of the arena.

I shift my focus away from my family and Queenie—the latter is more difficult than the former—and get my head in the game. It's intense since we're playing one of the best teams in the league, but I manage to keep the puck out of our net during the first period, and Rook scores a goal. In the second period our opposition gets lucky with a rebound off the bar, but Bishop scores for Seattle, keeping us ahead in the game. In the third Corey gets back-to-back penalties, putting us at a serious disadvantage. Offense has to work twice as hard to keep the puck on the other end of the rink, and the defensemen are all over it, protecting the net. We take the game 3–2, so it's still a win, but I blame Corey and his chippy playing for the close score.

Regardless, we won, my family is here, Queenie's divorce is finalized, and we're in a good place, which I'm taking as a positive sign.

Half an hour later I'm showered and dressed in my suit, ready to meet up with everyone. Bishop and I arrive at the bar together. My phone is blowing up with messages from my family, and I have a bunch from Hanna, which I assume is her letting me know she's here. I hear my family before I see them.

"Oh, man, you ready for this? Sounds like Gerald is already three sheets to the wind." Bishop's expression is somewhere between a cringe and a smirk.

"It would be cause for concern if he wasn't." I shake out my hands, almost like I'm preparing for a fight. My family in public can be a lot to deal with. At least my cousin Billy didn't tag along, as he sometimes likes to do. "You see Queenie anywhere?"

"Stevie messaged a while ago and said they're waiting for the bathroom, and there's a line or something. Sucks to have to sit to pee."

It's at that moment that Gerald spots me from across the restaurant and yells my name. My entire family turns around as if they've been practicing a choreographed dance move. My mother pushes through the crowd, not gently either. She elbows at least three people out of the way. I love my family, but man, they can be a rowdy bunch.

"King! What an incredible game! Kept me on the edge of my seat. I'm pretty sure your father nearly peed his pants a couple of times; it's a good thing he wears Depends when we go to events like these." She pats my cheek and smiles, then hugs me. She may or may not be joking about the Depends. "How are you, honey? I know the last week has been a struggle."

"I'm actually doing fine. I wanted to—"

"That's great. I'm so glad! And I brought you something that's going to brighten your day even more than a family visit! Come on, let me show you!" She grabs my hand and pats Bishop on the chest as we pass. "Hi, Bishop. I just need to steal our baby boy for a few minutes."

"Do whatever you gotta do." Bishop waves us off, and I follow my mom through the crowd toward my family, who all seem to be wearing slightly strained smiles. Hanna is at the end, beside Gerald, who's holding a beer in each hand. Her eyes are wide, and she's mouthing something at me, but I'm not adept at reading lips so I have no idea what she's trying to say.

Not that it matters, because the moment I get close enough, my dad and Gerald step away from each other, and my surprise appears.

Jessica.

My ex.

# CHAPTER 28
## WHAT THE H-E DOUBLE HOCKEY STICKS?

*Kingston*

"Surprise!" Jessica hurtles herself at me, which is as much of a shock as she is. She's more of a kiss on the cheek and an arm squeeze kind of woman, especially in public places.

I turn my head in my mother's direction, which is a good thing because Jessica's lips connect with my cheek. My mother looks gleeful, and Hanna, who's standing beside her, looks helpless and apologetic.

I scan the bar, searching for Queenie. This is not ideal at all. I can't introduce my girlfriend to my family when my ex has shown up for whatever reason. I pat Jessica on the back once before I take her by the shoulders and disconnect her from me. "What're you doing here?"

Her smile falters, possibly because of my harsh tone. "Your mother invited me as a surprise." She glances at Mom and then back at me, her expression shifting from excitement to uncertainty. "She said you'd be happy to see me, but you don't really look all that happy."

I blow out a breath and try not to take my frustration out on Jessica, because it's not her fault that my mother is a natural-born meddler. She generally has good intentions, but she misses the point. And now, despite the fact that I've told her repeatedly that Jessica and I are not getting back together, here she is.

"It's not that, it's just—" I spot Queenie across the bar. Her eyes lock with mine and shift quickly to Jessica, whose shoulders I'm holding on to. She also has her hands on my chest.

I have to assume Queenie knows what Jessica looks like. There are eight years' worth of photos of us together at various events, and just because we broke up doesn't mean I'm going to erase her from my life.

She scans the faces around me, gaze bouncing around my family— it's rather obvious that they're mine, since they're all wearing hand-knitted sweaters with my face on them. Apart from Hanna, since she's sane, and also she didn't fly in with the rest of them. Even Jessica is wearing one.

When Queenie spots Jessica, her expression shifts to something that looks a lot like defeat. She doesn't make a move to come to me; instead she gives me a small, sad smile, inclines her head toward the exit, and starts moving in that direction.

"I need to deal with . . . someone important," I mutter, and I try to step around Jessica.

She grabs my arm. "I came all the way from Tennessee to see you."

"I know, and I'm confused as to why, so we'll have to talk about that, but after I speak with my girlfriend." I shake her off and pin my mother with an unimpressed look. "This is a step too far," I tell her as I make my way through the crowd, following Queenie. My phone buzzes in my pocket as I reach the door and push outside. It spits me out into the alley behind the bar. It smells like garbage and urine. Queenie is standing there, phone in one hand, her face half-masked because it's buried in the crook of her elbow.

"Oh God! This is horrible!" I turn to find Jessica with her hand covering her mouth and nose, gagging, but her delicate sense of smell really isn't a priority right now.

"Can you please go back inside, Jessica? Your presence is the opposite of helpful at the moment."

She lowers her hand, and her mouth drops open. "You aren't being very nice to me right now." But her mouth clamps shut just as quickly, and the hand comes back up to shield her from the smell.

"I'm aware." I move past her and gently take Queenie by the elbow, guiding her away from the noxious odors.

She waits until we're not breathing in garbage before she lowers her hand. "Your family brought your ex-girlfriend with them."

"I didn't know until now. I'm sorry."

I reach out to . . . I don't know . . . touch her, hug her, reassure her. Something.

But she raises her hand and takes a step back, shaking her head slowly.

"Queenie, please understand. I had no idea."

"I believe you." She turns her head to the side and looks up at the sky, and a single tear cascades down her cheek. "But it's a pretty strong message, don't you think?"

"I don't—" I shake my head, because I honestly don't have a good explanation for this at all, but I need to say something. "My mom meddles. She doesn't understand. Jessica and I were together for a long time, and I think she's having a hard time letting go."

"I get it, King. I mean, I don't really, but I can see how all those years would make it hard for Jessica to walk away, especially from someone as amazing as you." She sighs and rubs her temples. "But I can't go back in there. What are you going to do? Introduce me as your girlfriend when they obviously brought her along so that you two could reconcile?" She takes another step away from me and holds out her hand, flagging down a passing taxi.

"What are you doing?"

"I'm going home. I can only take so much humiliation in one week, and this situation puts me way over my quota."

"I'll come with you." I take a step toward her.

"I don't think that's a good idea, do you?" She looks past me, and I glance over my shoulder to find my parents bursting out into the alley, followed by Jessica, again. "Your family is here for you. You need to stay and manage . . . whatever this is." She brushes a tear away. "My battle armor already has enough dings in it today. I'm not sure it can take another round of hits from your family tonight. And honestly, I don't want to meet them with your ex-girlfriend as a witness."

I don't stop her when she gets into the cab and they drive away, because she's right: I have to deal with my family and their thoughtlessness, and Queenie has been through more than enough this week.

Jessica's heels click on the sidewalk as she approaches, several steps ahead of the rest, mostly because Gerald is drunk-weaving and Hanna and my dad have to keep him from veering into the brick wall.

"Ryan? What are you doing out here?" my mom calls from down the alley.

"I was dealing with my girlfriend, who left because she's obviously upset about my surprise." I motion to Jessica and then feel bad about how much of a jerk I'm being to her, but Queenie's had enough crap this week, and honestly so have I.

"Pointing is rude, Ryan," my mom tsks.

"I thought you said Ryan and that adulteress broke up after that whole scandal thing happened," Jessica says to my mom, looking confused.

"You said *what?*" I straighten and clasp my hands behind my neck, pacing the sidewalk. I'm honestly trying to keep it together, but it's getting more difficult by the second.

My mom throws her hands in the air. Dramatically. Since there is no other way with her. "It's not like you're going to keep dating her after that whole thing went public in the media."

"She *is* married." Jessica props a fist on her hip.

"*Was* married. She's divorced now."

247

Jessica wrinkles her nose. "You're not really going to date a divorcée, are you? That's just . . . not like you at all, Ryan."

Gerald drunk-weaves into the middle of the group. "What's goin' on?"

My dad looks tired—as is typical when dealing with Gerald—and Hanna is obviously as pissed off as I am, based on her pursed lips and angry glaring.

"Where's the limo? We're all going home!" I shout over them. I need to get us all out of here before we draw more attention and someone decides to record this ridiculous conversation.

"But we just got here!" Gerald throws his arm over Hanna's shoulder and uses her to help keep him from tipping over.

"I'm calling a family meeting that isn't going to take place in this parking lot," I snap. "The limo. Where is it?" I ask Hanna, because out of everyone, she's the one most likely to take my side on this. She's always had my back, and I'm banking on her having it now too.

"It should be parked over there." Hanna motions across the lot.

My family follows, although Gerald grumbles about having left a half-full beer behind, and Jessica and my mom are whispering loudly about my mood. I don't say anything because I'm afraid I'm going to go off on them, and that's not normally something I do. I'm always even. Levelheaded. But this is a new height of interference on my mother's part, and I honestly don't know what to make of it.

Everyone piles into the limo, and somehow, despite my getting in last, I still end up between Jessica and my mom.

"What's gotten into you?" my mom asks once we're on the way home.

"Why would you tell Jessica that Queenie and I broke up?"

"Because she's married, and you were rightfully conflicted about the entire thing when we spoke about this as a family. Besides, I know my son well enough to know that you wouldn't continue to date her."

248

Once again, my mom has found a way to spin a past conversation to suit her own purposes.

"Out of all of us, you're the last one I expected to hook up with a married chick," Gerald says through a loud belch.

"Shut up, Gerald" comes the nearly harmonious family reply.

"What? It's true. The golden boy never fucks up."

"Queenie is *not* married. She's divorced, and she would've been divorced six years ago if her ass of an ex hadn't screwed her over. So it was a technicality that she was still married," I explain through gritted teeth.

"But who gets married at eighteen unless they accidentally got knocked up?" Jessica says and then cringes. "Sorry, Hanna. But you weren't even old enough to get married, anyway, so it doesn't count."

"No, I just had a baby as a teenager. Totally doesn't count." Hanna is all sarcasm, which Jessica misses.

"We're not debating who's allowed to get married when," I snap. "If there's a family who should *not* be judgmental about people's mistakes, it's damn well this one!"

"There's no need to raise your voice, Ryan. And we're not being judgmental: people make mistakes all the time. We know that, and I thought you'd finally realized that you made a mistake when you broke up with Jessica, so I took it upon myself to help set things right." My mother smiles nervously, hands clasped in her lap.

There's a murmur of agreement from Gerald, and my dad grunts when my mom kicks him in the shin.

Jessica puts her hand on my knee and squeezes. "I forgive you for that."

I rub the space between my eyes and grind my teeth. "No offense, Jessica, but I'm not asking for your forgiveness, because I didn't make a mistake."

"Ryan! You two have nearly a decade together! You don't throw that away because things get tough or something shiny and new catches your eye for a few minutes. You're lucky Jessica has been so understanding about all of this."

I love my family, but they're crazy. Apart from Hanna, anyway. I remind myself that I didn't get where I am today by losing my temper every time I get angry. This whole situation is seriously pushing my buttons, though. "Queenie is not something shiny and new. We've been dating each other for months, and I love her."

"Ryan!" my mother exclaims, and she flails her hand out toward Jessica. "Consider someone's feelings other than your own!"

That gets a round of mumbling from my family. Although this time not everyone seems to be 100 percent in agreement. Hanna looks like she wishes she were anywhere but here. Which makes two of us.

"Like you considered mine when you brought my ex-girlfriend as a surprise right in the middle of a particularly difficult time in my new relationship? Or maybe a better example would be when you kept the fact that my sister is actually my goddamn mother from me for thirty fucking years because it was better for you!" I shout.

Since we're in a limo, it's more like a roar. Also, I'm angry. Possibly angrier than I've ever been in my entire life.

And suddenly the vehicle is pin-drop silent. Everyone's eyes are saucer wide.

Gerald slaps his thigh. "I won the bet! Everyone owes me a case of beer! I told you King would lose it eventually and drop an f-bomb!"

"Unless you would like to know what it feels like to be on the receiving end of my fist in your face, I suggest you shut up," I growl.

"Yeah, but then you'd have to pay for the dental work." I launch myself at him, and it takes my dad and Hanna to pry me off. Hanna insists I calm down, because I'm going to hurt more than just Gerald if I can't get a handle on myself. I realize she's right, and that my mom and Jessica look terrified, so I sit back down.

We arrive at my house a minute later, thankfully, and everyone piles out, putting space between them and me. I punch in the code aggressively and usher everyone inside.

"Jessica and I need a minute alone, please," I say through clenched teeth.

"Whatever you have to say to me you can say in front of your family." She tips her chin up, almost defiant, and like maybe she thinks if I have to say it in front of them, I'll choose my words more carefully.

I've always been considerate of everyone else's feelings. Always treaded very carefully with my family and friends to avoid offending people or hurting their feelings, but this is really more than I can take after the week I've had.

"Why do you want to be with me?" I ask Jessica.

"What?"

"It's a straightforward question. What is it about me that makes you want to be with me?"

"Oh, uh . . ." She bites her lip and chuckles nervously. "Well, obviously you're very handsome."

After a few seconds of her staring at me, I ask, "Is that it?"

"Of course not. You're very put together and organized, which I appreciate, and you're very stable most of the time . . . apart from tonight, anyway."

"So I'm nice looking, I'm organized, and I'm stable? Those are my best traits?" The whole stable thing is questionable right now. I feel anything but level.

"You're also kind," she rushes on. "And you're good at following the rules, although you do tend to drive slow, but that's not a big deal, and you're very generous."

I jam my hands in my pockets. "Is that it?"

She looks around, maybe slightly panicked, and chuckles. "Um, I guess? I mean, you're putting me on the spot here."

"What about in bed? How's that for you?"

"Ryan!" my mother scolds, and the rest of the family either coughs or snickers.

Jessica's eyes flare and her cheeks turn red. "Excuse me? I don't think that's an appropriate question in front of your family."

"You're the one who invited them to this private conversation, and I think it's a legitimate question." I cross my arms. It might not be appropriate, but it's sure as hell pertinent. Part of me also hopes she'll either ask for privacy or my family will take it as a cue to leave.

"You're very attentive," she whispers.

"So would you say we're compatible in that capacity?"

"Um, yes, I guess."

"You guess?" I'm pushing for a reason.

"You can be very . . . chatty. I don't really see why this is relevant." Her eyes bounce around the room, and her face looks like it's about to burst into flames.

"I knew it! King's a dirty talker! I figured he couldn't be buttoned up all the time."

"Shut up, Gerald," everyone says in unison.

"And how do you feel about hockey?" I figure she's embarrassed enough, and I have the answer I need. Jessica is beautiful, nice, and friendly, but our relationship has always been flawed, and I see that so much more clearly now than I ever did before.

"What?"

"Hockey. How do you feel about it?" I ask gently.

"It's . . . fine."

"Fine?"

"Well, it takes up a lot of your time, but you're not going to play forever, and I've always had your family to keep me from getting too lonely, so I've been able to deal with it. At least I was able to deal with it until you broke up with me," she replies.

"I don't want it to be something you deal with, Jessica. Hockey is my passion. I love it. I'm excellent at it, and it's always going to be part of my life, even when I'm not playing professionally anymore. I don't need someone to love the sport the same way I do, but I need a partner who is at least going to understand my passion and help me foster it, not wait for my career to be over so I can fill my time with something else."

"But we've invested all these years together." She frowns. "And I'm already part of this family." She glances around the room, her sudden panic obvious as she sends an imploring look to my mother.

And there it is, the truth neither of us wanted to face, and clearly she's still struggling with it. Jessica's family is exactly like she is: poised, proper, a little cold, and emotionally unavailable. My family might be a bunch of lunatics, but they love fiercely. And I realize that this is the reason Jessica is here. That, and I think this is my mother's way of trying to stay in control of her family in the face of so much change. Of course she'd try to keep pushing Jessica and me back together, even though we're two mismatched puzzle pieces.

This is a conversation Jessica and I should've had a long time ago. And it's the primary reason we stayed together for as long as we did. I felt bad taking my family away from her when I knew she was so attached to them. And they were just as attached to her. I didn't want to rock the boat. I wanted to make my family happy, so I stayed in that relationship for more years than I should have. And then I met Queenie, and she turned my entire world upside down.

"It's not really me you're here for, though, is it?" I ask softly.

"I-I—of course I am."

I shake my head. "But you're not. It's not me you want back: it's my family. We hardly saw each other except for a month in the off-season. And even then, we spent that month with my family. Otherwise it was once every six weeks, if that. You only ever attended games when they were in Nashville. And you always came with my family." I take one of her hands in mine. "Look, Jess, I care about you and I always will, but being in love with my family isn't the same as being in love with me."

She exhales a long, slow breath. "I do love you, though."

"I know, and I love you, but it's not the kind of love that's going to help us build a life together."

She's quiet for a few long moments before she squeezes my hand, bottom lip trembling with the threat of tears. "We've been a part of each other's lives for so long, Ryan. I don't even know who I am without your family."

"I'm not asking you to give them up."

She sighs. "But you have a new girlfriend. I feel like I don't even know where I fit in anymore. I just . . . in my head I always believed eventually you'd be more focused on me than on hockey, and until then I could count on your family, but now that I've had time to reflect on it, I think it's more that I'm afraid to be alone. But that's not a reason for us to be together, is it?"

I shake my head and give her a sad smile. "It's really not. Neither of us would be happy in the long run. I'm sorry, Jess. I never wanted to hurt you."

"I know." She pats my cheek. "You don't have a mean bone in your body." She looks around the now-empty room, a little embarrassed. Apparently my family finally got the memo and gave us the privacy Jessica didn't think we needed at first. "I'm sorry it took me so long to finally see what you seemed to know all along."

"I think we both held on longer than we should have. It can be easy to become complacent when you're comfortable with someone, which is what we were." I don't want to bruise Jessica's ego any more than I already have. I'm just as responsible as she is for the way things have turned out between us.

"I'm going to go upstairs and pack my things and see if I can book a flight back home."

"I can help with that if you need me to."

"I wouldn't mind a few minutes alone, and you could probably use a little time to talk to your family." She inclines her head toward the living room. "Thank you for your thoughtfulness; you're an unfailing gentleman. And for what it's worth, I want you to be happy, even if it's not with me."

"I want the same for you."

She kisses me on the cheek and heads upstairs.

Since it was an afternoon game, I'm able to get her on the last flight out tonight—first class, obviously. I give her a few minutes to collect herself and then take her luggage from my bedroom out to the car I called to take her to the airport. I would drive her myself, but I don't want to make the situation more awkward than it already is.

I feel bad about the whole thing, but it's been a long time coming. And I'm glad she now realizes, just like I have, that our relationship didn't have what we needed for it to last a lifetime.

My family is sitting in the living room, murmuring among them-selves. Gerald has found the scotch I never drink, and everyone else is holding a cocktail or wineglass. So nice of them to make themselves comfortable while I deal with the mess they've made for me.

Gerald holds up a mason jar. "You have to put fifty bucks in here."

I should ignore him, but I don't. "Why?"

"Because you swore."

"It's a dollar a swear, not fifty bucks."

"Yeah, but it's you, so there's a markup."

I don't bother answering, because anything that comes out of my mouth is probably not going to be nice.

"I can't believe you threw away your relationship. Jessica has been part of our family for eight years." My mother's disappointment is clear in her tone and her expression, but for once I don't want to placate her.

"He did the right thing!" Hanna snaps before I can speak my mind.

"How can you say that?" Mom's hand goes to her heart, and she looks aghast.

"He wasn't happy with Jessica, and he hasn't been for a long time. It was right for him to end a relationship that wasn't working for him, for either of them."

"But he loves her and she loves him, don't you, Ryan?" Her expression turns imploring.

"I care about Jessica, but I'm not in love with her, and she's not in love with me either," I say.

"Of course she is. It's just a phase. Every relationship goes through this; you'll see. A little more time and you'll both come back around." She wrings her hands anxiously.

"That's not going to happen, Mom, and the sooner you come to terms with that, the better it's going to be for all of us." I'm frustrated that she's still harping on this point for reasons I don't understand.

"It's King's life," Hanna adds. "And it's his decision if he wants to pursue a relationship with someone he feels is better suited to him. Which is exactly what Queenie is."

"How can you say that?" Mom retorts.

"He's been happier and far more settled over the past few months than he ever was with Jessica, and the way he talks about her tells me everything I need to know. He's an adult, making adult decisions, and out of all the children you've raised, he's certainly turned out the best."

"Hanna—" I try to cut in.

"Let me finish, please," she implores. "He's the most successful, the most grounded, and he has never, ever been a pain in your ass. You've never had to bail him out of jail; he's never borrowed money. Even as a kid he didn't get into trouble, so have a little faith that he can make a good decision when it comes to finding someone who balances him out."

That seems to shut everyone up for half a second. Until our mother changes the subject, which is something she likes to do, especially when she's wrong. "Are you going through a rebellious phase?"

"I'm thirty. I make seven million dollars a year, I live in a house that's totally paid for, and I drive a Volvo. No, Mom, I'm not going through a rebellious phase."

She purses her lips. "I don't know that this girl is right for you."

"With all due respect, Mom, you've never even met her, so whatever opinion you think you have is based on tabloid garbage, and it's not your responsibility to make those kinds of decisions for me since I'm an independent adult."

"Burn," Gerald mutters.

No one tells him to shut up, because he's right.

She purses her lips, clearly unhappy with the direction this conversation has taken, so she switches gears. "Are you doing this because we didn't tell you about the adoption? You know, we decided as a family to raise you and Hanna and your brother as siblings, because it was better for Hanna, and for you. Both of your lives would've been so much harder otherwise. We were trying to save you from the stigma all of that would have brought with it."

I should've known we'd come back to this. We've already had a family meeting about this, but it was right after I found out. I've had months to process it, to think about it, reflect on it. Months to let it eat at me and fester, and suddenly, in the face of all this drama, I realize I might not be over it quite the way I thought I was.

"I get that when she was fifteen, that might have been true, Mom. But you uprooted the entire family, cut her off from all of her friends, and homeschooled Hanna for a year so no one would know that she was pregnant. Then, after she gave birth to me, you sent her to a new school with no friends and no social circle once you deemed her ready." I pace the room, my frustration and anger mounting. "You talk about it being a family decision, but Hanna was too young to fight you on it and Gerald isn't exactly a fan of taking responsibility for his actions. And for Christ's sake, who lets their fifteen-year-old go away for a month with her boyfriend on a cross-country camping excursion?"

"They were in a trailer with the entire family. How would they have an opportunity to—" She makes flailing motions instead of finishing that sentence.

"They were in the woods! For four weeks. Opportunities obviously abounded, since I'm here."

"He does have a point," Gerald says.

I pin him with a glare, and he sinks deeper into the couch. "I understand that we grew up in a rural town, with ideas of what was appropriate and what wasn't. I also understand your motives for raising us like siblings as a result of that. But I think you need to ask yourself this: Was it really good for Hanna, *for all of us*, in the long run? I get that maybe you were doing what you thought was best, but wouldn't it have made more sense to tell me eventually, when I was old enough to understand, rather than have me find out from Hanna's ex-asshole?"

"We were trying to protect you."

"Are you sure it was me and Hanna you were trying to protect? Or was it yourself?"

Her head snaps back, as if my words are a physical slap. And I realize I've hit a nerve. I sigh, and some of the anger fades like vapor. "You know that I'll always look at you as my mother, right? That's never going to change."

She blinks a bunch of times, and her chin trembles. My mother is a lot of things: high on self-righteous conviction, a meddler, a cheerleader, the dominant parent, and passionately maternal. What she rarely is is contrite; even less frequently is she emotional to the point of tears. I drop down, crouching in front of her, and take her hands in mine, seeing exactly how profound an effect this has had on her. I'm still angry, but it's tempered with understanding I didn't have before. "You will always be my mom, no matter what. Now I have two amazing women who want what's best for me." Three if I count Queenie.

She smiles but it's sad. "I was scared to tell you. I didn't want things to change or for me to lose you. And I thought if you and Jessica were back together, I could keep us closer because she already loves us. She loves me." She lifts a shoulder and lets it fall, her vulnerability leaking through. "I don't know this Queenie woman, and what if she doesn't like me?"

"Well, I love you and she loves me, so I think as long as you can give her a fair shot, she can give you one too. But in order to do that, you have to stop basing your opinion of Queenie on a highly slanted tabloid news story meant to incite public rage, by a person who might be a few face cards short of a deck. That woman who was busy dragging Queenie's name through the dirt also tried to blackmail the captain of our team almost a decade ago by using a plaster cast of her sister's baby belly and posting pictures online."

"Wow, now that's some crazy," Gerald mutters into his scotch.

"She faked a pregnancy?" My mom seems taken aback. She also tends to take anything on TV as gospel.

"Yes. It was a very elaborate ruse. Rook had to file a restraining order." I leave out the part where she also asked him to ejaculate in a cup so she could turkey baste herself.

"Oh."

"Yeah. Oh. So do you see now how this biased opinion you have of Queenie is based on nothing but slander?"

Mom squeezes my hands. "I'm so sorry. I've been very selfish about this whole thing, haven't I?"

I squeeze back. "We're all allowed to be selfish sometimes."

"I only ever want what's best for you," she says softly.

"I know. And Queenie is what's best for me. Now I need to go fix things with my girlfriend, because currently she believes that my whole family thinks I'd be better off with someone other than her. So I'm going to see if I can set things straight." I kiss my mom's forehead, then push to a stand, winking at Hanna as I cross the room. "Don't wait up."

# CHAPTER 29
## GOOD ENOUGH

*Queenie*

Today has been one hell of a roller-coaster ride, full of ups and downs and loop the loops, ending in a massive derailment.

Seeing Jessica pawing at Kingston was like a backhand to the face with a cactus mitten. She's so perfect, and blonde and willowy and Barbie-like, but with normal proportions. And he's so put together and gorgeous and perfectly *him*.

On the surface they look like they match.

But now that I know Kingston, I'm aware that there's a lot more to him than just a polo-and-khaki-wearing Boy Scout.

I've spent enough time over the past week looking through his social media. Kingston isn't the kind of person who would delete his memories, or the people he made them with. So I've had a front-row seat to the progression of a fresh-faced Kingston with Jessica posed sporadically at his side all the way up until midseason last year.

I can understand exactly why his mother would want them to be together. They are definitely a picture-perfect couple. Until you really look at the two of them together and compare those pictures to the ones he's been posting of us over the past few months. The sheer quantity alone speaks volumes.

I can see it in the way they orient themselves around each other: familiar but formal, posed but never relaxed, smiling but always a little tight lipped. And then there are the pictures of him and me together—which totally clog his feed and have replaced more than 50 percent of his pregame skate and workout videos. Kingston's smile is brighter, his posture is more relaxed, and the expression he wears when he's taking one of his silly selfies while trying to look at me instead of the camera tells me everything I need to know. That despite how different we are, or maybe because of it, we fit. The way he wants me is the same way I want him.

I get that his family's perception of me probably isn't the greatest if they've been listening to the gossip mill. But come on, everyone knows 90 percent of that stuff is bullshit based on a grain of truth.

And now I'm annoyed, frustrated, and kind of pissed off. Because his ex is here—probably in his house right now—and the woman who raised him as her son is the one who brought her. I'm not pissed at Kingston; he needs to deal with the situation. But in that moment when I saw them together, with his family standing and watching the whole thing, his mom beaming rainbows of happiness, I realized there was clearly a disconnect. And if I'd stuck around, I wasn't going to make an awesome first impression. Or second impression, if I'm counting the whole tabloid explosion.

Especially since I sort of want to tell his mom off, which isn't a good way to handle the family-intro business.

So instead I'm pacing the length of my kitchen, trying to figure out how the hell I'm supposed to deal with this. My group chat with Stevie, Vi, and Lainey is blowing up. They're appropriately outraged right along with me, which is validating.

A knock on the door startles me. A bubble of hope forms in my chest but then pops just as quickly when my dad lets himself in.

"Oh, hey."

He frowns, taking in the pile of used tissues and me. "I didn't expect you to be here tonight."

"Me either." I toss my phone on the counter and cross over to my fridge, pulling out a couple of beers.

"What happened? Why aren't you with Kingston?"

I twist off the caps and hand him a beer. "He's with his ex-girlfriend, because his mother brought her along."

"Wait. What? His momster or his mom brought her?"

"His mom, not momster." If it had been Hanna, I'd be a lot more upset, I think.

My dad sets the beer on the counter, obviously confused. "Why the hell would she do that? Why would Kingston let her?"

"Kingston didn't know she was coming. She was supposed to be a surprise." I rub the space between my eyes. "I didn't think a family introduction with his ex-girlfriend there was in my best interest, or anyone's, really, so I came home, and he's dealing with the situation."

"Dealing with it how?"

"Likely in his very diplomatic way." I glance at the clock. I've been home for forty-five minutes. That's a considerable amount of time to stew. And contemplate whether I made the right choice in coming home instead of standing up for King and myself and our relationship.

"Shit." I slam my full bottle on the counter, making it foam like a volcano.

"What?"

"I did it again."

"Did what again?" My dad's brow is furrowed, and he's clearly confused again, since I'm speaking out loud but explaining nothing.

I prop my fists on the counter and shake my head, annoyed not just with Kingston's mom but with myself now. "I ran away from the goddamn problem instead of facing it."

"You mean by coming home?"

A Secret for a Secret

I slap the counter, barely missing my beer. "Yes. I should have stuck it out and stood my damn ground."

"Well, in your defense, you've had a pretty rough day, let alone week. It's kind of understandable that you might need some time to gather yourself."

"The awkward level is pretty freaking high," I agree. "But I managed to get through dealing with Corey and his loon of a fiancée and a bunch of media BS, so I sure as hell should've been able to deal with an ex-girlfriend and some misinformed parents, regardless of the level of awkward. I mean, I can't expect Kingston to fight for us if I'm not going to, can I? Well, I guess I could, but where's the balance in that?" I grab my purse and phone and kiss my dad on the cheek. "Thanks so much for the talk, Dad."

"Uh, you're welcome?"

Just as I throw the door open, a set of headlights blinds me.

My dad brushes by me, squeezing my shoulder on the way out. "That's my cue to leave."

He claps Kingston on the shoulder and mutters something I can't hear as they pass each other in the driveway.

"Hey." He notes my purse hooked over my shoulder and my phone in my hand. "Are you going somewhere?"

"I was going to your place." I take a step back and allow him inside.

"My place?" He hooks his thumbs into his pockets, as if he's unsure what to do now that he's here.

I lift a shoulder in a half shrug and motion to my living room. "I can't fight for what I want from here."

He moves in closer until he breaches my personal-space bubble. I can smell his cologne, the faint hint of shoe polish and leather, feel the hum of energy that's always present between us. "You don't have to fight for anything. I'm yours unless you tell me otherwise."

"And I'm yours." I trace the collar of his polo. "I figured the best way to prove that would be to stand by your side no matter what. So I decided not to wait and just go to you instead, but now here you are."

"Here I am." He smiles softly and skims my cheek with the back of his hand. "I'm sorry about my mother's meddling. She misinterpreted our conversation last week and had it in her head that you and I were broken up, hence the surprise."

"Well, it certainly was that."

"This wasn't how I wanted tonight to go, at all."

"Me either. Gotta say, makes meeting the parents a little more awkward."

"I promise I've taken care of that. Jessica's already on a plane home, and there won't be any more misunderstandings where she's concerned. She's very clear on the fact that we're not right for each other." He runs his palms down my arms and takes my hands in his. "The only person who thought it was a good idea to bring Jessica was my mother, because half the time her head is up her butt. And my brother, Gerald, loves that there was some family drama that finally wasn't focused on him for a change." He brings my knuckles to his lips and kisses them. "I hated seeing you upset tonight and not being able to fix it."

"You had to deal with your family, and in that moment I wasn't prepared to face them, but I am now."

King grins down at me. "Feeling feisty tonight?"

I return the smile. "I think I might be starting to get the hang of this whole confronting the problem thing."

"Well, I like it. And I think my family deserves to stew for a bit. Besides, Gerald is drunk off his ass, and I don't feel like being the one who has to manage him tonight." He dips down and brushes his lips over mine. "I can think of a few good ways to capitalize on that feistiness, though."

I clasp my hands behind his neck. "Would that include nudity and orgasms?"

"See? We're totally in sync." His mouth crashes down on mine, tongue sweeping my mouth in a wet, furious tangle. He picks me up, and I wrap my legs around his waist. He carries me across the room, shouldering open my door. "Tomorrow we deal with my family. Tonight I get my fill of you."

◆ ◆ ◆

Awareness trickles in at the feel of a finger trailing along the edge of my jaw. I stretch, and my muscles ache deliciously. Cool air hits my chest when the covers slide down. A light tickle along my collarbone follows, and I moan at the wet warmth and suction when soft lips close around my nipple. The sensation is amplified by the sweet sting of teeth.

My lids flutter open, the haze of sleep drifting away as King's profile comes into view, long lashes fluttering as his palm curves around my other breast and squeezes gently.

I run my fingers through his silky hair, pushing it back off his forehead. It's damp.

He tips his head in my direction, freshly shaven cheek rubbing over my wet nipple. "Morning." He glances at the clock on the nightstand. "Well, afternoon."

The clock reads half past twelve. "Oh wow." My voice is hoarse, so I clear my throat, but it's still scratchy and soft. "How long have you been awake?"

"Awhile." He circles my nipple with the tip of his tongue. "I was trying to be patient, but I got hungry."

"We can make breakfast, or maybe brunch would be better."

"I didn't mean for food." His palm smooths down my stomach, fingertips circling sensitive skin, causing me to jerk and moan.

Half an hour later I'm wearing his discarded shirt from last night—mostly because I don't want him to put it on—and he's wearing his khakis and a very satisfied smile.

I hop up on the counter, sucking in a breath when the cold marble meets my bare butt. Kingston stops chopping pineapple and uses his pinkie to lift the bottom of my shirt. "Where are your panties?"

I shrug. "I never know when you're going to get hungry again."

He sets the knife on the counter and pushes the cutting board aside. Moving into my personal space, he taps on my knees, a silent request to open for him. I've already come twice since I woke up. And I lost track last night once we got to my bedroom. Apparently King loves my feisty.

"I'm always hungry for you." His palms ease up the inside of my thighs, and he parts me with his thumbs on a low groan.

"Not sure this is a particularly hygienic location for kitty snacks."

He smirks. "Don't worry, I'll clean up if I make a mess of you."

He leans in for a kiss, and we both startle at the loud knock on my door. "Shoot, that's your dad." He shifts to the left and makes a quick adjustment in his pants.

I don't consider the fact that I should probably be wearing more clothes, or that Kingston should be wearing a shirt, when I call out, "The door's open!"

Kingston gives me a *What the heck?* look, but it's too late, because my dad's let himself in.

"You should probably wash your hands, Boy Scout." I cough as I jump off the counter. At least the shirt is long and hits midthigh. "Hey, Dad." My voice is nice and pitchy.

"Morning, Jake." King's face is the color of a beet. "I mean, good afternoon."

My father's eyes bounce from a shirtless King to me, in King's shirt. Yeah. It might've been a good idea to remedy the clothing situation before telling him to come on in. "Looks like you kids made up just fine, huh?"

"Yuppers." Well, this is awkward.

"Well, uh, I hope you're being safe."

Annnnd now it's more awkward.

266

If my dad means Kingston painting my chest every time he pulls out, then we are definitely being safe.

"Of course, sir." Kingston dries his hands on a towel. "We were just about to prepare some brunch, if you'd like to join us."

"Oh, uh, before you do that, you might want to call your . . . momster? Hanna?" He holds up Kingston's phone and keys.

Kingston feels his back pockets. "Did I drop those in the driveway?"

"No, you left them in your SUV. I was passing by about an hour ago and noticed the keys in the ignition and the phone on the seat. The door was unlocked."

I don't bother asking why he didn't knock an hour ago because I already know what we were up to, and I'm pretty sure, based on how red his face is, so does he.

"Oh, wow . . . uh, thanks. I was pretty distracted last night."

"I accidentally answered a call a few minutes ago. I was trying to turn off the ringer but hit the wrong button." His face continues to heat up.

"No big deal. I'm guessing you told Hanna I'd call her back?"

"Well, uh, she said there wasn't a rush, but family dinner is at six, and everyone is excited to meet Queenie, so she's hoping you two don't have plans. And that cocktail hour is at five." My dad sets the phone and keys on the counter, pushing them toward Kingston. "I told her you could probably make it, but I'd get you to confirm."

"Oh, uh . . . ." Kingston's eyes flare, and he glances at me. "Okay?"

It's phrased like a question. I respond with the same upturned lilt. "Sure?"

"Great." My father smiles and rocks back on his heels. "She also invited me to come along too."

Kingston's brows lift. "Oh?"

"Are you two okay with that?" my dad asks uncertainly.

"Oh yeah. Totally. It'll be fun, right, King?" I'm not sure if *fun* is the word I would use to describe meeting my boyfriend's parents and having my somewhat overprotective dad tagging along, but if nothing else, it will be an adventure.

Kingston nods, eyes wide. "So fun."

"Okay. Well, great." My dad claps his hands together and startles everyone with the noise, including himself. "I'll run out and grab a bottle of wine or two. And I can meet you there, since I know where you live, King." He moves toward the door. Pointing a finger at King, he makes some kind of odd clicking sound with his tongue. "You kids play safe." And then he's off, with a bounce in his step.

"Sooo . . ." I turn to King, whose expression I'm having trouble reading. "I guess this is happening."

He nods slowly. "Looks like. Are you nervous?"

I shrug. "Maybe a little." I don't think the news has had enough time to sink in for me to process it.

He glances at the clock. "We have a couple hours before we have to head over. I have a few ideas as to how I can keep your mind occupied until we have to go."

# CHAPTER 30
## THE KINGSTONS

*Queenie*

We pull into Kingston's driveway just after four thirty. My dad was all about getting there early for whatever reason, and I felt weird about him arriving and us not being there, so we left at the same time; however, since Kingston drives like a ninety-year-old on a Sunday, my father is already parked and standing beside his car when we arrive. He keeps checking his hair and he's wearing a tie, which is probably overly formal, but then my dad sort of likes to dress up.

"Fair warning: my family is a bit . . . off the wall," King says to me as he puts the car in park.

"You mean compared to you?" Kingston is the least off-the-wall person I've ever met. He's the definition of zen—well, except in the bedroom.

"No, I mean in general. They're just . . . a lot to handle."

"Kind of like me?"

"You're not a lot to handle, Queenie." His gaze moves over me in a hot sweep. "You're the perfect amount of chaos, especially when we're naked."

"Focus, Kingston. We're not talking about sex right now; we're talking about your family."

"Right. Yeah." He shakes his head, like he's clearing it. "They're just a little . . . excessive."

"Excessive how?"

"I don't know how to explain it. You'll see, though." He gives my hand a squeeze and then cuts the engine.

I get out of the car before he can open my door for me. And suddenly it's not me who looks nervous anymore; it's Kingston.

"You two get stuck at every red light?" my dad asks as we walk up the front steps.

King doesn't even have a chance to key in the entry code before the door swings open.

"Gerald found your good scotch two hours ago," Hanna says by way of greeting. "Queenie. Hi! Hello! You're even more beautiful in person than you are on video chat!"

"Momster."

"Sorry." Her nose wrinkles. "It's so nice to meet you. I'm going to apologize in advance for whatever happens this evening." She pulls me in for a hug and says quietly in my ear, "Just remember that you love Kingston, and it's not his fault we're his family."

"What are you whispering about?" Kingston asks suspiciously.

"Oh nothing!" Hanna releases me from the hug and smiles brightly at Kingston.

Up until this point my dad has been hanging back. He steps up and extends his hand. "Hi, I'm Jake, Queenie's dad. We spoke on the phone earlier."

"Oh, yes." Hanna's eyes move from his face all the way down to his polished dress shoes and back up, slowly. "Hello, Jake." She slips her fingers into his open, waiting palm. "I'm Hanna, Ryan's momster . . . I mean sister. I mean mom. I'm actually both. Well, biologically I'm his mother, but we were raised as siblings." She grimaces. "I am so sorry for

270

that excessive overshare and terrible introduction. There's a reason I'm not a public speaker and work in an office most of the time."

My dad laughs and winks. "I can imagine it's not necessarily the easiest thing to explain."

"No. Definitely not."

They're still shaking hands, staring at each other.

"So . . . should we go in and introduce Queenie and Jake to the rest of the family, or . . ." Kingston trails off.

Hanna drags her gaze away from my dad. "What's that?"

Kingston motions past her. "We should come inside."

"Oh! Yes! Of course!" Hanna's eyes go wide and her cheeks flush pink, but she finally releases my dad's hand and steps back to let us in.

The noise level in the house grows exponentially as we walk down the hall. Kingston jams his hands in his pockets and blows out a breath, rolling his shoulders back. The first thing I notice when we enter the kitchen is that it's not neat and tidy like Kingston usually keeps everything. In fact, it's pretty much bedlam. And his family is congregated around the island, talking over each other.

"Hey, guys!" Kingston says, but they're so loud they don't notice him.

Hanna brings two fingers to her mouth and lets out a shrill whistle.

Kingston's brother—I'm assuming, based on his age—drops to the ground and covers his head with his hands. "I didn't do anything wrong!"

"Get up, Gerald. Hanna, was that really necessary?" King's mom-not-mom props a fist on her hip. "You know how much Gerald hates whistles. Oh! Hi there!" she says when she notices us.

I lift my hand in a wave, and my dad mirrors me. I don't know what to think about the gong show that is currently happening in my boyfriend's kitchen. I'm not sure what I expected from his family, but this sure isn't it. Maybe I thought they'd all be polo-and-khaki-wearing rule followers. However, it appears as though Kingston might be the only one who fits that bill.

"Mom, Dad, Gerald, this is my girlfriend, Queenie, and her dad, Jake."

271

Kingston's mom-not-mom looks from me to Jake and back again, clearly assessing the age difference between us. Or lack of age difference.

"It's so lovely to meet you both!" Kingston's mom-not-mom pulls me in for an aggressive hug. She then holds me at arm's length, like she's performing some kind of inspection. "Oh yes, I can see why Ryan is enamored with you. I'm so sorry about Jessica. I thought I was doing the right thing, but as it turns out I'm actually pretty good at doing the wrong thing. Like not telling Ryan I'm not his mother until the cat was already out of the bag." She grimaces and squeezes my shoulders.

"But in my defense, he's always been such a good boy. And I was really quite worried about how he would take the news. Gerald has been to jail more than once: not for anything serious, but still. And, well, you know all about the Hanna situation, so . . . I'm sorry. I should know better than to question Ryan's judgment."

"Uh, Mom, this isn't a therapy session or confessional. It's dinner and an introduction. You can save some of our family secrets for another day." Kingston rubs the back of his neck, cheeks red and his expression reflecting his embarrassment.

Over the next several hours I discover that Kingston is the most normal member of his family. I have no idea how he turned out the way he did. Gerald has been to prison not once but twice for stealing semis while intoxicated. Hanna is probably the second-most grounded in her family—teen pregnancy and recent divorce aside, which is ironically very familiar.

I'm regaled with stories of Kingston from his teen years. Apparently, he was frequently friend zoned by girls in high school because he was so hyperfocused on hockey that he failed to realize they were interested in him until it was too late.

I also find out why Kingston doesn't usually drink, thanks to his brother, Gerald, who seems to be the most off the hook. "When King was seventeen, me and our cousin Billy took him camping and fed him all kinds of drinks," Gerald tells me, wearing a huge grin.

"I thought it was just soda." Kingston swirls his white russian around in his glass, making the ice tinkle. "Not spiked with copious quantities of alcohol."

"You were so drunk you couldn't even stand." Gerald starts laughing and slapping his knee. "And of course he thought he could go for a run and burn off the alcohol, because King is nothing but practical, even when he's so shit faced he can't see straight."

"It seemed logical at the time," Kingston grumbles, cheeks flushing.

"I'm assuming that didn't go well," I press, imagining a drunk, teenage Kingston trying to sober up by going for a run.

"He kept stumbling around; ended up in a raspberry bush and scratched himself all to hell. Broke out in hives too."

"Because whatever you were feeding me had strawberries in it." Kingston rolls his eyes.

"We didn't know."

"All you had to do was read the ingredients."

"Oh my God, that must have been epic!" I snicker.

Kingston shoots me a look. "I was underage, and they got me blind drunk. Don't look so gleeful over this."

I pat his thigh. "I'm just picturing how you'd react, especially as a teenager."

"He tried to make himself puke, but King hates throwing up, so he started begging me to help him." Gerald is practically rolling on the floor laughing at this point, tears streaming down his cheeks.

"I think Queenie's heard enough of that story. Luckily I didn't die of alcohol poisoning."

"You had four drinks, and you weighed almost two hundred pounds even back then. You weren't going to die of alcohol poisoning."

"I didn't know that, though. And those four drinks consisted of mostly rum."

"King made himself puke, and he passed out in one of the lawn chairs. Ended up being bitten by, like, a thousand mosquitos. He looked like he'd come down with the chicken pox." Gerald turns to Kingston, wiping tears from his eyes. "Remember how you thought you'd fallen in a patch of poison ivy when you woke up?" He slaps his thighs, snorting through his laughter. "He was covered in hives and bug bites and he couldn't stop scratching himself."

"No wonder he never wanted to go camping with you again." Hanna shakes her head, but she's smiling.

"Maybe we should talk about the time I had to use the find my phone app because you were so messed up you had no idea where you were. Or the time I found you passed out on the front lawn at five in the morning wearing only a pair of women's underwear," Kingston fires back at Gerald.

"Those were some of the best nights of my life, even though I don't remember them at all," his brother says wistfully.

"Which is why you're still single."

"Or maybe it's because I'm asexual. Thanks for making me out myself in front of your girlfriend and her dad. I'll bill you for the therapy sessions." Gerald winks at me. "I'm not asexual. I'm commitment phobic; see the rest of my messed-up family for details." He motions to his family, lounging around Kingston's living room, no one apparently scandalized by the stories they've shared about each other.

"I'm not messed up," Kingston says.

"Dude, you drink more milk than infants do, and your entire wardrobe consists of khakis and polos. That's not normal."

"Whatever. Someone has to walk the straight and narrow. And I'm the most normal out of the rest of you." He kisses me on the temple and whispers, "Please don't break up with me because my family is insane."

Eventually Kingston has to fire up the barbecue for dinner.

I can practically feel the anxiety seeping out of him every time he walks into the kitchen where his mom, Hanna, Gerald, my dad, and I are helping prep for dinner. Hanna gave my dad the job of cutting buns open for burgers and sausages, and Gerald's role seems to be playing chicken with cutting board knives, since he's constantly reaching for cut pickles and cheese.

Based on the stories I'm told, Kingston used to drink a gallon of milk every two days. I'm not sure much has changed.

Hanna decides that dishes are too much work, so she goes in search of paper plates and disposable cutlery, and my dad offers to help. Gerald disappears outside with a beer, leaving me alone with Kingston's mom.

She wipes her hands on a dishcloth and turns nervously toward me. "I owe you an apology."

"I know how it must have looked from an outsider's perspective, and I can fully understand why you would have concerns about Kingston dating someone like me."

"I appreciate that you're letting me off the hook here, Queenie, but I'm the one in the wrong, and I should know better than to believe the media." She tosses the dishcloth on the counter, and I instinctively spread it out over the edge of the sink like Kingston prefers.

"Sissy spins a compelling tale."

"You're not wrong about that. It's still not an excuse for bringing Jessica here and creating problems where there didn't need to be any. Or for making you feel judged. Lord knows I've let other people's perceived judgment cloud my own vision more than enough times over the years. Ryan has always been the perfect child, and when he found out about Hanna being his mother . . . well, he was rightfully upset. More upset than I'd ever seen him before. I didn't want my role in his life to change, so I tried to control the situation, because that's what I've always done. But I see now how very wrong I was." She smiles softly. "I've never seen him smile more than he does when you're at his side. Thank you for being brave enough to come here today to meet all of us despite how uncomfortable it must have been."

"I love King. I'd brave just about anything for him."

She hugs me, and suddenly I understand what a real mother is supposed to be. Not perfect, but protective. Willing to make mistakes and own them because sometimes love outweighs logic.

# CHAPTER 31
## GREAT IDEAS

*Kingston*
*Three months later*

"I have never been more excited to see a white polo in my entire life. Eight days is far too long for you to be gone." Queenie fists my shirt and tips her head back, pulling my mouth to hers.

"I missed you too," I murmur, but I keep my teeth clamped together so she can't get her tongue in my mouth. "But we have an audience."

She backs off right away, smoothing out my shirt. "Oh, right. Yeah. Sorry." She cringes and looks around. Thankfully there aren't that many people milling around to witness the PDA.

Queenie was accepted to the University of Seattle, so she can now finish her degree. Last week her conditional acceptance to the master's program in art therapy came. On top of a full course load, she volunteers at the art center, in addition to working one-on-one with Lavender at least once a week, if not twice. She's amazing and focused, and I love watching her flourish like this.

I arrived home early this morning from an away series. It was a bit of a drama-filled week away. Sissy had the baby just before we left. Corey insisted on a paternity test, which was a wise move on his part, since it turns out the baby is most definitely not his. He found out right before a game and lost it on the ice, ending up with a twenty-game suspension. I have a feeling management will be negotiating for a trade at the end of the season.

I'm relieved to be home, and I've been waiting all afternoon for Queenie to be finished volunteering so I can take her home and show her exactly how much I missed her. Which is why I'm picking her up instead of waiting for her to come to me.

I wrap my arms around her in a PG hug and bend until my lips are at her ear. "As soon as we're home I'm going to spread you out on the dining room table and eat you until you're begging to ride me."

She sucks in a soft gasp and pushes back. For a second I think maybe it was too much, especially since we're in a public parking lot. She bites her lip, and a coy smile flirts at her lips. "Is that a promise or a threat?"

"Whatever gets you in the car faster."

"I'll take the threat, Boy Scout." She pats my chest. "And you better drag those orgasms out until I'm damn well delirious, or I'll be hella disappointed." She nips my chin and then flits around to the passenger side of the car and practically throws herself inside.

I grin and take my time getting in and make sure the mirrors are the way I like them, while Queenie crosses and uncrosses her legs. "Seriously, Kingston? You can't tell me you're going to make a meal out of me and then pull this whole seventy-five-point check deal."

"I just want to get you home safely."

"You mean you want to get me all worked up and tell me how much you love it when I've already soaked through my damn panties before you've even laid a finger on me."

She's absolutely correct about that. It's an incredible ego boost to be able to make her come within minutes of getting her naked, but I don't tell her that since she already knows. "Someone's testy."

"Yeah, well, that would be your fault, wouldn't it?" She fastens her seat belt aggressively.

She's more worked up than usual. I put the car in gear, and signal out of my spot. "How is it my fault you're testy?"

"You show up here, looking all delicious, whispering naughty things in my ear, and now I have to try and sit here and be patient while you drive like a grandpa on a Sunday afternoon. It's been eight damn days, Kingston. Eight days without you, or your tongue or your color commentary, or our mutual-gratification competitions. There will be no sweet and gentle tonight. I better have a hard time walking tomorrow morning. And teeth marks on my ass."

My erection kicks behind my fly. "I'll certainly do my best to ensure the difficulty walking and the teeth marks, if that's what you'd like."

"It's exactly what I'd like. And to ride your face," she tacks on.

"That's a given. Is there anything else you'd like to add while you're creating your list of demands for the evening?"

"I'm sure I can think of a few things." She shifts around in her seat.

On the drive home Queenie provides a very extensive, descriptive list of what she'd like to happen once we're naked. I'd like to say we make it to the dining room table, but that would be a lie. We don't even make it out of the garage. In fact, I end up on my knees on the concrete floor with Queenie wrapped around me. The floors are heated, so it sounds a lot worse than it is.

She's wobbly on her feet, and half her clothes are missing, by the time we're finished, so I offer my assistance in getting inside. "Want me to piggyback you?"

"Please." I give her my back and she climbs on, clasping her arms around my neck.

Her lips part against my neck. "You're salty."

"Not as salty as you were when you got in the car."

"These eight-day away-game stretches suck," she mumbles.

"There aren't a lot of them." I grab her messenger bag and close the passenger-side door, then carry her through the garage.

"Oh crap. I didn't even think to pack an overnight bag."

"I stopped at your place before I picked you up today and grabbed all your toiletries."

"You're so thoughtful." She kisses up the side of my neck.

"I try." I carry her through the mudroom and down the hall, past the staircase leading to the bedroom.

"Where are we going? Aren't you taking me to bed?"

"In a minute. I have something to show you first."

She perks up when she notices a new painting hanging on the wall. "Whoa, wait a second; let me down." I let go of her thighs, and she slides down my back. I feel her face mash into my back for a second, and she wobbles a bit as she steadies herself, still gripping my arm as she glances down the hallway, the walls no longer bare. "Are these all mine?"

I can't read her expression. "They were all just sitting in a corner in your place. I thought they should be where someone could appreciate them." Queenie's chaos is reflected subtly in all her art. She creates these amazing watercolors, half in pastels and the other half in dark, contrasting colors, the calm and the storm in everything. They're stunning, and the last place they should be is covered by a drop cloth.

"How many of them did you put up?" Her fingertips follow the edge of one raw canvas.

"Whatever was hanging around your place." She's been sleeping here more and more over the past few months, leaving things behind every time she stays over, which is every night when I'm not off on an away series.

She turns to me, her expression soft and warm. "When did you have time to do this?"

"This afternoon." I link my pinkie with hers. "There's more; come on."

"More?"

My palms start to sweat as I lead her farther down the hall. While I was away, I hired a decorator to come in and renovate one of the main-floor rooms, hoping it would act as an enticement.

I kiss her temple. "Close your eyes."

"What're you up to?"

"You'll see. Just keep them closed until I tell you to open them."

"Or what?"

"Or you'll ruin my surprise." I open the door and guide her to the center of the room. I stand directly in front of her, taking in her stunning face, bottom lip caught between her teeth. I skim her cheek with a fingertip. "Okay. You can look now."

Her lids flutter and I step to the side. "What do you think?"

Her mouth drops open, and her hands come up to cover it. "Oh my God, King, this is incredible." She turns a slow circle, taking in what was once an oversize workout room. It has amazing natural light, with huge windows that face the garden in the backyard.

One wall has been painted black with chalkboard paint. Another boasts giant blank Post-its that can be changed out regularly. A few of Queenie's gentler watercolor paintings that remind me of childhood fairy tales line the far wall. A desk and a drafting table have been set up, as well as adult- and child-size easels. There's even a pair of lounge chairs.

"It's pretty multifunctional. I thought it would be a good place for you to study, and I figured it might be good for you to have a space to work in case you wanted to bring Lavender here some days."

She smooths her hands over my chest. "This is amazing. I don't even know what to say."

I run my palms nervously up and down her arms. "I know we talked about you moving in with me at the end of the semester, but my place is closer to the university, and you always stay here when I have home games, and I'd really like it if you were here all the time."

"Are you asking me to move in now?"

"You're already halfway there, and now you have your own art studio. It makes sense, don't you think?" God, I'm so nervous.

"I'm kind of messy."

"I don't mind."

"Yes, you do."

"I'll deal with it. I don't mind coming home to your bras hanging off the back of the couch, as long as it means you're wandering around with perky nipples. I want to know you're sleeping in my bed, *our bed*, even when I'm not there."

"Sleeping *naked* in our bed. Don't forget that important detail."

"Obviously. I thought that was a given." I brush her hair away from her face. "Is that a yes?"

"Yes. It's a yes. I'll bring my chaos into your calm."

I place a soft kiss on her lips. "There's no place I'd rather be than the eye of your storm."

# EPILOGUE
## MY KING

*Queenie*
*Six years later*

The doorbell rings at 3:45 p.m. I put my paintbrush in the mason jar of water and walk as quickly down the hall to the front door as possible, which isn't very fast, since I have a small bowling ball hanging off the front of my body and it's slowly becoming more of a waddle than a walk these days.

Kingston has knocked me up for the second time in two years. Scout, our son, is currently having his afternoon nap, but I'm sure he'll be up soon and looking for entertainment. Thankfully, I have the perfect source standing at the front door.

I throw it open, smiling widely, excited for today's session. "How was your first day of school?"

Lavender's long auburn hair is pulled up in a haphazard ponytail with flyaways blowing around her face. She's dressed in her eclectic style of homemade clothes sourced from old items she tears apart and puts back together again with more flair. Lavender is going to be a very talented seamstress one day.

However, right now she looks more sullen teen than happy-go-lucky ten-year-old. "Boys are stupid."

"Uh-oh, that doesn't sound good."

"Eh, it's whatever." She bends and pats my rounded belly. "Hello in there. I hope if you're a boy, you end up being nothing like the ones in my school."

"Do you want a snack, or do you just want to get down to it?" I ask.

"I'd like to paint, if that's okay."

"Of course it's okay." When Lavender's hands are busy creating, she's the most chatty; all her feelings and thoughts are channeled into whatever she's making. She would probably sew her way through our sessions, but the sewing machine is loud and makes it tough to talk, so she generally uses paints or pastels when she comes here.

In the past six years I've finished my degree and have gotten my master's. Kingston and I got married the summer after I graduated.

He was mine and I was his, and he wanted it to be official. He wanted to see me walk down the aisle in a gorgeous dress and recite our vows in front of our friends and his crazy, wild family. And so we did. Then we spent a month traveling, just the two of us.

And now here we are, about to be parents for the second time, and I have my own art therapy studio. Lavender doesn't always need the weekly sessions, but it's become our thing over the past few years.

Instead of picking up a paintbrush, she goes over to the massive sheet of paper taped to the wall and gets out the finger paints. Which tells me everything I need to know about her day. The finger paints rarely come out anymore.

I don't push her to talk right away, allowing her time to warm up and settle in.

"River and I are in different classes."

Ah, here we go. "And how do you feel about that?"

She swipes her fingers across the page, thin yellow lines converging and twisting before she moves on to red. "Guilty."

"Why guilty?"

"Because I'm as relieved as I am disappointed." She drags her red fingertips through the yellow and then swirls up and around. It looks like sunlight and angry wind on fire.

"It's okay to want space and the opportunity to be your own person."

"I know." She pushes her glasses up her nose.

"But?"

"It's hard when everything is new and different. I want him to be more than my shield from the world."

"So being in a different class this year will be good for you, maybe?"

"Maybe, probably."

We spend the next hour talking about her new teacher, her classmates, and the girl in her class who likes the same graphic novel series as she does. She's made such huge progress over the past six years, and honestly, so have I.

I considered pursuing my PhD, but then I got pregnant again, and as much as it's a goal for the future, I don't want to add more to my plate until all my babies are in school. And I have a feeling Kingston isn't going to want to stop at two, and neither am I.

Scout has been a dream child, and this pregnancy has been amazingly smooth. So if things keep going the way they are, there's a good chance we'll end up with a hockey line's worth of babies.

Kingston arrives home a few minutes after Lavender leaves, her steps a little lighter, her smile brighter. I'm in the art therapy studio, putting away supplies while Scout babbles in his playpen.

Kingston's huge body fills the doorway of my studio. "How's my beautiful wife?"

"Great, just tidying up, and then we can start on dinner."

Scout's arms shoot out, and he does the cute little toddler dance where his feet move to a beat that's only in his head. "Dada!"

"How's my man?" Kingston pauses to kiss my temple and pat my belly. "Did he have a good day?"

"He was fabulous. As always. Ate all his vegetables at lunch, napped like a champion, and finished off the afternoon by showering his cuteness and love all over Lavender."

"Making girls fall in love with you already, huh?" Kingston scoops him up out of the playpen, gives him a tickle, and kisses his cheek.

"I saw her walking home when I was coming down the street. She doing okay?"

"She is. She's growing up, fast."

"They do that."

We head for the kitchen, put Scout in his playpen again, and get to work on dinner. Kingston feeds Scout while I prepare our meal. Later we get Scout ready for bed together, which is how it always is when he's home and not on an away series.

I watch my husband tuck our son into bed, kiss his forehead, and tell him he loves him. We don't go back downstairs after we put Scout to bed. I'm well into my second trimester, so the exhaustion isn't as profound, but Scout is an early riser, which means I'm often in bed before ten these days. Instead we head to the bedroom, where Kingston helps me into my pajamas, but not before he makes slow, gentle love to me while whispering politely dirty things in my ear.

Afterward we cuddle, me tucked into his side, his hand splayed protectively over my baby bump. I rest my head in the crook of his arm and lay my hand over his chest, feeling his heart beating steady beneath it. Calm, strong, constant.

"I've been thinking." Our best conversations tend to happen in bed, postsex, when I'm cradled in his protective hold and my brain and body are the most settled.

He kisses my temple, and I can feel his slight smile. "About what?"

"With baby two on the way, I thought it might be a good idea to scale back my hours at the clinic and start working from home more."

He stills and then shifts, tipping my chin up so he can see my face. His is passive, questioning, ready to hear me out. "Okay. Would you like to talk about the why behind the idea?"

"There will be lots of time for me to work as the kids get older, but I want to be here, with them and you, as much as I can right now. They're where I want my focus. I'll adjust my hours so I can keep my current clients, but I really want to be a mother first." Scout was a bit of an accident. I always wanted children, but being raised the way I was, without a stable mother in the picture, made me hesitant. So when I missed a period, panic mode set in. All the what-ifs and the insecurities bubbled to the surface.

Fortunately, I have King, always calm and rational. Always here to help me up when I fall, to remind me that I'm worthy, I'm more than just enough, I'm his everything and he's mine, and I would be the most amazing mother in the universe. It helps that I have his family, and the wives of his teammates to rely on, as well as my father, who finally found a love of his own. But that's a whole different story.

Kingston gives me a soft, warm smile. "I'll support whatever you want to do. I know you've worked hard for your career, though." He kisses my fingertips, nailbeds forever outlined in a rainbow of paint. "And I would never want you to give up what makes you happy."

I love this man so much. For the better part of four years he was the center of my entire world, and I never thought that would change . . . until Scout came along. He's become the sun we orient ourselves around. And Kingston is exactly the kind of father I expected him to be: all in, devoted, present, and fully invested.

I'm not afraid of failing anymore, because no matter what, I have the most amazing man at my side. He's always there to catch me when I fall and to celebrate every success, so making this choice is easy, because I know it's what's best not just for me but for our family.

"I'm not giving up what makes me happy; I'm adjusting my path so I can do *all* the things that make me happy, without compromising any of them. I want to give our kids what I never had, and the more hours I work, the less I can be here with them and you. And I honestly don't want to split my time more than I already do. I want time with you and Scout, and eventually this little peanut." I cover the hand on my belly with my own. "More than I want anything else."

"If that's what you want, then I think it's exactly what you should do. And not just because it means I'll get more of you." He pulls me in closer, lips moving across my cheek and toward my mouth.

"I could always use more doses of my personal Valium," I mumble against his lips.

He chuckles at one of my many nicknames I have for him and the almost sedative-like effect he has on me at times.

"And I can't get enough of your chaos, so I think this arrangement is going to work well for both of us."

And I don't doubt for a second that it will.

He's the calm to my storm.

My still lake at dawn.

My king.

# ACKNOWLEDGMENTS

Hubs and kidlet, you are forever a source of inspiration and support. Thank you for always being my cheerleaders. I love you both endlessly. Mom, Dad, and Mel, thank you for being my family and for always supporting me.

Every book takes a team effort, and this one was no different. I've been so fortunate to have such a wonderful, supportive team of people to help bring this series into the book world. Kimberly, as always, I'm lucky to have you in my corner, always pushing me (gently) to do better and dig deeper.

To my Montlake team: you've been amazing cheerleaders and partners. Thank you for making this such a wonderful journey.

Debra, after more than a decade and a combined thirty-plus releases between us, you are forever the pepper to my salt. Thanks for putting up with me.

Tijan, you are such an incredible human being and genuine friend. Your kindness is unparalleled.

Leigh, thank you for being such a solid friend, for your insight, your positive words, and, of course, the magic that is the insult "boner killer."

Sarah Pie, thank you for being so much more than a PA; you're my friend, my sounding board, my organizer, and the leader of my teams. I could not do this without you. Hustlers, the same goes for you; I'm honored to have you with me every single time I release a book, holding my hand when I'm freaking out.

Beaver Den members, I'm so lucky to have such a wonderful group of readers. You're always there to share in the excitement, try new things, and fall in love with new characters. You're amazing, and I'm eternally grateful for you.

Sarah F., you, ma'am, are a rock star, and I adore you. I'm so glad we can be TMI with each other without even a second thought, or any kind of postshare regrets. My team at SPBR, you're amazing, and you make every release that much easier to handle.

Gel, Sarah S., and Angy—thank you for your amazing graphic talent. You bring these books to life, and I'm so grateful for your incredible imaginative skills.

Bloggers, bookstagrammers, and readers: your love of words, of stories, of romance and happily ever afters is the reason I get to do this thing I love so much. Thank you for your continued support.

Deb, Tijan, Leigh, Kellie, Ruth, Erika, Teeny, Kim, Kelly, Marty, Karen, Kat, Angela, Jo, Julie, Marnie, Krystin, Laurie, and Lou, thank you for your unfailing friendship. I'm a lucky person to have so many amazing, talented, caring people in my life.

# ABOUT THE AUTHOR

*Photo © 2018 Sebastian Lohnghorn*

*New York Times* and *USA Today* bestselling author Helena Hunting lives on the outskirts of Toronto with her incredibly tolerant family and two moderately intolerant cats. She writes contemporary romance ranging from new adult angst to romantic comedy.